STORIES · FROM · THE
SIX WORLDS
MICMAC · LEGENDS

RUTH · HOLMES · WHITEHEAD

ILLUSTRATED BY
KATHY · KAULBACH

NIMBUS PUBLISHING LIMITED

Published by:
Nimbus Publishing Limited,
P.O. Box 9301, Stn. A
Halifax, Nova Scotia
B3K 5N5

Designed and illustrated by Kathy Kaulbach, Halifax.

Canadian Cataloguing in Publication Data

Whitehead, Ruth Holmes

Stories from the Six Worlds

ISBN 0-921054-06-8 HC ISBN 0-921054-14-9 PB

1. Micmac Indians—Legends. 2. Indians of North America—Maritime Provinces—Legends. 3. Tales—Maritime Provinces. I. Title.

E99.M6W54 1988 398.2'08997 C88-098585-2

Printed and bound in Canada

In memory of
Ruth Holmes Walker Gadsden
and
Fern Everett Luker

Nsi's kjikitpuoin, ktui'katikn.

CONTENTS

THE WORLD ABOVE THE EARTH
THE WORLD ABOVE THE SKY

GHOST WORLD

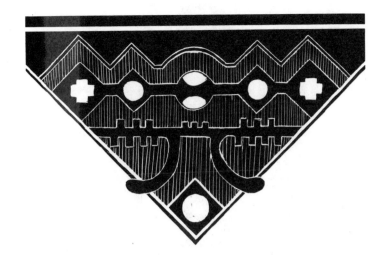

INTRODUCTION:
THE WORLD
OF
THE PEOPLE

INTRODUCTION: THE WORLD OF THE PEOPLE

The People are the Micmac, and their world is eastern Canada and northern New England. In 1500 A.D., when their history first begins to take written form, they were reported living in what is now Nova Scotia, Prince Edward Island, northern and eastern New Brunswick and portions of the Gaspé Peninsula of Quebec, territories their ancestors had occupied for at least two thousand years.

Their name for themselves was *Lnu'k,* the People. Their traditions say they came into this land from somewhere to the southwest. They greeted the Europeans who began venturing into their world in the sixteenth century, and writing about it, as *nikmaq,* which means 'my kin-friends.' It is this term, which the Europeans learned to use when speaking to the People, that became the modern tribal name Micmac.[1]

Long before their world began to be described in writing, and their history set down in books, the People described it, remembered it, and by word of mouth passed it on to the generations which were to come after them. "What was my amazement ... at discovering, day by day, that there existed among them, entirely by oral tradition, a far grander mythology than that which has been made known to us by either the Chippewa or Iroquois Hiawatha Legends, and that this was illustrated by an incredible number of tales."[2] The Micmac histories were songs and stories.

Archaeology can tell us where the People lived, and much about their imperishable materials, like stone. It can show us the rocks of their hearth-fires and the bits of bone or seeds in the ash. None of this, however, can tell us much about what the People thought or felt, the conversations they had while they cooked and ate their moose and ground-nuts. Archaeology cannot show us their hearts, and neither can recorded history.

1

While the available historical documents do give us flesh on the archaeological bones, such records and reports were largely compiled by Europeans, most of whom knew relatively little about the people whom they were describing. Few of these 'outsiders' spoke Micmac, to begin with, and even with some knowledge of the language, their understanding was limited to concepts which were readily demonstrable and common to both cultures—cooking and eating, for example. Any deeper understanding of the Micmac world was slow in coming, for when ideas and world-view radically diverge, the differences may be so great that neither side is even aware that there is anything *to* misunderstand. Comprehending the way another culture looks at the world is probably one of the most difficult intellectual and spiritual exercises, even without the language barrier.

Truly, then, it is their surviving stories that are the great historical and cultural wealth of the Micmac. For only in their stories do we hear the People themselves speaking about their world; only in their tales are we given glimpses of how their universe arose, in all its fascinating Otherness, and how the Persons living therein were expected to conduct themselves.

To the Old Ones of the People, Creation itself was fluid, in a continuous state of transformation. Reality was not rigid, set forever into form. Here form changed shape according to the will and whim of the Persons manifesting those forms, at any given moment. This Creation is clearly depicted in Micmac stories: not only through their content, interestingly, but through their basic structure and the language in which they were told.

Within the framework of the traditionally long story-cycles, individual storytellers often transferred elements from one cycle into another. The intent or whim of the teller was the string onto which episodes, actions, characters and messages were threaded like beads. Such 'beads' could change their colour and form as well, so each retelling of a story, even by the same person, might be different. The structure was fluid, accommodating itself to the teller's will. All its elements could change their shapes, their content.

The Micmac language, the original medium for these stories, is equally fluid. Its use of verb phrases, with hun-

2

dreds of prefixes and suffixes, means that there are very few fixed and rigid separate words in the language. "The full conjugation of one Micmac verb would fill quite a large volume," wrote Rand about a language he found "copious, flexible, and expressive."[3] In a very real sense, the speaker creates the vocabulary as he goes along, minting verb phrases to meet the needs of the moment, to give the very finest detailed shades of meaning. Words, in Micmac, are shape-changers as well, following the intent of the speaker.

In their transformational properties, both Micmac language and Micmac tales have the same structure as does the Micmac universe. As stories hold many levels of meaning, the cosmos holds many levels of existence: the World Beneath The Earth, the World Beneath The Water, Earth World, Ghost World, the World Above The Earth, the World Above The Sky. These are the six worlds of the People which their legends depict, all of them strange to any twentieth-century eyes looking at them through the lens of a European mind-set. They make up a universe which forms itself out of Power. To understand it, and to understand the stories themselves, one has first to comprehend what the People meant by Power.

▲

Modern science maintains that all matter is energy, shaping itself to particular patterns. The Old Ones of the People took this a step further: they maintained that patterns of Power could be conscious, manifesting within the worlds by acts of *will*. They thought of such entities as Persons, with whom one could have a relationship.

"Kji-kinap made the world," says one of the tales in this collection.[4] *Kinap* is a Micmac word which means power, strength, force. (It is also used as the term for the *kinapaq*, those humans who use power, those whom we would call supernaturally strong.) *Kji* is a prefix, meaning 'great.' So in this creation myth, the Great Power forms the world. In a variant from Maine, Kluskap creates himself by an act of will, from dirt left over after the Creation. He then has a conversation with the Creator, the Great Power, who tells him, "Behold here, how wonderful is my work, all I created by my wish of mind: the existing world, ocean, rivers, river-lakes."[5] Kluskap and the Creator next strive with each other to see who can will things into existence best. Kluskap

wills a wind; it tears trees out by the roots. Then the
Creator wills a wind, and this wind is so strong that it tears
Kluskap's hair out by the roots. But this wind is also so
subtle that Kluskap doesn't realize what it has done until
he touches his head and all his hair comes away in his hand.

Power is the essence which underlies the perceived
universe; it gives rise to it, transcends it, energizes and
transforms it. It is everywhere at once, and yet it is also
conscious, particulate: it is Persons. Through word-end-
ings, the Micmac language catalogues elements of the
created world in two ways: as animate or inanimate.
Persons are those manifestations which are animate, and
they include humans, animals, trees. Persons are themselves—a Clam, a Dog, a Birch Person—yet they take
human shape as well. Each form contains the other. In
some ways, they are seen as being both at once. They can
also take other shapes.

Within the six worlds live a number of such Persons.
Muini'skw—Bear Woman—is just what her name implies:
a Bear Person and a Woman, a human woman singing
lullabies, sewing moccasins, living in a wigwam and making fire. Kwimu is a Loon Person, an animal spirit-helper,
yet he is also a man, a husband, a hunter. Other stories tell
of Plant Persons, who visit as humans, to instruct the
People in the use of their plant forms and properties.

These worlds also contain beings in animal forms not
found in modern bestiaries, such as the Horned Serpent
Persons, the Jipijka'maq. In their snake shapes, they
travel about under the earth, swimming through the layers
of rock; the ground trembles as they pass. Sometimes they
come up to the Earth World, and carve great ruts in the
land as they move across it. They live as humans in the
World Beneath The Water. Sleeping, they can seem mountains. All Jipijka'maq have one red horn, one yellow horn;
these horns are Power-objects, and stories about their use
are known westward all the way across northern North
America and through the centuries, back into northern
Asia.[6] The Kulu'k take the Power-shapes of Giant Birds.
They sometimes prey on humans, yet they are the beings
who fly between Earth World and the World Above The
Sky; they are strong spirit-helpers. In one tale, it is a Kulu
who brings animals down from the Sky World so that men
may hunt them and live.

In the Micmac language and the Micmac universe, however, much more than trees or animals is regarded as

4

animate.[7] Stars are Persons, for example. They hunt through the sky. The Thunders are Powers of the natural world and Persons, the Kaqtukwaq. And as Thunders, they live both in human form and bird shape. It is the beating of their wings that creates the noise and great winds of storms below them as they fly.

Winds themselves are Persons, as are Seasons and Directions. The very geography is animate in the six worlds. Mountains are alive, and lakes, and the icebergs floating on the sea. Strange features within the landscape are Persons thought of with affection, or placated with gifts. Boulders and cliffs are sometimes revealed in stories as Shape-Changers who choose those forms when they wish to hide or to rest.[8] Such rocks could be potent and terrible beings, as Ki'kwa'ju discovers when the boulder he has disturbed begins to rumble after him, crushing the forest in its path. It is challenging him and chasing him; it is trying to kill him.

"I once asked an old man," wrote Irving Hallowell, " 'Are all the stones we see about us here alive?' He reflected a long while and then replied, 'No! But *some* are.' "[9]

How does one know which ones these are? One knows by the way they *feel*.

> The forest sings itself to darkness
> and the stone holds a light
> he can feel in his palm;
> it is the same light animals leave
> on the stones along the river
> where they have passed the night.[10]

Stones are the bones of the earth; like the white powerful bones of animals, they are alive. They can be dangerous. They must be treated with respect.[11]

The Mn'tu'k also inhabit the six worlds. *Mn'tu* is another word for Power—one which seems to refer more to its conscious aspects than does the term *kinap*. The closest English translation of the word would be 'spirit.' *Mn'tu'k* are Persons, entities who do not necessarily need to take form, although they can and do, as it pleases them. The worlds shimmer with their presence.

Other beings live in these worlds as well: the Kukwesk are giants, covered with hair. They crave human flesh. The sound of their screams can kill. The Mi'kmwesu'k are beautiful and strong—flute-players whose music enchants. Male and female, they appear to humans lost in the woods.

They themselves are thought to have once been People, having become through Power the ultimate realization of human potential. "I am becoming a *mi'kmwesu*," says a man to his wife in the story "Skun." His wife is puzzled.

"What is a *mi'kmwesu*? Is it a *mn'tu*? Is it good or bad?"

"I am not sure," says the man. "I think it is like a human Person. It is not bad."

Time runs differently in a Mi'kmwesu wigwam: one night with them, and a year has passed in the camps of the People. Time, as well as space, is elastic in the six worlds.

▲

In Micmac stories about these six worlds, it is always the forest where such beings and events are encountered.[12] The further into the forest, the stranger the encounter, for it is the forest where reality becomes fluid. Within the Micmac universe, the forest is Chaos—the unconscious, the unknown, the place where the map ends. In only one tale, the story "Skun," does the sea play this role: out on the ocean, lost in fog, a man and a woman see the shadow of strangeness coming toward them across the water. Usually, however, it is deep inside the forest that Persons come face to face with Power, and a story begins to unfold.

Within this forest-heart, the image of the Tree is one of great importance, an image "essential to the beliefs and ritual practises of shamanism because it connects the three fundamental zones of the shamanic cosmos; its roots penetrate the Underworld, its branches rise to the Sky."[13]

Micmac shamans, the *puoinaq,* prepared for their rituals by erecting outside their tents a tree, a pole, or a branch, often decorated or hung with gifts. This was an outward and visible manifestation of the World Tree, on the *essence* of which the shaman climbed up or down. As healer and diviner, a shaman of the People often needed to seek answers and Powers in all the six worlds. On such journeys, he or she used the Cosmic Tree as a ladder.

His blood pulsing to the drum, he passed through the cries of ravens, the rising thunder of hooves, the enormous silences of empty valleys, of ages and seasons like a river flowing over the land. Swimming beneath the earth or climbing to the sky-world, he embarked on a journey fraught with dangers.[14]

In the story "The Man Who Married Jipijka'mi'skw," a practising shaman makes and uses such a Tree from a tree. The Weasel Women, in "Ki'kwa'ju and Skusi'skwaq," travel down from the World Above The Sky on a Tree. Unfortu-

6

nately they open their eyes—come out of the trance-state—
too soon, and discover themselves still up in its crown,
unable to get down. In the tale "Lamkisn," a baby comes
into Earth World out of a phosphorescent log. And in
"Wsitiplaju," Wijîke'skw pulls up her wigwam door-post
and "cries herself" down its hole into the World Beneath
The Earth. This door-post is also a Tree image, and she is
chanting and climbing down its roots in the traditional
shamanic way.

To enter the trance-states necessary for their journeys,
then, shamans of the People withdrew into the forests of
the mind, the place where transformation begins. And deep
within this forest-state, they found the Tree that was both
actuality and symbol of the road on which they travelled. In
stories, this is represented by having the characters with-
draw deeper into the physical wilderness.

Living in the forest, dressing in leaves and mosses, is also
a Micmac metaphor for antiquity: it is the way the very
Oldest Old Ones are seen, and their presence in a story
announced.

> There was a woman, long, long ago
> She came out of a hole.
> In it dead people were buried.
> She made her house in a tree;
> She was dressed in leaves,
> All long ago.
> When she walked among the dry leaves
> Her feet were so covered
> The feet were invisible.
> She walked through the woods,
> Singing all the time,
> "I want company; I'm lonesome!"
> From far away a wild man heard her....[15]

The woman "long, long ago," whose home was a tree, and
whose clothing was leaves, is an archetypal First Woman,
walking through the forest when the world was still very
young. There are echoes of her in the story "Kwimu," where
a girl is dressed in a robe of leaves; she walks the lake-
shore, calling to the Loon Person who one day will become
her husband.

▲

How did this Micmac cosmological view first take form?
A creation story from the seventeenth century says that the
worlds were made by the sun. The People saw the sun as a
Person, addressed him as "Grandfather," a term of respect.

They say that when the sun ... created all this great universe, he divided the earth immediately into several parts, wholly separated one from the other by great lakes: that in each part he caused to be born one man and one woman, and they multiplied and lived a very long time.[16]

The People were born from the body of the earth, their mother. In the eighteenth century, prayers to the sun and the moon, a Person of the female gender, acknowledged the role of both in the creation of the world.

[To the Sun:] The father of the day can never fail us.... It is plain that we are thy children; for we can know no origin but that which thy rays have given us, when first marrying ... with the earth we inhabit, they impregnated its womb, and caused us to grow out of it like the herbs of the field, and the trees of the forest, of which thou art equally the common father. [To the Moon:] How great, O moon! is thy goodness, in actually, for our benefit, supplying the place of the father of the day, as next to him thou hast concurred to make us spring out of that earth we have inhabited from the first ages of the world.... Thou regardest us, in truth, as thy children.... Beautiful spouse of the sun![17]

Sun and Earth and Moon are the ancestors of the People, and the People too are Persons. Ordinarily, they live on the Earth World, but these and other stories recount their journeys elsewhere: diving into the World Beneath The Water, climbing down the door-post hole to the World Beneath The Earth, willing themselves into the World Above The Sky, or flying to the World Above The Earth on the back of a Kulu. After death comes the journey to Ghost World, but once, just once, some few brave men accomplished it in their living flesh.

All the People, being animate, *are* Power, in a sense. As such, they can manipulate Power just as Kji-kinap does, creating the world by an act of will. Yet as Kluskap ('Liar') himself discovers, the ability to use Power varies from individual to individual. Some can just naturally do it better. Stories are full of contests, where Persons match their Powers against each other, seeing who is stronger. All beings have a certain amount of Power; the classifications that follow are not formal, but arbitrary. A Person could be two or more of them at once.

8

The *kinapaq* are generally seen as those able to expand their strengths, their perceptions. *Kinapaq* appear in a number of tales: some of them born that way, and some acquiring or developing their abilities as the story progresses. They can outrun the wind. They dive deeper, hold their breath longer and let it out as storms; they tear trees in half and carry a ton of moose meat on their backs. When they dance, their feet sink deep into the earth with each stamp of a foot.

> One of them was a boy
> He was blind from his birth,
> But he frightened his mother by his sight.
> He could tell her what was coming,
> What was coming from far off.
> What was near he could not see.
> He could see the bear and the moose
> Far away beyond the mountains;
> He could see through everything.[18]

The *puoinaq* are those who use Power to heal: the curers, the shamans. (*Puoin* is also a word for Power, as are *kinap* and *mn'tu*.) They could also use Power to destroy, as the characters Plawej and Miskwekepu'j do, in the stories of the same name. *Puoinaq* were often feared, and many tales tell of how they are abandoned by their People or driven out or killed by other *puoinaq*, in a combination of fear and jealousy, precautionary measures, or revenge. *Puoinaq* are Shape-Changers capable of handling enormous Power, past the domestic magics of the ordinary mass of the People. They excel at manipulating reality.

Nikani-kjijitekewinu means 'one who knows in advance.' Quite a few Persons in the six worlds can foresee coming events, warn of dangers yet to be. Precognition plays a part in many tales, and various methods of divination are depicted. When Plawej falls on his face by the bowl of water, he enters a trance, empowering the water to speak to him. And it does. It becomes blood. The appearance of blood—in a bowl, in a tobacco pipe, or on a Power-robe—is a frequent device in Micmac stories. It is always an announcement of death.

▲

Death is common in the worlds these stories show us, yet death is not oblivion. It is simply another transformation, for the first law of this universe says, "Everything is eternal, yet nothing is constant." Form is continually chang-

9

ing. The entire landscape of the six worlds is a nexus of Power moving beneath the outward appearance of things like light: of Persons shifting in and out of form, of patterns recombining. Life is a kaleidoscope of Power, and Death is just a shifting of the glass.

In Micmac, the absentive case-ending "conveys the idea of existence, though apart for the time."[19] It is used in speaking of an absent person or a dead one—each still animate, but now out of sight of the speaker. So in stories, no one is surprised when the absent one returns, for death is not necessarily permanent. Kitpusiaqnaw calls his older brother back from the dead. Kluskap reanimates the frozen bodies of his grandmother and Little Marten; "Grandmother, get up!" he says, and she does. Skun transfers some of his Power to his slain son and revives him. A grieving hunter brings the soul of his dead child home to the Earth World, in order that he might awaken in his body once more.

There are other types of reanimation, of escape from death. A second law of the six worlds might read, "The part encapsulates the whole." And as long as a piece of it survives, the whole can be read out, reborn, from it. When Ki'kwa'ju[20] is about to be flattened by a rock, he screams, "Let my backbone be preserved!" And from that bone, his Power-core, he calls his body back into the material world. When he drowns, in another episode, and his old corpse washes up on shore, two little boys begin a catalogue of his symptoms of decay: "Look at the maggots in his nose, the maggots in his ears." Says Ki'kwa'ju, "That's nothing but snot, nothing but earwax." He reverses his manifestations of death by naming them as manifestations of life. Then he shakes himself, and stands up a healthy young man. All in all, Ki'kwa'ju is killed four times in this story, and none of these deaths lasts longer than he wants it to.

A further example is the chipmunk skin in "Lamkisn," which becomes the animal again and again whenever Lamkisn has need of it to gather news for him. When the

10

chipmunk has finished its task, it becomes a skin again, and is folded away until the next time.

Waisisk Ketu'muaji Ji'nm, in the story "Bringing Back Animals," causes the moose, the caribou and all the other creatures of land, sea and air to reincarnate from the bits of their bodies left over after humans have consumed the gift of their flesh. This ability for the part to become the whole again underlies the Micmac teaching that all the bones of animals taken by hunters *must* be treated with respect and preserved. Thus not only will the animal *wish* to re-enflesh itself in the immediate vicinity, but it will be *able* to do so, because the bone is there—a channel through which it can come once more into matter.

The converse of this is that every part of an enemy must be obliterated. Ki'kwa'ju tries to eradicate permanently his foe the Rock Person. He burns that stone, cracks and crushes it to powder. And even then there is life in it, but by flinging the grit into the air and transforming it into blackflies, Ki'kwa'ju prevents this Person from reassembling himself. In the same way, Kitpusiaqnaw grinds up the bones of his dead Kukwes father, to deny him further life. He scatters the ashes and the Person who was his father is dispersed. Yet the life-force survives. The ashes become mosquitos and flies. There are further ways in which death becomes life. A tree is spoken of as animate until it dies, yet its dead wood, shaped into something, lives again. Suffused in the Power of the shaper, and the Power of the *function* it will assume, it once more takes the animate case-ending. So such things as women's decorated hair-strings are animate—at least three tales tell of their magic. What happens is that the painted eelskin, the porcupine quills and sinews—formerly parts of living things—now combine their disjointed inanimacies into a new being: the hair ornament. A man's weapons are likewise animate, as are things like canoes or cups or clothing. In the minds of the People, all have the potential to change shape or speak, and in stories they often do. They are manifestations of Power which can wake

11

to consciousness. And yet they are formed—re-created—from "dead" matter.

▲

The six worlds are a universe of Shape-Changers. Micmac stories emphasize this over and over. The character Ki'kwa'ju is a wolverine, a young man, a vertebra, a pregnant woman, the rotting corpse of an old man, and a waterfall, all within one tale. He even attempts a Kulu shape, but the Kulu woman to whom he shows it has Power, and she feels that something is not quite right. Unfortunately for her, his Power is stronger, and he kills her.

In the same story, the Weasel Woman, Older Sister, is both a weasel and a human woman; she is wife to a marten, a star and a sea-bird. To escape a bone which is also a vampire, she turns herself into a man, and shape-changes her younger sister into a tiny human figure, whom she hides in her hair.

> We are the stars which sing;
> We sing with our light.
> We are the birds of fire,
> We fly across the sky.[21]

Stars are stars and singers and birds of fire. Yet stars are also men, as the tale "Ki'kwa'ju and Skusi'skwaq" informs us—both young and handsome, and old and wrinkled men. Animals on the Earth World were themselves once stars, now transformed. Stars are also the spirit-road. And none of these are metaphors—they are actualities, for Star Persons are Shape-Changers.

The tricky thing about Shape-Changers is that not only do they change their forms, they also change their minds. Thus in stories there are no Good Persons, the Heroes; there are no Bad Persons, eternally Villains in a European sense. There are only beings acting according to their natures and according to their whims, their emotional states of the moment.

Micmac storytellers used this to great dramatic effect. A good example is found in the story "Kitpusiaqnaw." The Kukwesk, Eaters Of Human Flesh, were universally feared and loathed by the People; yet the humanness of these Persons, the love which Kukwes has for Kukwes, is portrayed very movingly in this tale. Kitpusiaqnaw's Kukwes father loves him. His last thoughts are for him. As he burns in flames which his sons themselves have set for him, over and over he calls out to his older boy, "Save the young one! Save your younger brother." And Kitpusiaqnaw's grandfather permits his son to marry a human woman he cannot

12

live without; he refrains from eating her until his son gives him permission. This old Kukwes's wife loves him also. "My poor old man," she says, mourning him, "he had a very sweet liver." The Kukwes who marries a human woman, who entrusts his Power to her, and who has her killed when she fails him, is a complex, horrific and sympathetic character. Recognizing the good within him gives this story an extra dimension.

Because of this aspect that nearly everything in the six worlds—including the geography—can change both its shape and its mind, the universe is unpredictable, unreliable in a European sense. So how do humans and other Persons survive when nothing is necessarily as it seems? They survive by accumulating Power of their own, the ability to change their own shapes and modes as circumstances require. This is such an important tenet that almost every story of the People has Power as its central theme: how to acquire it, how to use it, how to lose it, and the consequences attendant on all of the above.

Some Persons are born with Power: the miraculous child of the stories "Kitpusiaqnaw" or "Kulu," for example. Some acquire it through death-transfer, as when Tia'm passes his Power to his sister as he dies, in "Tia'm and Tia'mi'skw." Others are symbolically reborn. Kluskap takes the young man who has soiled himself like a baby to wash him in the sea as babies are washed, and then he gives him new clothes to put on, as babies are dressed for the first time. This young man is born again into Power; he becomes a mi'kmwesu.[22]

Possession of the part confers Power over the whole and the Power *of* the whole. Miskwekepu'j, with his bag of snake bones and *jipijka'm* bones, holds the Power of those animals; it is his to use, through the law by which the part equals the whole. When Plawej steals the hair-string from the Seal Woman combing her hair on the ice, she must come to him and be his wife, for he has captured part of her, part of her essence.

By this same law, clothing is a protective mechanism, one which was used by the Micmac throughout their early history; so the Powerful nature of costume is yet another theme running through Micmac stories. For clothing, adornment and even tattooing or body-painting is armour: the cumulative Power-fields of all the materials and symbols used. Animal hide and fur, ivory, teeth, claws, horn, bone and feathers are Power locked into dress; dreams or visions encoded into painted or appliquéd designs lend it their energies. Light-mirrors like micas or quartz, sewn

13

onto costume or carried as amulets, capture flashes of the sun or quick glimpses of the landscape. All of these things—these beings—are potent protections.

This is why Wijïke'skw, in the story "Wsitïplaju," washes herself, paints her face with red ochre and dons her finest costume before venturing very far into the World Beneath The Earth. Belts which cover the solar plexus, the life-force, are particularly important articles of Power-dressing, so the mother-in-law in the tale "Kulu" ties her belt on before going out to wrestle with her enemy. And to put on the costume of a very Powerful Person, as the young man does in "Kluskap and Mi'kmwesu," or as the hunter does in the tale "Skun," is to assume that Person's Power-shape over one's own. Clothing, amulets and Power-objects in one's medicine pouch are a first line of defence in the six worlds.

Proper behaviour is also a protection; we see in the story "Papkutparut" what happens to those who have not conducted themselves as they should. Proper conduct is an interesting mixture of Respect and Insolence, Caution and Boldness, Compassion and Ferocity. A young man speaks respectfully to a strange old woman, and she befriends him. Younger Sister treats a bone disrespectfully and it tries to kill her. Little Marten urinates into the bowl of water he brings to his oppressor, an act of insolence which presages his liberation. Caution in dealing with the unknown seems to lie behind the habit of characters in stories replying, "Nothing in particular; nowhere in particular, nobody in particular," when questioned by those who might otherwise capture the speaker's essence from a particular, revealing answer. Boldness in dealing with a subtle attack saves those who, like the chief in "Kulu," throw their dinner in the face of the cook trying to poison them. Compassion must be shown to kin-friends, to those within the band; rejecting them means a loss of their potential Power-contributions, at the very least. Sometimes compassion is extended to enemies, as in "Kulu," when the last Great Bird Person is spared. However, the enemies of one's allies are assumed with the bond, so Youngest Son in "Nuji-Kesi-Kno'tasit" must slay with merciless ferocity all his prospective father-in-law's foes, even the women and children.

Ferocity and Duty To One's Kin combine to make Revenge one of the central tenets of Micmac life, and one of the great themes of Micmac stories. Revenge restores balance, by taking a life for a life, or giving cruelty for cruelty. Revenge also restores emotional balance, by providing a tangible outlet for grief and anger. It is both a lesson and a deterrent. One of the hardest concepts for Europeans to deal with was the belief held by the People that there was no individual guilt. There was only tribal (or band, or family) guilt, and therefore revenge could be taken on the 'innocent' members of the guilty individual's group, just as acceptably as on the actual offender. When the part *is* the whole, then the whole is equally guilty with the part. Therefore, any portion of the whole, any person, becomes a suitable object for revenge. That includes women, children, the elderly. Even in stories, this idea continues to be unacceptable to people from a European background, yet one must view it from the perspective of the People: revenge is balance, and balance is necessary for survival.

In stories, any character bent on revenge is therefore implacable and terrifying. The very act of doing as he should empowers him, so revenges in these tales sometimes amount to overkill. Proper conduct is a protection and a way to Power.

A major way of acquiring Power and defences is through alliances, through one's relationship with helpful empowering Persons. The People sought allies on every level; they adopted, married and bonded, creating reciprocities within the web of the world. Two of the strongest bonds seem to have been those between siblings—in stories, this is usually between an older sister and younger brother—and those between humans and their animal spirit-helpers.

The Beaver in "Kopit Feeds the Hunter" and the Loon Person in "Kwimu" exemplify the way spirit-helpers of this nature befriend, empower and teach their human 'kin-friends.' Animal allies such as Skun's dog, Lamkisn's chipmunk, or Plawej's pregnant squirrel are considered part of the Power of the owner. The stories present us with other alliances as well: Kluskap empowers a Mi'kmwesu, a Mi'kmwesu empowers an ugly young man, the giant Skun empowers a hunter.

Some of the more dangerous alliances were those of marriage, where one had to venture out of the immediate kin-group, and go among (relative) strangers. Stories reflect the anxiety of the moment, and the severe testing the prospective husband must undergo. His bride's family must see if he will be an addition to their communal Power, or a drain on it. The story "Wsitiplaju," for example, has six marriages in it, and none of them works out. The character Wijike'skw takes three husbands in that tale, and all of them end up dead. Other forms of alliance in that story are more profitable. The brother-sister bond is very strong, and both siblings are helped more by a Bear Woman and a Marten than by their respective spouses. The Moon in particular empowers them to the point where they can survive against impossible odds.

The tale "Sakklo'pi'k" presents its audiences with a step-by-step primer for the acquisition of Power. Basically, it is an account of how a lazy young man becomes a *puoin*. Because he treats the old woman he encounters in the forest with respect, she gives him a Power-object which enables him to get a wife for himself, and for the chief's son. This puts the chief's son in his debt, and also makes him a blood-relation, an ally. "They are as brothers," the story says over and over.

The chief's son is a *puoin*, and he begins to train this lazy young man, showing him how to do all those things which the *kinapaq* can do. He shows him the Power that the part—fur, feathers, bone, hair—has over the whole animal. He shows him Escaping, telling him to put rags on over his clothes, and to provoke someone to attack him. As soon as this lazy man is wrestling with his opponent, he slips out of his tatty costume, and his attacker, *imagining that he is still in it,* beats the costume and leaves it for dead.

Undergoing a ritual death seems to have been part of shamanic training in many cultures. The initiate dies to the old life and perceives in a new way. In "Sakklo'pi'k," the apprentice *puoin* precipitates the violence which, by putting him in jeopardy, will call up all his Power, perhaps latent until now. It may be that this part of the story is metaphorical: all the time safe in the "real clothes" of his essence, the shaman watches, amused, the death of the "rags" of his flesh. He no longer need fear dying. He has seen the escape of slipping out of form. He understands at last that it is his own will which is dressing and undressing him in matter.

As his Power grows, this lazy man begins to Dream. Ultimately he has a Power-dream about a Whale Person, and manages to call him in from the sea, to attract him as an ally. The Whale presents him with another Power-object, and becomes his spirit-helper, his *tioml.*[23]

Such then is the way a man or woman of the People might become a *puoin*. In the story "The Man Who Married

16

Jipijka'mi'skw," we see a
male shaman at work, and in
"Lamkisn," a female *puoin* instructs her son in Power. But what
are the consequences of having these
Powers, these abilities? There is a curious tension in Micmac stories. The People
seem to have been quite ambivalent about
Power, and those who wielded it. One of the
outcomes of acquiring Power is that the very
thing which enables one to triumph over enemies,
marry, hunt successfully, even to become beautiful—
and thus have much to offer the band—also makes one
feared and hated, shunned, marooned, driven into exile.
Gaining Power almost inevitably results in isolation.

In the tale "Kwimu," the children given Power by a Loon
Person are seen by their kindred as peculiar from the very
beginning. "Nobody can understand what they are saying;
all the People think that they are strange." Ultimately they
are rejected by the group; a second band of the People
attempt to kill them once they have seen the boy's Power.
As the story progresses, brother and sister move farther
and farther into the forest, farther and farther away from
other humans. In "The Man Who Married Jipijka'mi'skw,"
the hunter can only be reunited with his band by having his
Horned Serpent Power stripped away from him. His return
to the group is made possible through his once more
becoming ordinary.

Through such stories, one gets the very strong impres-
sion that to be alone in the forest, away from the camp, the
group, is to be imperilled. The need to belong—to have kin-
friends, to make alliances for Power—comes across time
after time. One is lost without supporters. But Power—
without which one is also lost—comes in stories primarily
to those who are already separate or individuated in some
sense. So to be alone in the forest is also to be empowered.

Joseph Campbell has said that great mythological sys-
tems have both a mystical and a social function. On the
social level, "... the whole sense of symbology remains
locked to local practical aims and ethical ideals, in the
function chiefly of controlling, socializing, harmonizing in
strictly local terms...."[24] The People attempt to control and
harmonize the use of Power for the survival of the society:
both *through* the myth and *within* the myth. This is the role
of 'he camp, the band, the group in Micmac stories.

The mystical level of myth, says Campbell, enables the

"recognizing *through* the metaphors [of] an epiphany beyond words."[25] On another level in stories, the People knew that such epiphanies—Power—will come only in silence, in isolation, alone in the mind of the forest, or the forest of the mind. Being alone in such a forest enables one to "hear" the metaphor in the first place, to live the epiphany—acquire the Power—which in turn becomes the myth. In the story "Sakklo'pi'k," when the young man slips out of his costume, his form, he is laughing—the only appropriate response to enlightenment.

The whole story "Sakklo'pi'k" can be considered a metaphor for the integration of both social and mystical (Power) concerns. For the two men in this tale avoid the difficulties attendant on the acquisition of Power by refusing to compete; each offers to defer to the other, each aids the other. This tale is unusual. It is one of the few Micmac stories to have a happy ending: wives, children, food, no enemies, the utter security of the group *and* the Power to ensure that it always will be so. It can stand as a metaphor for the integration of the individual, as well as one for the integration of the group.

The final lesson on the great theme of Power which Micmac stories teach is about the ways in which Power is lost. As a Power-user, one's conduct must be impeccable. Personal tabus and constraints must never be ignored. And a common constraint is that Power-objects are usually an intensely private matter, and any breach of the secrecy surrounding them has grave consequences. Here again, the trappings of Power make one an individual in a communal life-style. One acquires property along with Power: medicine bags, masks, amulets, even songs and dances or visions which cannot be held in common, or often even revealed. To reveal these things, to let another touch or see or use them, is to lose the Power, often with disastrous results. And yet secrecy creates curiosity, and a story begins to unfold.

In "Tia'm and Tia'mi'skw," a sister is warned never to let her medicine bag, made from her brother's skin, out of her possession. She leaves it under the fir twigs that line the wigwam in which she is a guest; another woman pulls it out of its hiding-place, and everyone in the entire camp perishes. In "Papkutparut," a father has the soul of his son in another medicine bag, bringing it home to put it once more in his body. He is warned not to let it escape, but he is diverted from his task by what he sees as the need to dance his gratitude. He hands the pouch to a nosey old woman. She opens it, and father and son are lost to the Earth World.

▲

The purposes of Micmac stories are complex and many. The People used myth to convey to their children their understanding of the way the world works, and such tales operate on several different levels at once. A single incident in a legend might give information about animal behaviour at the same time it explores social problems and their resolution, dramatizes tabus or provides comic relief. Quite frequently there are insertions in tales as the storyteller pauses to give an explanation of how something came to be, how the bullfrog got a crumpled back, how the White Birch's bark got covered with those little marks, how flies and other insects arose and covered the earth. Sometimes this may have nothing at all to do with the development of the plot. There are puns which make no sense in the English translation, and which therefore do not seem to fit into the story as it has been collected: "Where is your shoulder-blade?" "Not in my backside, but in my back." There are actions and characters which only make sense when seen as riddles, such as the final episode in the tale of Kitpusiaqnaw, when he kills a Person Who Walks Sideways, puts him up on his back to use as a door, and meets his family who have frogs and snakes coming out of their faces. Through such multi-layered composition of stories, Micmac children learned the things they needed to know in order to walk through the six worlds in safety.

The potency of these stories from the Micmac is still so great that even today, regardless of the broadened audience, the modern era, the language barrier, myth can still perform this teaching-magic. Myth taught the People as it also teaches us, for myth both awakens us to the world of the Micmac, and connects us to it. Myth establishes us within that world, at its very centre, and then we begin to learn it because we are living it.

We listen to the words, or read them, and then behind the words, something else begins to make itself known. It is the presence of Power, moving across the mind like shadows of clouds on the folds and falls of a mountain. Then suddenly we are seeing the clouds themselves—Power-shapes, drifting with the wind—and as their shadows touch that mountain below, it awakens. Jipijka'm, Horned Serpent Person, flickers into flame. The old, old eyes of Jipijka'm look deep into our own. Then serpent coils back into sleep, and once more becomes geography.

The story has finished, yet it still resonates within us. It is not merely that for a moment boundaries have dissolved and we most intensely have lived the legend, it is that the story changes, even if only slightly, the way we will forever after see the world. A new perception of things emerges. The words of the myth have invoked it, and the reality behind the myth reaches out to encompass all who will listen.

Na teliaq.
Here, then, are the stories.

Ruth Holmes Whitehead

NOTES

1. Whitehead 1987:19-20.
2. Leland 1884:iii.
3. Rand 1894:xxxiv.
4. See the story "Kluskap," above.
5. Speck 1926:186.
6. Phillips 1987:61; Brasser 1987:120.
7. Not all plant-life is considered animate. Usually, only trees take the animate case-ending.
8. See the stories "Plawej" and "Ki'kwa'ju and Skusi'skwaq," above.
9. Hallowell 1960:24.
10. Red Hawk 1983:34. The stories and chants of many North American tribes celebrate the mystery of stones; the modern writer Red Hawk's poems about stones, in *Journey of the Medicine Man*, are some of the most powerful.
11. Crystals and small stones are great repositories of Power. In 1675, LeClercq (1910:222) inventoried the contents of a Micmac shaman's medicine-pouch. In it was a "stone the size of a nut wrapped in a box which he called [its] house." The shaman used to press his stone against his solar plexus and will it to bring him good hunting.
12. As European elements begin to come into Micmac tales, the city sometimes replaces the forest as the dangerous fluidizing heart of the world.
13. Vastokas 1977:95.
14. Whitehead 1987:23.
15. Leland 1884:309. Uncited, but probably Micmac, from internal evidence in Leland.
16. LeClercq 1910:84-85
17. Maillard 1758:22, 25, 47-48.
18. Leland 1884:309. See Note 14; this is from the same poem.
19. Rand 1894:xxxvi.
20. See "Ki'kwa'ju and Skusi'skwaq," above, for all references to Ki'kwa'ju.
21. Leland 1884:379.
22. See "Kluskap and Mi'kmwesu," above.
23. This term for 'spirit-helper' is no longer in use, so the orthography given here is tentative. Rand writes it "teomul."
24. Loudon 1987:101.
25. Loudon 1987:101.

THE WORLD
BENEATH
THE EARTH

THE WORLD
BENEATH
THE WATER

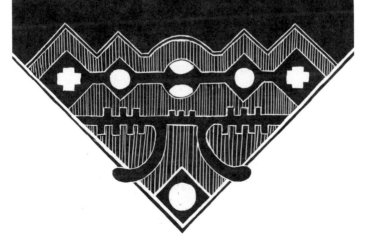

WSITIPLAJU

It is long ago, in the time of our Elders. Two families are living together in the forest. The first man, he is Plawej, Birch Partridge. The second man, he is Wijɨk, Spruce Partridge. Many children were born to each of them.

Now it is winter. This winter is very bad: there is no food. There are no animals to hunt, to eat. There are no birds to catch, to snare. There are no fish to net, to spear and eat.

"*Akaia,*" cried Wijɨk. His children began to die. "*Akaia!*" One by one they die, until there are only two left.

"*Akaia,*" cried Wijɨk, and he died too, his mouth empty, his stomach empty. "*Akaia,*" cried Plawej. His wife is dying. "*Akaia, akaia!*" His children are dead. "*Akaia!*" He buries them, hands empty, stomach empty.

Plawej takes the wife of Wijɨk, Wijɨke'skw; he takes the children of Wijɨk, the little boy, the little girl. He goes out to hunt again. He must find food for his new wife and her children.

But the hunt is difficult. Plawej is finding no game. So he does a thing: he cuts the flesh from his back. He cuts it off, he brings it home, and his family cooks and eats it.

The hunt is very difficult. Plawej is finding no game. So he does another thing: he cuts the flesh from the backs of his legs. He cuts it off, he brings it home, and his family cooks and eats it.

For a long time Plawej brings home from his hunting this old *muso'q,* this lean meat, without fat or bone.

"I want some fat to eat," says the new wife of Plawej. "My stomach needs greasing. Why is there never fat or bone?" She is feeling something wrong.

Plawej was tired; he weakened as his flesh was lost. Every night he comes home from hunting and lies down. He lies by the fire opposite his wife, and warms his back. Then he falls asleep.

This night his wife waits. She waits until he sleeps, then lifts his robe and sees: his back is stripped down to bare bones. All his flesh has been consumed.

In the morning, then, she followed him. He did not see her hiding. Plawej cuts spruce boughs. He breaks them into little pieces; he is spreading them on the ground. He takes his knife and cuts the flesh from his legs; he lays strips of his own meat on the branches.

Plawej has Power. He makes this flesh grow thick and long. It becomes a large pile of meat. He makes the meat grow back on his legs. Then he turns home.

"Ah," says his wife, from her place of hiding. "Have I been eating your flesh? I will leave you tomorrow."

It is day. Plawej leaves the wigwam. He is going hunting. Now Wijɨke'skw, Spruce Partridge Wife, his woman, she is leaving too. She washes herself. She puts on her best clothes, nicely painted, nicely quilled. She makes herself beautiful. Her eyes are red and sparkling. And then she pulls up the door-post at the entrance to the wigwam, and she sits down by the hole.

Wijɨke'skw sits by the door-post hole and cries out. She cries out until she has cried herself down into the hole. She goes into the hole and she passes through the earth until she comes out into a new world, the World Beneath The Earth. She has left her children behind.

"Put the door-post back into the hole after me," she calls up to them.

The new world is beautiful. Wijɨke'skw travels through it until she comes to running water. There by the water she stops. She must bathe. She must comb her hair. She must paint herself with red ochre. Then she will be strong. Wijɨke'skw has Power. She crosses the running water, she travels on through the beautiful world under the earth, following the water until it leads into a river. There she sees a camp, a large camp of the People. At the outer edge is a small bark wigwam. Wijɨke'skw calls out greetings, and goes in.

Little Marten lives here, Apistane'wj. He lives with his grandmother Muini'skw, Old Bear Woman. They are very poor. Little Marten runs all around the camp, asking for food to feed the strange woman who has come.

A strange woman has come, and every man wants her as his wife.

"I will marry," says Wijɨke'skw. "I will marry the first man to kill enough to make a big feast: fat, meat, marrow and blood."

26

The men go out to hunt, and the chief's son makes the first kill. He kills a moose, and brings it home.

"Go over to the chief's wigwam," Old Muini'skw tells Wijɨke'skw. "There you will be fed."

The chief's wife welcomes her. "Come in, my son's wife," she says. Now Wijɨke'skw eats moose meat. She eats moose fat; it drips down her chin. She stays in the wigwam as the wife of the chief's son.

Up above in another world, the Earth World, Plawej returns to his wigwam. There is no woman waiting to cook his food, his flesh.

"Where is your mother?" he asks the children.

"We do not know, *Ta'ta,*" says the little girl.

Plawej goes searching through the forest for his wife, and the little girl says to her brother, "Let us wash ourselves. Let us pull up the door-post and go to find our mother."

They sit by the door-post hole and cry out. They cry themselves into the earth and down, down, until they come out in the beautiful world. The river takes them to the People's camp, the *meski'k wutan.*

The little girl is clever. "If we find our mother, do not speak to her. Let us wait to see what she will do."

Before them is the little wigwam where Marten lives with his grandmother. They call out greetings. *"Pjila'si,"* answers Muini'skw, and the children are invited in.

"Yes," says Muini'skw, "there is a strange woman recently come. Now she is living in the chief's wigwam."

"That is our mother," says the little girl. "But do not tell her so."

"Hmm," says Muini'skw, Old Bear Woman. "I cannot feed you. But go to the chief's wigwam. There you may get something to eat."

The chief's wife tells them to come in. This little girl, this little boy, they sit politely by the door, saying nothing. Their mother is there. She says nothing. She does not notice them. But after a while, she rises, takes down some lean meat from the drying rack, takes down some fat, and gives it to them.

"Take this," she says. "Go away and roast it."

The children take this meat and return to Muini'skw. They cook their food and share it, staying there with Muini'skw. They do not go back to their mother.

Up above, on the Earth World, Plawej has come home. He sees the door-post pulled up. He sees the children gone. He sees the hole that leads under the earth. *"E'e,"* says Plawej. "Yes."

Plawej washes himself. He sits by the hole. He cries himself into the earth until he passes from the surface of this world into the beautiful world. He walks toward the camp of the People.

Wijɨke'skw, Spruce Partridge Wife, she has Power. When she sees Plawej coming, she sets the dogs on him.

"Kill this stranger for me," she says to her husband and his men. "Slay him and I will skin him. I will use his hide as my door-blanket."

The men of the People killed Plawej. The woman Wijɨke'skw flayed him and stretched his skin on a frame, to use as a door-blanket. But now the People by the river are feeling something wrong. The animals are turning their backs to the hunters. The birds are leaving.

"It is those two strange children, in the wigwam of Muini'skw," says Wijɨke'skw, their mother. "It is those two strange children who are doing this. I have seen such before, in another camp, in another time before. Two strange children came out of the forest. The people fed them, but these chidren had Power. They were *mn'tu'k,* Spirit Persons. They made the animals disappear. They made the birds fly away. They made the fish hide from the People."

The People looked at the wigwam of Muini'skw, with the two strange children in it. "What should we do?" they said to Wijɨke'skw.

"Catch these children," she said. "Take them by the heels. Tie them together and hang them from a tree. Do not kill them. Tie them up, and we will leave this place."

"E'e" said the People. "We must leave. We must find a place where there are lots of stars. We must find a place where the night is bright. We must find a place where there are lots of caribou and different kinds of meat."

They tie the children together by the heels, they bend down a tree and lash them to it. Then the tree springs upright again, with the children hanging from it high in the air, and the People prepare to leave. "Let no one throw away any food that those children might find and eat," says Wijɨke'skw, their mother, Spruce Partridge Wife. "Let no one leave them fire."

But Muini'skw has lighted a piece of touchwood. She holds it in flame until it glows red all over. She hides it to burn secretly, deep under the sand of her fire-pit. Little Marten watches her. When all the hunters are moving off, when all the women and children are moving off, he asks his grandmother Muini'skw to let him save the children.

"Can you gnaw through the straps that bind them to this tree?" asks Muini'skw, Old Bear Woman. She throws an old moccasin to Marten, and he bites it through.

"*E'e,*" says Muini'skw. "Yes. Good. Go."

"Hurry up," calls the chief's wife to Muini'skw. "You will fall behind."

Muini'skw says, "I must mend these moccasins for Marten. They are poor and rotten."

Little Marten digs out the touchwood. It still smolders. He makes fire. He makes fire all around the tree in which the children are hanging. And when the tree is burnt through and ready to fall, he makes a big pile of moose hair, a soft pile of moose hair, for them to fall into. Now that he has them down out of the tree, Little Marten begins to gnaw. He chews, he gnaws on their ropes with his teeth, until he has set them free. Then he runs to catch up with the People. No one must know the children are alive.

"Remember us," calls the small boy. "Pity us: when the heavy snows fall in winter, sweep them away from the wigwam door, and we shall benefit."

Now this little boy takes his name: he is Wsitiplaju, Hung Up By The Heels.

The People are travelling deeper into the forest. The chief's wife is feeling something wrong. "Where is Muini'skw?" she asks. "Why are we still waiting for her? Go and find her; she is acting strangely." Muini'skw and Little Marten are coming up the trail behind the People.

"What have you been doing?" they ask her.

"Oh," says Muini'skw, "Marten has such bad moccasins, I have to stop and mend them now and then." The People from the camp by the river kept walking away, away into the forest. They walked for three days, and then they set up camp again. They put up the wigwams, they are lighting the fires. But still they are feeling that something is wrong. No animals are coming to be taken by the hunters. Again they begin to suffer. *Kewisultijik.* They suffer from hunger.

Wijike'skw has Power. She will not speak of how the something-feeling-wrong is coming from her own self. She says it is

29

the fault of those two strange children. "See," she says. "I told you of their doings."

In the empty camp by the river, the two children are living, the little brother and sister, the children of Wijike'skw. They have the fire that Muini'skw left for them. They have the scraps of things left behind. The little girl takes moose sinew. She makes a snare for her brother to use. First he catches mice. The girl skins them. She cleans them. She roasts them for food. She makes their skins into a robe for her brother, Wsitiplaju.

Wsitiplaju has Power. He takes a mouse skin, he wraps it around his arrow. He shoots the arrow into the rising sun three days' journey, and it strikes the ground inside the doorway of the wigwam of Muini'skw.

"E'e," said Muini'skw. "Those children are alive. I am greatly pleased."

Wsitiplaju has Power. He calls the rabbits, and they come into the wigwam to be killed. The girl skins them. She cleans them. She roasts them for food. She makes their skins into clothing for the winter. She makes a better robe for her brother, Wsitiplaju.

Wsitiplaju has Power. He takes a rabbit skin, he wraps it around his arrow. He shoots it into the rising sun three days' journey, and it strikes the ground inside the doorway of the wigwam of Muini'skw.

"E'e," said Muini'skw. "These children are alive. I am greatly pleased."

Wsitiplaju has Power. He speaks to the beaver and they come out of their lodges to be killed. He shoots an arrow wrapped with fat beaver meat, three days' journey into the doorway of the wigwam of Muini'skw.

▲

Winter is coming. They are melting snow in birchbark dishes, melting snow to have water to drink.

Wsitiplaju has Power. He speaks to Keswalqw, the Hollowed-Out-Moon, the New Moon. He asks the Moon to shape him in the night, to grow him into a man. To grow him in strength, even as the Moon grows.

It is evening. Wsitiplaju drags two logs of wood into the wigwam. He drags in two logs: they are the size and height of a man.

"Nmi's," he says. "My older sister, when I lie down tonight and I am asleep, you must stand these logs up: one at my head, one at my feet. When morning comes, I will get up and make the fire. Do not look. Do not open your eyes.

30

When you hear me say to you, '*Nmi's*, the fire is all out,' do not worry. Lie still. Wait. After you have waited, then you may get up."

The morning comes, the sun comes. The boy is as tall as a man: he is a man. He is Wsitɪplaju. The little girl is glad. The daylight goes, the sun goes beneath the earth. The girl lies down, and her brother places one log at her head, one log at her feet. He speaks to the Moon for her. In the morning she has grown up, *staqe e'pite's*, like a young woman.

Now Wsitɪplaju makes himself weapons: killing weapons, man's weapons. A bow he makes, a spear he makes, and arrows with stone heads.

He makes his weapons, and he says to his sister, "*Nmi's, sapo'nuk eksitpu'nuk attukuliann, a'qatikiskɪk pkisintes, tlia'tlimulann, tuie; mukk tuiew.* My older sister, tomorrow early in the morning, when I go out to hunt and return at midday, although I shall say to you, 'Come out,' do not come out. I will call you three times. Then you may come out."

Day comes. Wsitɪplaju gets up early, and goes to hunt. At midday, *a'qatikiskɪk,* he returns.

His sister hears a noise. It is a great noise outside the wigwam, a noise of trampling, a noise of shouting. Wsitɪplaju is calling, "*Nmi's, tuie apoqnmui!* My older sister, come out and help me!"

She waits in the wigwam. She does what Wsitɪplaju has told her to do. She waits until he calls three times before she goes out to him. Wsitɪplaju calls once. He calls twice. He calls three times as loud as he can: "Come out and help me!" Then all is quiet, and still she has waited a long time. Finally she puts her hand to the door-blanket, and pulls it open.

Wsitɪplaju stands before her. His legs are astride a dead animal. The Boy Who Was Made A Man By The Moon is red. Blood covers him. He is red with it. It is the blood of moose. It is the blood of caribou.

Wsitɪplaju has Power. He has driven the moose and the caribou to his wigwam, and killed them before his door. No one will have to fetch the meat home. *Welta'sit e'pite's:* the girl is much pleased.

Now they are both working, skinning the animals, butchering, slicing the meat to dry it on the drying racks inside the wigwam, freezing it in caches outside. The girl cuts up the meat. She crushes the bones and makes a good supply of rich red marrow. She crushes the bones and boils them for *qamu*, their fat. She scoops the fat off the top of the water and lets it harden into little cakes. They will have food for the whole winter.

The earth is quiet and white under the snow. Every day Wsitiplaju goes out to hunt.

The earth is white and quiet under the snow. And every day the sister of Wsitiplaju must go out of the wigwam and make a journey of her own. She must walk a long distance from their camp. Something is calling her.

Every day that girl takes tallow, she pours it through her hair; it is stiffening in the cold. The Girl Who Was Made A Woman By The Moon is white. Tallow covers her. She is white with it. Her hair hangs a great white robe all down her shoulders, *mimey qamuey.*

Every day she must journey to a lake, a lake long and white under the ice. Someone is compelling her there. Now she is sitting on the boulders at the lake's edge. She looks out over the white ice, and sees her lover coming to her.

He is Muin Wapskw. He is the Person who is the Great White Bear: he has Power. His Power has called her, and she must answer it.

Very quietly she goes to him. Very quietly he licks the tallow from her hair. When he has finished, she returns to her camp.

She does not tell her brother.

Three days' journey away, in the camp of the People, hunger is all they have to cook and eat. Little Marten and Muini'skw must have food.

Wsitiplaju takes an arrow. He wraps it with moose meat and with fat, and he shoots it three days' journey, so that it falls before the wigwam of Muini'skw. Old Bear Woman hears the noise as it lands, and sends Little Marten out to see.

"It is meat," he says, coming in with it. "It is fat. Our friends have remembered us." Muini'skw is quick to cook it.

Now in the camps of the People, heads raise as the smell of cooking meat drifts along the smoke from the wigwam of Muini'skw.

"Where did she get meat?" they wonder.

Little Marten says they are boiling old leather.

In this camp lives Ka'qaquj, Old Woman Crow. Ka'qaquj is clever. She thinks she will fly back to the old camp on the river. The bodies of those little Partridge children will be hanging from the tree. She is wanting to eat them.

When she gets over the river, Ka'qaquj sees smoke! It comes from the old wigwam of Muini'skw. Huge piles of

32

meat lie on the drying racks. Those children are alive!

She does not greet them, she does not ask them, she lands on the pile of meat and begins to eat.

The Girl Who Was Made A Woman By The Moon came out of her wigwam. She saw Ka'qaquj.

"My brother," she called. *"Mijisit ka'qaquj kwijmuk.* A crow is eating outside here."

"My sister," says Wsitiplaju, *"piskwa'j.* Let her come in."

So Ka'qaquj is invited into the wigwam. The girl feeds Old Crow Woman. Then she begins winding entrails around her shoulders, *msuksi,* entrails turned inside out, so the good fat fills them up like sausages. Ka'qaquj can fly home with food.

"Ka'qaquj," says the girl, "here is food. Here is fat. Take it to your children. But no one must know where this fat comes from. You must gather mushrooms. You must cook mushrooms. You must say, 'I am only cooking mushrooms,' when the smell drifts like smoke over the heads of the People in your camp."

Ka'qaquj promises. She goes home. She picks mushrooms, and while they are cooking, she feeds her children meat and fat. The meat smell floats past the noses of the People. The fat smell drifts past the noses of the People.

"Where did she get meat?" they wonder.

The People sent a little girl to visit Ka'qaquj. "See what she is cooking." But the little girl sees only mushrooms.

Wsitiplaju is also feeding Muini'skw and Little Marten. He shoots his arrows full of meat and fat to them. He shoots into the rising sun, three days' journey. The arrows land before the wigwam of Muini'skw.

"E'e," says Muini'skw. "These children are alive. I am greatly pleased."

Wsitiplaju has Power. He hunts every day. There is always food in the wigwam. But he notices that the supply of tallow, the white tallow cakes, this is getting smaller and smaller every day.

"My sister," he says, "what is happening to the tallow?"

She cannot tell him. "My brother," she answers, "I am eating it." Wsitiplaju can smell the Power of something feeling wrong.

Day comes. The sun comes. Wsitiplaju goes out to hunt, and in his hunting he climbs to the top of a very high hill. This hill looks down on a lake, a long lake, white with ice. He sees his sister, walking slow and slow with her long hair white with tallow. He sees the Person who is Great White Bear.

33

"E'e," says Wsitiplaju. He watches. When the Bear is finished, his sister returns home.

Now it is evening; the sun has gone beneath the earth. Wsitiplaju pulls back the door-blanket and enters his wigwam.

"Nmi's," he says. "My sister. *Tala'teket net muin?* What is this bear about? Why do you allow him to lick your head?"

Now his sister can talk to him: "If I did not go to him, he would kill us both."

"Well, then," says Wsitiplaju, "Tomorrow I will go out with you, and we will see how it will be."

Day comes. The sun comes. Wsitiplaju gets tallow and melts it. He pours it over his sister's hair until it dries, stiff and white, a robe to cover her. Wsitiplaju takes his bow; he takes his stone-tipped arrows. Then they are walking, this brother and sister, walking toward the lake.

"Sit here, my sister," says Wsitiplaju, "here, where I can shoot into his heart. Sit, and I will hide."

Muin Wapskw is coming, White Bear Person. He does not see Wsitiplaju. He only sees the girl all white with tallow. He comes to her. He bends his tongue to lick her hair.

Ssssssss. An arrow strikes his heart.

But the Great White Bear does not die. He does not die when five arrows strike his heart. He looks at Wsitiplaju. Then he speaks.

"Do not shoot my body." His voice comes cold on the wind. "Wait until I lift my paw. Shoot the underside of it."

Wsitiplaju nocks his sixth arrow. He fires.

"Feed your enemies on my flesh," says the cold, cold voice of the Great White Bear. Slowly, slowly, he falls, he crashes down.

The ice cracks and groans under his body; a cloud of snow drifts up and then falls again. Muin Wapskw lies white and quiet under it. Wsitiplaju flays him. He cuts off his white fur, then he butchers him, Muin Wapskw, Great White Bear. They drag the pieces back to the wigwam, and there the girl cuts up the meat in strips, and hangs them up to dry, to smoke and to cure.

Three days' journey away, hunger is still strong in the camp of the People. Wsitiplaju sends arrows to feed Muini'skw and Little Marten, little Apistanew'j.

Wijike'skw is proud. She never goes to visit Muini'skw, Old Bear Woman. But now she smells meat cooking. Running up, she says, "Give me a piece. Where did you get that meat?"

Muini'skw looked at her. "I got this meat," she says, "from your children whom you left behind."

Wijike'skw says nothing.

But still Ka'qaquj is going every day, flapping her wings, going to the river, going to the old camp, going to the children who were left behind: taking meat and flying home with it. *Netuksiktmat.*

The People can smell it. "Wonder where she got that meat?" they keep asking, and one day, while she is cooking, they cannot bear it any longer. They burst into her wigwam and catch her. They catch her eating meat. They catch her eating fat.

Ka'qaquj flies up and crows: "Ka'! Ka'! Ka'! *Wsitiplajukik westa'sni'k!* Those two children you hanged on a tree are alive and safe!"

The People are amazed. *"Taluet?"* they ask. *"What* did she say?"

Ka'qaquj flies away. Those who have heard her explain it to the rest.

"There must be meat there," say the People. "There must be fat there. Let us return to our camp on the river."

So the People came back to the river. It was evening; the sun had gone beneath the earth. The camp was dark, but there is smoke coming out of the old wigwam of Muini'skw and Apistane'wj. Old Bear Woman and Little Marten call out greetings and enter. Wsitiplaju and his sister made them very welcome. *"Pjila'si,"* they both say. "Come up to the seat at the back of the wigwam."

Now Wijike'skw, Spruce Partridge Wife, she comes in too. They do not notice her. They do not ask her to sit down. They do not give her food. "I am your mother," says Wijike'skw. "I am your mother." She pulls open her robe to remind them that she has fed them from her breast. "I am your mother, I fed you."

'Yes,' they think in their hearts. 'And afterwards, you would have killed us if you could.' So they say nothing. Wijike'skw leaves them. She returns to her own wigwam.

Now Wsitiplaju, who was hung up by his heels: Wsitiplaju, the Boy Who Was Made A Man By The Moon: Wsitiplaju says to his sister, "Take some food around to the People."

Now the girl who was hung up by her heels, the Girl Who Was Made A Woman By The Moon, she does this. She takes down the Bear's meat, the flesh of Great White Bear, lean and fat she takes it down and sends it around to all the families of the People.

Inside the wigwam of Wsitɨplaju, Muini'skw and Little Marten are eating meat and fat. The girl cuts caribou meat and roasts it by the fire for them. She cuts moose meat and roasts it by the fire for them. She brings them fat to drink. They all eat and eat until they are so full they must spend the night going in and out of the wigwam.

Outside, all night long, in the camp of the People, everyone is gorging themselves on the flesh of the Great White Bear. The flesh works in them. After a while they begin to cry: "Akaia," cry the People of the camp by the river. "Akaia, akaia," cries Wijɨke'skw who left her children tied by the heels. "Akaia," cry the People who hanged the children on the tree. Their eyes are staring. Their mouths are open. In the morning, they all lie dead.

Wsitɨplaju and his sister are ready to leave the camp of the People by the river.

Muini'skw and Little Marten are staying behind in their old wigwam. Wsitɨplaju promises to hunt for them, to send them food. They will live and eat well.

▲

Wsitɨplaju and the Girl Who Was Made A Woman By The Moon walk into the forest. Now it is evening; the sun has gone beneath the earth. *Wela'kw ketkunijik:* they stop for the night. In the morning, early, they journey on.

It is the end of the second day; the sun has gone beneath the earth. Wsitɨplaju and his sister come out of the forest to the sea.

Here they will stay. Wsitɨplaju builds a big wigwam. Every day he goes into the forest to hunt. Wsitɨplaju has Power. He drives the moose to his door for butchering; he drives the caribou to his door for butchering. His sister cuts the meat into strips and dries it for them to eat.

Here by the sea, there is another camp of the People. And now their hunters cannot not find any moose; they cannot find caribou. Someone has been there before them! They can feel him. They can feel the moose being gone. "What shall we do?" they ask each other. Six young men set out to trail this Thing Which Has Taken The Moose Away, this Person who has disturbed their forest, this trespasser: they

36

will find him. And so they come to the wigwam of Wsitiplaju.

They call out greetings and go in. Wsitiplaju entertains them; he treats them well. His sister feeds them meat and fat. Now it is night, but the six young men will not stay. "We will return the next day," they say. "We will come back, we will return."

Back at their own camp, the six young men make report to the Elders. "It is Wsitiplaju," they say. "He has Power. He is taking the moose, he is killing the caribou. What then must we do?"

Now the old *puoin*, the Shaman, he is talking to them. "This is Wsitiplaju," the old one says. "He has Power. You will not be able to kill him, you will not able to capture him. We must trick him. Power must fight Power, and then, perhaps, he may be confined. We will bind him to a tree with the *jipijka'm wsmu'l:* the horn of Great Serpent Person."

"*E'e,*" said the men of the camp of the People by the sea. "Let us do that."

Now it is midday. The sun is high in the sky. The six young men went back to the wigwam of Wsitiplaju. They feasted, they ate meat, they drank oil. And when they had eaten, they sat with Wsitiplaju and smoked and talked.

Each of the young men takes out two horns from his own medicine pouch. They are talking, talking, and each young man has two horns in his hands: one red horn, one yellow horn. As they talk, they carefully place a horn in their hair, one on each side: one yellow horn, one red horn. Then, talking, friendly, they offer horns to Wsitiplaju.

The Girl Who Was Made A Woman By The Moon has been cooking meat and bringing food. Now she is feeling something wrong. She speaks to her brother, she warns him: "Do not touch them, the red horn, the yellow horn. Your death lies in these horns."

But Wsitiplaju is caught in the Power of the horns. He whispers, whispers to his sister: "*Nmi's,* my sister, *ejela'tu.* I cannot help it. *Ta'n tela'taqati'tij nikmaq, miamuj tela'tekey.* What my comrades do, I am surely doing."

Wsitiplaju places a *jipijka'm* horn in his hair.

He cannot take it out. The horn roots into him; it roots into his head, and then the horn tip begins to grow. Up, up it grows, piercing through the wigwam; out, out it grows until it finds a tree. Then this horn, *jipijka'm* horn, it winds around and around that tree tighter than any vine tendril, and it has Wsitiplaju caught fast.

37

The six young men exult. They have overcome Wsitiplaju, and they leave his wigwam.

The Girl Who Was Made A Woman By The Moon bursts into tears.

"Akaia, akaia, njiknam, ne'pa'ski'k: my younger brother, they have killed you!" Frantically she tries to set him free.

First she takes a knife, *waqan,* she tries to cut him free. But the knife is not leaving even a scratch on this horn, *jipijka'm* horn. She takes a stone to cut the horn; she cannot scratch it, she cannot cut him free. At last she tries a clam shell.

E'e, this clam shell is making a scratch, a little tiny scratch on *jipijka'm* horn. She saws and saws until she wears the clam shell out, and then she picks up another. Then another and another shell, sawing on *jipijka'm* horn.

Now she has used all the shells which lie on the beach at the edge of the sea where sits the wigwam of Wsitiplaju. Every morning she must travel far out on the point, *kwiewey,* gathering clam shells to cut the horn from Wsitiplaju. She fills her robe, she takes them home, she saws on the horn which binds her brother to a tree. And when these shells are all used up, she returns to the point for more.

This day it is very hot. The Girl Who Was Made A Woman By The Moon is walking out on that point of land, gathering shells, and she sees a rock out in the water. She wades out to it, through the water. Up there on that rock she loosens her hair. She is combing it up there in the wind, on that rock in the sea. The day is hot; she lies down on her hair and sleeps.

Something is coming toward her. Someone is coming to take her. It is Wipitimu'k in his canoe.

Wipitimu'k, Killer Whale Person, The One With Teeth, Long-Tail, Wipitimu'k.

Slowly, slowly, he slides his paddle beneath her. Slowly, slowly, he lifts her up off that rock. Still she is sleeping, and he lays her down gently in the bottom of his canoe.

When she wakes they are far out to sea.

Wipitimu'k speaks to her gently. "You need not cry. I am going to treat you well at home. I have a good mother. I have good sisters."

It was evening when they came to the island. Wipitimu'k beaches his canoe. There is a large wigwam on the shore, and sitting in front of it are his father and his sister.

"Welcome," says the father of Wipitimu'k. "Welcome, *ntlu'sue'skw,* my son's wife."

38

And so the daughter of Spruce Partridge Wife, this Girl Who Was Made A Woman By The Moon, she is caught. She is the wife of Wipitimu'k, Killer Whale Person. And she bears him a son. For two years she stays with him, but every day she goes down to the seaside and gazes over the sea. She is looking across the sea to where her brother lies, imprisoned by *jipijka'm* horn, held fast to the tree which rises above their wigwam.

The sister of Wipitimu'k is curious. "Why do you weep when you look out to sea?"

At first the wife of Wipitimu'k will not tell her.

"Why are you weeping?" her husband's sister continues to ask her, and one day, down by the sea, the Girl Who Was Made A Woman By The Moon tells her of her own brother.

"He has the Power. He is Wsitiplaju. But they trapped him, and I cannot get back to him to cut the horn from his head."

"Ah," said her husband's sister. "But *could* you cut the horn from his head before?"

"I was using clam shells. I cut a little thin line."

"Ah," said her husband's sister. "I can help you. I know how to get that horn off."

"My brother has no wife," says Wsitiplaju's sister to the sister of Wipitimu'k. "He is a good hunter. He has Power. But he has no sons."

The sister of Wipitimu'k smiled. "It is red ochre," she said. "The circle of red must be made around this horn. Then it will come off. *Weukuju.* Red ochre. It is hard to get. It comes from a far-off place. We will have to be very clever."

The little son of Wipitimu'k, the son of his wife whom he took from the rock in the sea, this little son was just beginning to talk. His father gave him everything he asked for. His father gave him his heart; he would do anything to please him.

Now this little boy's mother and his father's sister are sitting with him. They make him See something. It is red. It is beautiful. He wants it.

"*Weukuju,*" says his mother. "That is *weukuju,* the red ochre."

He wants it.

"It is not here," says his father's sister. "It is far away."

All day long the little boy cries for this beautiful red thing. "*Weukuju, Weukuju! Weukujuuuu....*" He is crying for it when his father comes home from fishing.

The father wonders what is wrong. Why does his son cry

so? Wipitimu'k speaks to his wife: *"Tala'teket mijua'ji'j teltemit?* What is the matter with my baby, that he cries so?" "He is crying for some red ochre," says the Girl Who Was Made A Woman By The Moon.

Wipitimu'k picks up his little son. "Stop your crying," he says. "I will bring you some *weukuju* tomorrow."

The baby likes the red ochre; he plays with it. But then his mother and his father's sister show him something: they show him the red cloud in the western sky, the red cloud at sunset. And when his father comes home from fishing, his son is crying for it.

"What is the matter with my baby, that he cries so?"

"He is crying for a piece of that cloud, the little red cloud in the sky at sunset."

"Ah," says Wipitimu'k, "that will be more difficult. But do not cry; I will go get you some of it early in the morning."

Wipitimu'k and his father are going to get the red cloud. They start early in the morning, as soon as it is past midnight. It is a long distance to that red cloud.

As soon as their canoe can no longer be seen, the two women get into the other canoe. They are paddling fast in the other direction; they are paddling long and hard. The baby lies sleeping in the bottom of the canoe.

They are paddling long and hard, and at last they see the land, rising like a bow in front of them. But something is coming. Something is coming from behind. It is Wipitimu'k and his father, swimming after them. Wipitimu'k has Power; he comes very fast in his Killer Whale shape.

They paddle faster, faster. *E'e,* the next time that Killer Whale comes up to breathe they can see from his spouting that he is much closer. *Aji-kikjiw, aji-kikjiw:* he is much nearer, he is much closer. He breaches, rising up out of the water; he is almost upon them.

The Girl Who Was Made A Woman By The Moon takes her baby's clothes, she takes them and flings them overboard: his moccasins she flings over, his little robe and leggings.

Wipitimu'k sees them fall and sink. He must stop to gather them up. He swims round them again and again, weeping bitterly, then he leaps through the water, chasing after the canoe. He calls out, he cries out, he is almost upon them.

40

The Girl Who Was Made
A Woman By The Moon takes
her child's cradleboard, the *atke-
naqn;* she takes his cradle wraps,
his *kopesunul,* she flings them over
the side. Wipitimu'k comes up to them
as they sink in the water. He swims round
and round them; the old whale too swims
round and round them, uttering cries and wail-
ing for his grandson. Now the canoe with the son
of Wipitimu'k, the canoe with his wife, the canoe
with his sister, it is about to touch land. Wipitimu'k
swims like an arrow shot, he swims like a spear cast, he
leaps at that canoe. Just as it touches the earth, his teeth
catch the stern. He seizes it. But the women with the child
have leaped ashore.

Wipitimu'k crushes the canoe; he breaks it with his
teeth, but he cannot come on land to take the two women
back.

"Come home to me, my wife!" He calls her with all the
Power of his voice. "Come into the sea to me." But she is on
her own land now, and she will not go.

"I never loved you," she said. "And I will not come."

"Give me back my son," cries Wipitimu'k in a frenzy.
"Give him back to me!"

"He is my child," says the woman he took from the rock
in the sea. And she walks away.

Her brother's wife follows her; she does not listen to the
voices of the two Killer Whales calling her. Those two
women left that place where the land sticks out into the sea,
and they went to the wigwam of Wsitiplaju.

The sister of Wsitiplaju says to the one who will be her
brother's wife, "*Nilmus, Wmaqtaml,* do not go in to my
brother. Make a fire here, and warm the baby. He is cold.
Let me go to my brother first." She walks toward the
wigwam.

Inside is Wsitiplaju, hanging from the horn which rises
through the smokehole and fastens around the tree above.
He is still alive; there had been plenty to eat in that
wigwam. He is still alive; Wsitiplaju has Power. But he and
the wigwam are covered with filth.

"My younger brother," says his sister, going to him. "I
have brought you something. I have brought *weukuj,* the
blood-red ochre. I am going to cut you loose."

The Girl Who Was Made A Woman By The Moon opens
her pouch. She takes out the red ochre and she is making

41

a circle around that *jipijka'm* horn. She makes the red circle around it, and instantly it snaps. It snaps right off his head, and Wsitɨplaju is free.

Wsitɨplaju has Power. But now he is so weak he can hardly stand. His body is covered with filth. His sister helps him into the sea and bathes him. His strength is coming back, it is coming back fast. His sister gives him new clothes, and then she tells him: "Someone is here. Come up to the fire."

Wsitɨplaju sees the sister of Killer Whale, the sister of Wipitimu'k, and he wants her for a wife.

"Will you stay with me?" he asks.

"I will stay with you forever," says Killer Whale Woman, "if you can keep me away from the shore. You must take me into the forest. You must never again let me see the ocean. If you do this, *mu la'liwn wkta'nuk, mu la'liwn sitmuk,* although it be for thirty years, so long will I be your wife: *tlia' nesinskekipunqek teli pkiji-wikmatitesnu.*"

"Very well," said Wsitɨplaju, "I will do so."

So'qa'tijik; na so'quita'jik. Now then, they go from the shore even deeper into the forest.

Now they are living in the forest. Wsitɨplaju hunts as before; he drives the animals up to the wigwam to kill them. The women slice up the meat and hang it to dry. And Killer Whale Woman gives a son to Wsitɨplaju.

The son of the Boy Who Was Made A Man By The Moon, and the son of the Girl Who Was Made A Woman By The Moon, they are growing up together. One day these two boys are playing together.

"I have a father," says the young Killer Whale to the son of Wsitɨplaju. "I have a father just like you do. He is living in the sea. *Ni'n nutj apaqtuk eyk.* My father is out on the ocean. *Ki'l kutj kiknaq.* Your father is here, in the wigwam."

The son of Wipitimu'k remembers his father. He remembers him, and one day, when Wsitɨplaju and his family are moving camp, travelling through the forest, a great storm comes.

The rain is drowning them, the fog is tricking them, the noise of the wind is fooling Wsitɨplaju. He has Power, but he is lost in this great fog, this terrible storm. At last he speaks to the women.

"We will stop here. Build a shelter, and let us see if we can light a fire. Let us see if we can sleep out this storm."

So they make camp, they eat, and then they lie down to sleep.

42

In the morning, it is Killer Whale Woman who wakes
first. The wife of Wsitiplaju wakes first, and she stands up,
she makes her way to the door, and she goes outside.
What does she see?
It is the ocean, it is the waves beating on the shore, it is
wind and the smell of salt. The Power of Killer Whale
Woman comes up in her. The sea calls to her and she must
answer it. Her marriage promise no longer holds her, for
Wsitiplaju has brought her to the shore.
Quietly she goes into the wigwam. Quietly, quietly she
wakes her son and her nephew, and takes them outside.
There is the sea.
"We are Killer Whale Persons," says the woman to the
children. "We are the Killer Whales, and we must return to
the sea. *Mtoqitaiek.*" And then she plunges into the waves.
The children follow her.
Wsitiplaju awakens. It is dark inside the wigwam. It is
quiet. Wsitiplaju has Power. He senses something feeling
wrong. His wife is gone. His son is gone. His sister's son is
gone.
"Wake up," he says. "The children are gone. My woman
is gone." And so speaking, he runs outside. He runs down
to the shore; his sister runs after him.
Out to sea, swimming in the water, they see those three:
those three Whales, leaping and spouting, going away from
Wsitiplaju and the sister of Wsitiplaju.
Wsitiplaju screams. He cries out to them: "Come back!
My wife, come back to me. Come home to me, to live on land.
My son, bring your mother back! My little boys, come home
to me."
His Killer Whale son turns in the water to look at him.
"*Nu'*. Father. *Telimisk nkij, 'mukk la'liew sitmuk.'* My
mother said to you, 'You must not take me to the sea shore.'
You have not kept your word, and we are now going home.
My mother is returning to her mother, she is going to her
father. My cousin has a father of his own; he swims now to
meet him."
And the three Killer Whales moved off into the open sea.
Wsitiplaju gazes after them with longing; he has given
them his heart. "*Akaia,*" mourns Wsitiplaju. And as he
grieves, he sees Wipitimu'k surface, spouting, far out to
sea. He sees the son of Wipitimu'k surface by his father's
side. And he watches them as they swim off together,
toward their distant home.

THE MAN WHO MARRIED
JIPIJKA'MI'SKW

In the time when the Old Ones are alive, two brothers go out hunting together.

They are in the forest, tracking game, when they see a thing. It is a deep cut in the surface of the earth, a long cut like a trench. Something has worn the earth away like this, passing back and forth through the forest.

One of these men lies down in this trench. He wants to see how big the strange thing is that has made this groove in the ground. But this place is full of Power, it is the trail along which Jipijka'm travels.

Jipijka'm. Horned Serpent Person.

There is Power in this serpent track, and it begins to change the man. His body thickens and lengthens. He becomes strong and terrible, he is changing into a *jipijka'm* himself. And as he does so, he can smell the track. It is the track of a woman of the Horned Serpents, Jipijka'mi'skw.

Jipijka'mi'skw. Horned Serpent Woman. He begins to move in her track, moving in his serpent shape, following her smell down to the water. In his serpent shape he passes into the World Beneath The Water, and his brother cannot save him.

Underneath the water, he sees a wigwam. Inside it are an old man, an old woman, and a girl. They are Horned Serpents, and the girl is she whose smell he has been following.

The old woman speaks. "Come in, my daughter's husband," she says. And later, when the girl's brother returns, the old woman tells him, "Your sister's husband has only now just come in."

"All right," says her son. And their words make it so. This hunter stayed with the Horned Serpents as their daughter's husband.

But this man and his brother were of the People. And in their camp was a *puoin,* a shaman, a man whose Power was great. And this man's brother comes running to him. "In the forest," he says, "in the forest, we found the track of a Jipijkami'skw. And my brother lay in her track, and it began to change him. He changed, and he moved and he went on this trail until it went under the water."

"*E'e,*" says the shaman. "He has gone to her. And if he has slept with her under the same blanket, we cannot bring him back. But if he has not, then we can call him up to us again."

And he rises to go into the forest, to the place where this has happened. He digs a trench; he puts water in it. He puts Things of Power, medicine, he puts these in it, on top of the water. Then he climbs a tree, and as he climbs, he cuts off the branches below him.

There he waits, in the top of this tall tree, this Tree With No Branches.

Something is coming. Something is making a noise in the forest. It is a terrible noise; it is the noise of two Horned Serpent Persons, two *jipijka'maq.* One of them comes to the tree where the old *puoin* is sitting, and coils around and around it, sticking up his head in the middle of the coil.

"This is your brother," says the shaman to the second hunter, who is coming out from his place of hiding. "It is all right." But his brother cannot get near this Horned Serpent.

Now the shaman is coming down the tree trunk. He takes a wooden knife, and with it he cuts off the head of this Jipijka'm. Out of the Serpent's carcase he pulls the entire body of the lost hunter. The hunter's wife is crazy with happiness. She jumps, she shouts, she sings and begins to dance, because her husband is saved from those Horned Serpents.

Now the *puoin* gives medicine to the man taken from the Horned Serpents. It is powerful medicine, and it makes him vomit. His brother tells the People, "When I first tried to talk to him, he was making a noise like a *jipijka'm.* He could not speak properly."

If he had stayed with the Horned Serpents for another day in the world under the water, he would not have been able to come back. This is true. We know it because the Old Ones have passed it down to us.

THE WOMAN WHO
MARRIED JIPIJKA'M

In the old times, there was a family with a daughter who was very proud. She would not sit down where anyone else sat, and when she combed her hair and oiled it, when she bathed and painted her face, she would not do it with the others of the People, but by herself. When young men came to the wigwam, she would not talk with them. She refused to marry.

An old man says to her father, "You better be careful. Something is feeling wrong. Unless you make her marry the next boy who comes, some bad thing will happen."

Now this girl is going to the spring to get water. She takes the bark bucket with her, to carry home the water in. She kneels before the spring, and begins to dip out water. And there, deep in the water, she sees a man. He is very beautiful. And he sits under the water, cross-legged as any hunter sits who has killed his first moose, and with his arms folded across his chest.

The heart of this girl goes to him.

The man from under the water rises out of the spring. He smiles at her, and he carries home her bucket of water. When he comes into the wigwam, her mother greets him as "daughter's husband," and so the thing is done. This girl is wed.

And when the time comes that this girl has had a son, her husband says to her, "Come. Let us go to my home. My parents would like to see the baby."

All the People went with them to the lake. There this man from the world under the water tells his wife to remove the clothes from the baby. And there, before all the people, the three of them begin to change. Their bodies thicken and lengthen, lying upon the ground. They become Horned Serpent Persons, *jipijka'maq:* the man, the woman and the child.

46

"Goodbye, you of the People," calls the man as he changes. "Do not look to see us any more." Then he and his wife and child slide into the lake, into the world under the water.

The People never found that girl again.

This is what pride will do.

EARTH
WORLD

THE CHILD FROM BENEATH THE EARTH

Out in the forest, all by themselves, an old man and an old woman are living. There is a Noise that they are hearing. It is a sound of knocking, a sound like the birchbark drum makes. It is a sound like the beating of a heart.

"Where is this coming from?" asks the old woman.

They look everywhere, inside the wigwam and outside the wigwam. And after a while, they know. They know that this is a sound coming from under the ground.

The old man and his wife begin to dig. They dig away the ground, and there under the earth is a small boy. He has come to them from the World Beneath The Earth.

They take up this child and carry him home to the wigwam. The old woman washes the earth from his body; she makes him clothes. The old man goes out to hunt, to get something to feed the baby. And even though they are very poor and very old, and it is hard for them to hunt, they are very glad to be doing this for the little boy who has come to them from the World Beneath The Earth.

And after a while, it is good that they have fed him. He grows. He grows very fast. Soon he is helping. He hunts for them. He fishes for them.

One day it is almost winter. The boy says, "I will go out to fish."

He goes out to fish, and after a while, he returns. "I have caught a whale," he says. The old man and the old woman rush down to the shore to see this whale. There it is on the shore: it is a large pile of *mn'tmu'k,* oysters.

So they sit down, all three of them. The old man takes out his knife. The old woman takes out her knife. The child who has caught this whale takes out his knife, and they all have a feast. These are very big oysters.

All of a sudden the old woman stands up. The need to dance is filling her. She begins to move. She dances around

those oysters, those *mn'tmu'k,* back and forth, winding around and around them. She dances faster and faster. The dance is filling her with something; she has the Power in her. Power is filling her, and as it does, one of those oysters begins to change its shape.

This Mn'tm, Oyster Person, it begins to grow. It grows high. It grows wide. It fills the whole space of a whale, *nusknik ika'luj,* thirty widths of the elbows-placed-on measure. This oyster is shaping itself into a whale. The old woman's dance is calling it.

Now the whale is lying there before them, on the beach. The old man begins to butcher it. The old woman helps him. The boy who has come to them from the World Beneath The Earth helps him. For days they are slicing up and drying this whale meat, setting it to freeze in caches for the winter, hanging some of it to smoke above the wigwam fires. They eat whale blubber and rejoice. There is enough food for the whole winter.

Now it is winter. And the old woman dies. The old man washes her body. He wraps her in the birchbark shroud. He puts her knife in with her, and her dish. He gives her whale meat, so she will not be hungry.

"Come," he says to the boy who came out of the earth. They put the body on a toboggan, and they carry it to a place where it can rest until spring, when the ground is not frozen. They carry it to the place where the dead ones of this old man's band are always buried.

When spring comes, the old man goes back to visit his wife. He is going to bury her. But he wants to see her again. He pulls the bark sheet away from her face. He looks. He sees her once more, and he is happy. He begins to dance....

❀

LAMKISN

Long ago this is happening. An old woman and an old man are living in a wigwam. The old woman goes out to get pine bark for the fire. She is walking through the forest and she sees a long log of foxfire, a long log of *lamkisn*. And then she hears something.

"*Kwe, kwe, kwe!*" Something is crying. Something is making a noise. The old woman thinks it must be *skite'kmujk*. She thinks it must be ghosts. This noise is coming from that log of *lamkisn*.

But this old woman has Power. She goes and looks inside that log of *lamkisn*, and she finds a child. A boy child, *mijua'ji'j lpa'tu'ji'j*. She takes him out of that foxfire log, she wipes off all the moss, and she takes off the little moose-sinew string that has been tied around his neck to kill him.

This old woman puts that baby in the hood of her robe, the *kini'skwejkiktuk*, the pointed place, and then she takes him back to her wigwam.

"I have found a baby," she says to her husband. "I am going to keep him."

"*E'e,*" says the old man. "All right. What are we going to feed him?"

That old woman has Power. She knows what to do. "We will feed him on moose brains," she says. And the old man goes out to kill a moose for her, so that she can feed the baby.

She names this child Lamkisn, because she took him out of the *lamkisn* log. She feeds him on moose brains until he is a year old.

This old woman has Power. She is a *puoin*, a shaman. She is very strong. She can See ten days into tomorrow, she can See what is to happen. And when her son is two years old, she begins to make him strong, too. She begins to give him Power. She makes him one of the *puoinaq*.

This old woman takes a chipmunk and skins it. She stretches the skin and pounds it, pounds it to make it soft. And all the time she is doing this, she is speaking to it, she is singing to it: "Chipmunk, do all I tell you to do for my son Lamkisn. *Nkwis* Lamkisn. My son Lamkisn."

When it is done, she gives the skin to her son, her son Lamkisn. She says to the skin, "You must go ahead of him. You must always See ahead of him. And whatever you see, come back and report, so that he may know."

▲

Now the People of that band are going to war. They want to take Lamkisn with them, to cook for them, and to See for them. They want to travel in the heart of the country of their enemies. They want to go into the country of the Kwetej.

Every morning, when the sun has come from beneath the earth, the war chief speaks to Lamkisn. "Have you dreamed in the night? What have you seen? Have you dreamed any danger, anything ahead of us?"

And every morning, Lamkisn says no. There is no danger.

But now there comes a morning when he says, "Today we will know."

They travel on, all that morning. And when it is time to rest, the war chief says to Lamkisn, "I want you to find out what lies ahead."

"*E'e*," says Lamkisn. He has his medicine bag, his *puoinoti* with all the things in it that he will need. He takes out from it his chipmunk skin and he strokes it. He speaks to it, "I want you to go out now, go out ahead of us, and See. I want you to See what lies ahead, what dangers are before us. Go!"

And that chipmunk skin takes on its shape and runs. It runs ahead, it Sees into the tomorrows, and then it returns and crawls into the boy's robe. It crawls up on his shoulder and speaks into his ear.

"There is danger. This war chief will die. He will lose his head in two days' time."

And that same day, these men of the People reach the fighting place. It is a large mountain, levelled out on top. The war chief stops down below the mountain. He will not fight until the following day, the day that is yet to come.

But Lamkisn says, "I am going up on the mountain now. I am going to dance the War Medicine Dance, the *nskowaqn*. I will dance it on the top of this mountain."

Lamkisn goes up on the mountain and he dances. The whole time he is dancing that *nskowaqn,* that Power Dance, the Kwetej are shooting at him. But they cannot kill him. And when he comes down, his whole robe is filled with the lead musket shot which they have fired at him. They are sticking in his robe, but they have not gone into his skin. They have not gone into his body. He shakes them out.

Lamkisn says to the war chief, *"Nsi's,* my older brother, you must go now. It is your time to dance."

This war chief goes up on the mountain, and it is as the chipmunk skin has said. The Kwetej kill him, and cut off his head.

Lamkisn dreams. He tells his dream. "They are coming," he says. "They are circling around us from behind. And they are wearing caribou feet, so that we may not spot their tracks."

"They are coming now," says Lamkisn, "but they will not see us."

Those Kwetej passed all around the war-band of the People, but they could not see them. And as they passed them, they lost all their caribou feet.

Lamkisn and the men of the People got those caribou feet, and now that they have them, they can go wherever they want.

And *kespi-a'tuksitkik,* that is as far as it is told about them.

MIMKÍTAWO'QU'SK

Away in the forest a young girl is living all alone. She had no family, she has no kin-friends. She must do everything for herself, and her life is very hard. She gets her own wood and water, she hunts for herself, she prepares her own food and makes her clothing. And this young girl is often very lonely and sad.

One day this girl is out gathering wood for the fire. She cuts a stick to make a *nu'se'kn*, a stick for poking up the fire. She cuts it from moosewood, from *mimkitawo'q,* and she carries it home with the rest of her wood. She sticks it into the ground outside her wigwam and leaves it standing up out there. And then she goes into the wigwam to eat and fall asleep. For it is evening; the sun is going beneath the earth.

Deep in the night, she hears a sound. It is the sound of a human voice, complaining about the cold.

"Nmi's," says this Voice, "my older sister, I am cold. *Kewji.* I am cold."

"Come in and warm yourself then," says the girl to the Voice.

"I cannot come in. I am naked. I have no clothes to wear."

This girl gathers up fur robes. "I will give you some," she says, and she puts the clothes outside the door-blanket.

And now the Person Who Has Been Speaking comes into her wigwam. She sees him. It is a man, a tall strong man, and he seats himself in the seat of a younger brother. *"Nmi's,"* he says to her. "My older sister."

He is the *nu'se'kn* which she has left outside the door. The moosewood stick has become a man. He is Mimkítawo'qu'sk, Moosewood Person. And he lives with her and hunts for her. He is a very good hunter, and her life becomes much easier. She no longer has to work so hard.

Yet this young girl is still lonely. She is still sad. Her younger brother is often away hunting, and she has no one

to talk with. So after a while, she speaks to him about this. "I am lonely," she says. "I am lonely when you are away. I wish for you to marry, so that I may have a sister to stay with me, to be my company, when you are out hunting."

"*E'e*," says her brother. "I will do this for you."

His older sister tells him which way to go, to find another camp of the People. She tells him of the dangers which he will encounter between this camp and that one.

"There are nests of Serpent Persons," she says. "Do not try to fight them. Do not try to overcome them or meddle with them. Take your bow and use it like a pole. Use it like a pole to jump over their nests."

Now the sun has come from beneath the earth, and this man is setting out on his journey to find a wife. And after a time, his sister is feeling such a lonely feeling, that she determines to follow him. She sets out as well, going after him. But in order to show him that it is she who follows him, and not some enemy or other thing, she begins to sing.

Her Power comes up in her, and she sings to him. And all that distance away, he can hear her.

He speaks: "*Moqwe, nmi's*," he says to her. "My older sister, do not follow me. You must remain in the camp and wait."

"Very well," she sings to him. "I will go home and wait for you to bring me a sister."

He goes on a long journey, and he does as his sister has told him. He jumps over the snake nests and escapes them. And finally he comes to a large camp of the People. There is a wigwam there, on the edge of the camp. It is a poor small wigwam, but this is the one into which he goes.

Inside are sitting an old man and an old woman, with all their daughters. All these daughters are beautiful, but the youngest is the best. And so Mimkitawo'qu'sk takes his seat by her side. She stays sitting by him. She does not get up and move away. Her parents stay silent. They do not ask him to leave. And so it is done. They are married. Mimkitawo'qu'sk has found a wife. "*Nmi's*," he says, "I have found a sister for you."

Mimkitawo'qu'sk is a strong man, a tall man, a beautiful man. This family likes the way he appears. But the other young men of this camp of the People do not like him. He has gotten the most beautiful of their women, a woman who would not look at them. They are jealous. They decide to kill him.

They decide to kill him, but they will wait for the wedding feast. They will kill him then, in a contest of strength.

58

Now that girl's father speaks to Mimkɨtawo'qu'sk. He
tells him to hunt food for the wedding feast. All the People
will eat his kills. They will see his successes as a hunter.
They will recognize the marriage.

So Mimkɨtawo'qu'sk takes his wife. He takes the canoe
belonging to his wife's father, and he goes up the river to the
best hunting grounds. He and his wife build a little shelter
to live in, and he begins to hunt.

Mimkɨtawo'qu'sk has Power. He is a great hunter. And
soon he has killed many beasts. He has meat to eat. He has
fat and marrow to feed the People at his wedding feast. He
has furs to give his wife's father. So he and his wife prepare
to return to the camp of the People further down the river.

But the young men of this camp have other plans. Some
of them are *puoinaq*. Some of them are Shape-Changers.
They come up the river, and prepare to move against
Mimkɨtawo'qu'sk. They cannot attack him openly. They
recognize his Power. So they wait until it is night, and then
they do a thing.

One of these young men is changing his shape. He
changes himself into a Mouse Person, and he creeps into
the wigwam. He will crawl into the sleeping-robes and then
he will stab Mimkɨtawo'qu'sk in the heart, before he can
wake or call up his Power.

So into the wigwam crawls this mouse. But
Mimkɨtawo'qu'sk is awake. His Power is strong. And when
the mouse gets into his robes, he pretends to roll over in his
sleep, and he traps that mouse between his knees, and he
begins to squeeze it.

The poor Mouse Person begins to scream and holler.
"*Ai'e, ai'e, ai'e,*" squeals this mouse. The wife of
Mimkɨtawo'qu'sk tries to wake him up.

"You are lying on someone," she says, shaking him
gently. "Move a bit and let this Person up."

But he pretends to be asleep. He mutters like a man
having a dream; he rolls over some more, and he begins to
squeeze that mouse harder.

"*Ya ya ya,*" screams the mouse.

Mimkɨtawo'qu'sk smiles, there in the darkness. He presses
harder, and then he moves his leg.

That Shape-Changer scoots away as fast as he can go.
Mimkɨtawo'qu'sk has almost killed him. He tells his friends
that they must return to their camp and wait for the feast.
Perhaps they may be able to overcome him some other way.

Mimkɨtawo'qu'sk looks at his wife. It is morning, and the
sun has come from beneath the earth.

59

"It is the day of our wedding feast," he says to her. "I want to fetch my sister to see it. Can you take the canoe and all this fur and meat, can you take it alone, back to the camps of the People, while I do this thing?"

"Yes," says his wife. "I can."

Mimkɨtawo'qu'sk watches her leave, then he goes for his sister.

In the camps of the People, they are amazed at all the animals he has killed for them to eat. They are amazed at all the furs he has gotten, as a gift for his father-in-law. They help his wife carry it up from the canoe. Then the women begin to cook, and the People wait for Mimkɨtawo'qu'sk to return.

Now they see him coming. He is coming into the camp, bringing his sister with him. The feasting and the playing are going to begin.

First the young men race. Then one of them challenges Mimkɨtawo'qu'sk to dive with him. They will compete, to see who can stay the longest underwater.

"What are you?" says Mimkɨtawo'qu'sk to the Shape-Changer who has challenged him.

"I am Kwimu," says that one, proudly. He changes shape. He becomes a Loon. "And you, what are you?"

"I am Jikmui'j," says that Moosewood Person, Mimkɨtawo'qu'sk. He changes shape himself, into the Sea-Duck. Then he dives.

They are underwater for a long, long time. And then Kwimu, the Loon, he floats up to the top of the water, dead, and drifts off down the river. The Jikmui'j is still down there, under the water, and all the People wait for him. For hours they are waiting for him. Finally he comes up. He flaps his wings in triumph, shaking the water off them, and comes to land. He has won, and all the People know it.

Now comes another Shape-Changer. "Let us try a game of growing," he says.

"What will you choose to be?" asks his rival.

"I will be a Pine Tree, a *kuow*."

"Very well," says Mimkɨtawo'qu'sk. "I will be an Elm."

And they begin. They change, they grow, they are seeds, then seedlings. Now they are young trees. Now they are growing tall and taller. That pine tree has grown huge, with many limbs. That elm tree is even taller, but it is a Tree With No Branches. And when the great winds come, they catch the branches of the pine tree, and push it over. The great winds kill that shape-changing pine.

But the elm bends in the wind, and does not fall. When the wind dies away, Mimkɨtawo'qu'sk has won.

Mimkitawo'qu'sk wins all the contests, and returns to his own wigwam. The marriage feast is over. His wife's father is proud of him. But all the young men are jealous. And all his wife's sisters are filled with envy.

When his wife gives birth to a son, her oldest sister asks to nurse it. "I can take care of my baby myself," says his mother. She is afraid they will harm the child to hurt Mimkitawo'qu'sk.

Her father takes his son-in-law outside to talk. "I am afraid of what may happen here," he says. "I think it would be best if you returned to your home. Take my daughter and the baby away from here. Take your sister away from here. I will give you a canoe and weapons. And if they attack you on your journey, defend yourself against my People."

Mimkitawo'qu'sk agrees. He takes his wife, his son and his sister, and he leaves that camp of the People. But they pursue him and attack him.

"I am getting tired of all this," says Mimkitawo'qu'sk. His Power comes up in him and he slays them all. And then he takes his family back to their own home, deep within the forest.

Here the story ends.

THE COMING OF PLANTS

Long ago, in the time of the Old Ones, seven men were journeying across a steep mountain. They came down the sheer cliff-face of this mountain into a meadow. And in this meadow was a long, long narrow lake.

In the lake was a tiny island. These seven men used that island as their boat. The island had a pole on it, and they used this to push themselves and the island through the water. When they came to the other side of the lake, they saw the wigwam of Skunk Woman, Apuḳjilui'skw.

Skunk Woman cooks for these seven men, but she will eat nothing. And one of these seven men, he laughs at Skunk Woman.

Now Skunk Woman has Power. She picks up her bladder bag, her *wisqoti* for storing grease, and she begins to dance a small dance, just a little swaying dance, and she begins to sing:

> *we'kwaptmɨk mekwa'sikek*
> *we'kwaptmɨk*
> *we'kwaptmɨk*
> *we'kwaptmɨk mekwa'sikek*

This is her song. "As far as you can see," sings Skunk Woman, "it has turned red." She dances a little more. "As far as I can see, red clouds are coming, dangerously."

This man throws his axe at her to stop her calling up her Power. It hits her bladder of grease and cuts a little chunk of it off. He picks it up and keeps it.

Now these seven men decide to cross water again and visit the Wild Persons who live on the far side. "We will go and see these good dancers," they say. These Wild Persons are fierce, they will kill the People as soon as they see them. None of the People has ever crossed that water, none of the People has ever been able to go to their camps.

So these seven men are plotting how they can get across the water, when they see something swimming through it. It is Ki'kwesu, Muskrat Person.

"*Ankam!*" screams Ki'kwesu. "*Lnu'k!*" He bobs up and down in the water, screaming. "Look! People!"

The man who has cut off a bit of Skunk Woman's grease container takes some fat out of it and throws it to Ki'kwesu. Ki'kwesu likes anything fat, and he is quiet while he gobbles it up. But as soon as he finishes, he begins yelling "*Lnu'k! Lnu'k!*" to warn the Wild Persons that People are near.

"You want more fat?" the men say to Ki'kwesu. "Go swim across to the other side, and steal for us one of the canoes of the Wild Persons. Bring it here, and we will give you all the fat that is left in this container."

So Muskrat, he swims over to the other side and he steals that canoe and brings it back.

One of these seven men is Tities, Jay Person. He says to the others, "I am going over there. It is night, it is dark; they won't see me. I want to watch them dance."

Ki'kwesu says, "I will go with you. I can bite holes in all their canoes. I can bite holes in all their paddles. Then I will get an old stump and drag it through the water. They will see it, and think it is a Moose." So Muskrat Person, Ki'kwesu, he is biting holes in all the Wild Persons' canoes, while Jay is paddling across the water.

Jay cannot wait. He wants to see the dancing. He finds his way in the dark to a large wigwam. The sounds of dancing are coming from inside. There is a hole in the cover of this wigwam, and Jay sticks his nose in through that hole.

There were some nice girls sitting inside there. And there was an old woman in there too, with very clever eyes. This old woman says, "What is that sticking in through the hole? It looks like a nose. It looks like a nose of one of the People. I will burn it with this brand, and if it is a nose, then it will move."

So she burns Jay's nose, his beak, Jay Person. And he could not move. But when she has given up and gone away, he flees back across the water to his friends. And they are all laughing at him.

Now the moon comes from beneath the earth. Moonlight is shining on the water, and Muskrat is pulling his old stump through the lake. One old woman of the Wild Persons sees him, swimming along the path of the moon.

"There is a moose over on the island," she tells the dancers. So all the Wild Persons stopped their dancing and went off after that moose.

Now there is a secret that these Wild Persons are guarding. This is why they are so fierce, why they kill all the People who try to spy on them. They have a summer garden, a place of plants, and this place is guarded by two old women. These two old women are guarding all the plants in the world. All the plants are in that garden, there are none in the world yet, except in that garden.

So when all the Wild Persons are out chasing that stump, that moose which Muskrat has made, and while all that water is leaking into their canoes from the holes Muskrat has chewed, and while their paddles are snapping from all the bites Muskrat has bitten in them, the seven men of the People pass over the water and they find that garden.

They get past the Power of those two old women, and they take plants of each kind out of there. Before then, there were no plants in the world. And after that was when the People began to make gardens.

These seven men of the People returned home across the water, across the island, across the lake, over the meadow, and up that steep mountain. That is the way they came home, bringing plants with them. And *kespi-a'tuksitkik,* that is as far as it is told about them.

BRINGING BACK ANIMALS

Long ago, in the time of the Elders, a big camp of the People was nearby, on the river. This *meski'k wutan* was a good place, and the People stayed there all the time. They went torch-fishing in the river, from their canoes. At night the whole river was bright with the light of their torches, bobbing up and down, while the People speared salmon and trout and eels.

In the forest on either side of the river were many moose. The People hunted them, dried the meat, smoked it, toasted it over the fire until it was nice and brown.

The river is a good place, and the People live there content.

In this camp are two young men. They have Power. They are *puoinaq,* shamans. Something is calling them. A journey lies before them. They have heard something calling, and they must go.

"We are going to see if there are any other People in the world," they say to all the camp.

"When are you coming back?"

"Ah," they say. "We will come back after we have found some."

These two young men are talking about which way to go.

"South," says one of them. "We will go south."

So they take their weapons, their bows and quivers of arrows. And they walk. They walk and they walk on, going south. They walk for seven days and then they walk for seven days more. Their Power protects them. Nothing can kill them.

Now one of those young men is sitting down. He takes out his stone pipe and packs it full of *nespipaqn* roots. He sucks in the *nespipaqn* smoke and he Listens. He is Listening for signs, he is Listening for sounds. His Power comes up in him as he smokes.

"I taste People somewhere close," he says, blowing smoke out into the air around his head. Slowly he raises his arm, and points. "We must go down that way."

And there before them is a wigwam. These two young men approach it. They call out. *"Pjila'si,"* says a voice from within, and so they enter. Inside there is a man and a woman.

"Where are you from?" asks the man, after they have smoked and sat a while. "Where have you come walking from?"

"We have come from a camp where many of the People live, a *meski'k wutan,"* says one of the young men. "There are many wigwams there. Here I see only one."

It is a long wigwam, with a door at either end. The man inside that wigwam says, "I have lived here since the world began."

He says, "I have my grandmother living with me. She has been with me since the world was made. This is a wigwam where much is done."

"What kind of work do you do here?" asks one of the young men.

"You will see. You will see this evening, when I begin. I cannot work now," says the man. "It is not yet time."

Then that man turns to his grandmother. He speaks to her. "Grandmother, please cook something for our guests to eat, quickly. The sun is about to go beneath the earth."

The old woman is cooking moose meat and ground-nuts for them. She is hurrying as fast as she can. The man is restless. He urges them to eat, and when they have finished, his grandmother gathers their bowls and spoons, she gathers her pots, and she puts them all away.

"Now, my grandsons," she says to the guests, "you may lie down here, close up against the walls of the wigwam. Do not lie with your feet toward the fire now. We need space. We need room to work." And she puts out the fire.

The sun is going beneath the earth. And the man inside the wigwam begins to beat on bark, and to sing. The sun has gone beneath the earth. He beats on his birchbark drum, and he sings.

He says, "I am Waisisk Ketu'muaji Ji'nm, I am Man Singing For Animals. I am singing for the animals, for all the animals, the *waisisk,* to come alive, to come back to life, from all those parts of them, all those wings, heads, feet, all those bones, meat, marrow, all those parts of them that have not been eaten by the People, all those parts of them that have not been eaten by other animals, all those parts of them that have been thrown away."

67

He sings. He sings, *"Nekanisunku'l pesikwiaku'l:* what belongs to my feet I am losing." That is how his Song starts. He sings and beats on the bark drum. All night long he sings, as the stars rise and pass across the dark sky above the wigwam, to sink once more beneath the earth.

Now it is morning. The sun has come from beneath the earth. The man inside this wigwam stops singing at daybreak. He says to his visitors, "This is my work every night. I do not like to see the People waste anything, any part of the animals. They should treat those things with respect. They should save everything, they should save eel skins. They should save all the parts of the animals. What they cannot save and use, they should bury with respect. They should not waste any hair or anything."

Then this man rose to his feet. He stretched himself and wriggled around a little bit. "My canoe is down on the shore," he said to his visitors, and they all went down to the shore with him.

"Do you want to see the fish come?" says this man to his two guests. He takes out a whistle, a whistle made of shell, and he begins to play on it. The bottom of the sea here is very clear, and they can see all kinds of fish, coming to hear the music.

"These are my fish," says the man. "They come from all those parts of fish which the People throw away on the shore. I sing for them and they come back."

Then they went back to the wigwam. "Are there any more of the People around here?" they ask this man, and he tells them yes.

"Well," they say to him, "we can go home now. We have found People."

And every night this man is singing. The bones of the animals the People have put in the woods, he is singing for them to come back to life. He puts out the fire, and he sings in the dark. He takes out a moose bone and sings over it. The moose jumps out of the bone, and runs away. He takes out a caribou bone, he beats the birchbark drum, he sings to it. The caribou leaps up and runs away. He takes out the bones of mink and beaver and bear, and while he is singing, these bones burst into animals, and the animals run away. All of them come back to life. This man, Waisisk Ketu'muaji Ji'nm, the Man Who Sings For Animals, the Man Who Brings Back Animals, he makes them all live again.

FETCHING SUMMER

Saq, saq, so long ago. The People are living in twenty wigwams, down below the mountain. Above them on the mountaintops, are the camps of the Bear Persons. Above them on the mountaintops are the camps of the Kukwesk Persons. But the People live down below.

They are working all the time. They hunt moose, they hunt deer and fox and all kinds of animals with furs. The People make canoes and moccasins and baskets, snow-shoes and tools and the wooden cradles for carrying the babies. The People are working all the time.

And the People die. When they die, their kin-friends smoke their flesh and cover them with birchbark. Every bit of them is covered with that birchbark, all sewed up, so that not a hair can fall out, so that nothing can get in. Then they would bury them. Their kin-friends would put sticks of *lamkisn* foxfire, near them, so that they would have light in the dark.

Down below the mountain is a family of the People. The old man dies. The old woman dies. All that is left are the children: one daughter, three older boys, and a small baby boy. This little boy grows to be about four years old, and one evening he is talking to his sister. He is saying, "Where is our mother? Where is our father?"

And at last his sister tells him, "Our mother is dead. Our father is dead." She tells him about death, she tells him what happens when death comes to the People.

Now this little boy is getting very sad. He is lonely for his mother and his father, and he begins to cry. This little boy cries for two days without stopping. And at last his sister says to one of his older brothers, "You had better go up on the mountain, and fetch Muini'skw. Fetch one of those Old Bear Women. Tell her we need her to come down and make our little brother stop crying."

69

So the older boy climbs up the mountain. He finds one of the Muini'skwaq, and he says to her, "Come down to help my sister. The baby will not stop crying about our mother and father."

"*E'e,*" says Muini'skw, "I will come."

That Muini'skw comes down off the mountain. She leaves her own two little boys behind up there, and she comes to the wigwam where the human child is crying. She takes that child up in her lap and begins to rock him.

Muini'skw is singing, singing to the human child. She sings:

Pa pa po
Pa pa po

And that little boy finally falls asleep. But in the morning, when he wakes up again, once more he begins to cry. It is the middle of winter, and all across the drifts of snow and the patches of ice around that camp of the People, everyone can hear that little boy crying.

"Make him a little bow," says Muini'skw to his older brothers. "Make him some little arrows to play with. Perhaps that will dry up his tears."

So they get wood and shape it. They smooth it and shape it. They make a tiny little bow and string it with sinew. They make him some tiny little arrows. But still this child will not stop crying. Muini'skw is rocking him on her lap, and finally she says to him, "My little son, what would make you stop crying?"

"I want it to be warm," he says to her. "I want it to be summer. If you made it be summer, with little birds and flowers, then I could stop crying."

Muini'skw calls his three older brothers. Tities, Blue Jay. Kwimu, Loon. Kiunik, Otter. She calls them, all three of them, and she tells them, "You must go and fetch Summer to your younger brother."

"How shall we do this thing?" they are asking her.

"I will tell you," says Muini'skw. Muini'skw has Power. "You must take three big hide bags. You must travel far to the west, to the place where the Sky is burning, where the air is hot. You must ask Sky to help you."

Those three brothers are journeying far to the west. It is getting hotter and hotter. The air is burning, the Sky is burning. These three brothers open their hide bags.

"Help us, O Sky," they call out. "Give us Summer. Give us *Nipk* to take home with us."

Now a Voice is speaking to them. It is Sky. Sky says, "Close your bags quickly. Tie them up tightly. Go to my

70

wigwam over there, and take a few of the plants you see with you. Take a pair of birds of each kind. Take all these things home with you, and when you get there, open your bags again. All my hot air will come out. If you have snow, it will go. If you have ice, it will go. Wherever you are, there will be no snow. *Kesik,* Winter, it will be gone.

"After the snow is gone," says Sky, "take out all the little plants and birds and spread them around. Then you will have Summer."

These three brothers have made a long journey, and now they have come home. They open the hide bags and all the warm air rushes out. The snow begins to melt. Soon it is gone. The ice is gone. Summer has come to the People in that camp below the mountain.

These three brothers make a nice garden, with all those plants and all those little birds, nice little summer birds. Pretty little flowers begin to bloom. And the child comes out of the wigwam and begins to smile.

Old Bear Woman, Muini'skw, she says, "Now I must go home. Your little brother is smiling; he forgets about his mother and father. He will not cry any more."

That little boy learns to use his bow and his arrows. The People stay in that camp at the foot of the mountain. They go hunting every day, and that little boy grows up.

That little boy grows up. He learns war, he becomes a chief, he wears the shell medal. His People have canoes, they cross the ocean, they are fighting and killing lots of enemies.

KOPIT FEEDS THE HUNTER

The Old Ones of the People are camped in the forest by the sea.

Now it is the moons of winter. The dead time. Hunting is bad. No one has anything to eat. The hunters do not bring home any meat. They cannot find the moose. They cannot find the caribou or the beaver. No one has seen bears, or any little animals like rabbits or partridges.

There is a woman living in this camp of the People, and she says to her husband, "Go out once more. Maybe you will have good luck if you try just one more time." So he puts on his snowshoes and goes out into the snow.

After he has walked for a long time in the white forest, he sees something. He sees the tracks of other snowshoes. It looks as though a number of other hunters have been that way. "Well," he thinks, "there are so many people in this part of the forest, I may not get any game. But perhaps they have something to eat." So he follows their tracks.

By and by he comes to a lake, and at the far end of it he sees something. He sees a wigwam sitting all by itself. Smoke is drifting out of the smokehole at the top. When he gets up to it, he calls out and goes in.

An old man is lying asleep on the other side of the fire. A caribou head is roasting over the coals, dangling from a long twined string, which slowly twists and untwists. Fat is dripping onto the coals. The hunter's mouth waters, but he says nothing.

The old man wakes. "Greetings," he says, "come in and welcome. Did you see any young men in the forest?"

"No," said the hunter. "I saw only tracks."

But by and by, the old man's sons returned. They had brought home great sled-loads of caribou meat. Their father wants to know why they are so late. "The caribou head has been done a long time," he tells them. They are soon sitting around the fire eating it, and their visitor shares it with them.

72

After they have eaten and smoked, the old man asks politely where the stranger is from, and that one tells him a little of his camp: how the hunting had been so bad, and how all the people were so hungry. "We are in great trouble," he says, and the older man is quick to reply.

"We must help our friends back there in the forest; you boys tie up for him a good back-load of meat for him to take home." So it is done, and then this man leaves to bring that welcome food back to his own band as soon as possible.

When he reaches his own wigwam, he drops the load of meat outside, as is the custom, and goes in. His wife is sent out to fetch it in: "There is a small bundle of something outside," he says quietly.

But when she unwraps it, behold! It is not meat at all. It is *mitiey maskwi,* poplar bark! It is food for beavers, not for humans.

This hunter has not been with People at all—he has been in a beaver lodge. He has been visiting Kopit.

Kopit. Old Beaver Person.

This man has seen Kopit.

Kopit has Power. He has shown this man his human shape. He has shown him a wigwam of the People. He has shown him his children hunting, and shown him a caribou head to eat.

This man has eaten with Kopit. And Kopit has sent food home with him.

But this man is not happy. He feels he has been tricked.

"*E'e,*" says this man, "I have eaten poplar bark, and brought it home to my family; I think next time I will eat BEAVER." He says to his kin-friends, he says to the hunters of the People, "I have found a beaver lodge."

And in the morning, all the men of that band set out to hunt those beaver.

But this man has eaten with Kopit. Now he has Power. He is back-trailing himself, following his own tracks, when he finds a bear's den. There is a bear in it. And so these men kill that bear. They kill that bear, and then they stop to take the meat home to their families.

Once more they set out for the lake of the beaver's lodge. This hunter has eaten with Kopit. And now Kopit will show him something.

Kopit makes them walk for a long time through the white forest.

Finally those hunters reach the place in the trail where the man's tracks had crossed the tracks of the other snowshoes. But these other tracks are no longer there. Before them, still clear, lie the tracks of the man, but the other snowshoes' marks are gone. That Old Beaver has Power.

Kopit is going to show that man something. For at the lake, there is no wigwam, no smoke, no fire. There isn't even a beaver's lodge there. Kopit is gone. He has been there, he has not been there. Kopit has Power. So the hunters return to the camp without beavers.

The man who was shown things by Old Beaver Person has Power. He has no beaver to eat. Instead, he has caught a bear. So for a while there is something to eat in that camp of the People.

The Man Who Visited Kopit is feeling something. He calls his kin-friends, he calls the hunters of the People. He asks them to go with him to hunt whales. But they do not want to go with him. They want to go after white bears.

"White bear's meat is poisonous," says this man. "It will make you sick to eat it. We must go looking for whales. It is the right moment."

"But the wind is all wrong. The wind blows; it is no weather for catching a whale."

"You will not need your canoes," says this man. "You will not need your spears. You will not need to worry about the wind. I am telling you. I am feeling whales."

So they go with him down to the shore.

The wind drops.

The sea becomes as smooth as the oil on top of soup.

The wind drops, and this man takes up his alder-wood pipe and begins to play the music of whales calling to one another. Nothing happens. There are no whales. So everybody turns. They turn from him, and they all go home. But this hunter has eaten with Kopit, and he knows. He has Power. He stays playing his whale-music on the shore.

At last. Far out on the edge of the horizon, a whale is spouting. It listens to the pipe-music, the whale-music. It thinks it hears the singing of its kin-friends, the Putupaq, and so it comes. Closer and closer it comes, under the Power of the music. Finally it is so near the beach that it grounds itself on the rocks and sand.

This is the hunter's moment. He runs for camp as fast as he can, calling the news. Everyone races out to help him. The whale is taken. For days they are cutting up the meat and the rich blubber, and carrying it home to eat and to cache. Piles of it are sent round to all the families.

And after this no one is hungry, all the rest of that winter.

SKUN

In the time of the Old Ones, a man and a woman are living at the edge of the sea. This man and this woman have many children. Most of them are still small children. They live all alone with their children by the edge of the sea, and they are very poor.

Often this man and his wife must be out in the canoe, fishing and catching birds to feed their family. They have to leave the children at home all by themselves.

Now one day, this man and his wife are fishing far out to sea when a big fog comes up. And they are lost in it. They do not know where the land is. They do not know where home is. They do not know how to get back to the children. They must wait for the fog to go away.

So they are floating on the sea, waiting and worrying about their children, all alone at home, when the man sees a thing. It is a large dark shadow, coming toward them. This shadow is looming up in the fog, and it is coming fast. What is it? It is a canoe, a *kwitn*. But this canoe is enormous. And there are giants in it. Eight giants, paddling along in a giant canoe.

And now they see another, and another canoe. Three canoes, all filled with giants.

A Voice speaks to them. It is the leader in the first canoe; he has seen them. "*Njiknam,*" he calls to the man. "My younger brother." Because he has politely recognized them as kin-friends, the man and the woman know that he means them no harm, and this makes both of them feel better.

"*Njiknam,*" calls the giant, "*tami wejien?* Where have you come from?"

"We are lost in the fog," replies the man from down below in his little canoe. "We cannot get home, and all our children are left on their own without us."

The leader hears the sorrow in his voice, and leans down from his giant canoe. "Do not be sad. Let us take you up into our canoe. Come in with us, and I will take you home to the camp of my father. My father is the chief there, and I can promise you that you will be well treated. You have nothing to fear."

So the man agrees. He will go with the giants, with his wife and his canoe.

Now the other two big canoes come up on either side of the little human canoe. Two men in each big canoe take their paddles, and place them under the bow and stern of the tiny canoe. Then they lift it aboard the leader's canoe. And once their guests are safely within, the giants begin to paddle off.

Now they are coming out of the fog. Ahead of them, they can see the land, rising up out of the water. And there on the shore are three giant wigwams.

A very large giant is coming down to the water's edge to meet them. He calls out greetings to the leader in the first canoe. "*E'e*, my son," he says, looking into the boat. "Whom have you got there? Where did you find this little brother?"

"*Nu'*, my father, I found him lost in the fog, far out to sea."

"Very well," says the chief, "bring him up to the wigwam."

The giants beach their canoes, and then they lift the little canoe, with that man and woman of the People still sitting right in it, and they carry that canoe up to the wigwam and inside. They put it down in the eaves at the back of the wigwam, where the chief squats down to talk to them.

This chief is a kind Person. He orders that food be made for them to eat.

"I am Skun," he tells them. "That is my name, Skun. Liver. The one who brought you here is my son."

He sends his men out hunting soon after. And now the man and his wife can see how strong these giants really are. For when they come home from hunting, each of them has many caribou strung hanging from his belt, just like men of the People string and hang rabbits or partridges. Each giant has beaver hanging from his belt as well, and otters. These giants are out hunting often, and they always come home loaded down like this.

Now this giant chief is *puoin;* he can See many days ahead, into the tomorrows. And he tells them that soon they are going to be attacked. "A Jenu is coming," he says. "We must prepare for the fight. I want some of you to go out to meet him. He must be destroyed before he reaches the camp here."

So they choose four fighters to go out to kill Jenu. Two sons of the chief and two others are to go. And on the morning of the third day, these four giants set out to fight.

Now it is nearly midday. Skun comes to that man of the People and his wife, and he bends down to speak to them. "You are in danger," he says. "The screaming of a Jenu can kill. So you must melt *qamu,* moose fat, and pour it in your ears. You must cover the sides of your heads with fat, so that you do not hear it. Then roll yourselves up tight in these sleeping-robes here and wait. This Jenu will scream three times as he begins to fight."

So they do as they have been told. The woman melts fat and pours it in the ears of her husband. She covers both sides of his head with a thick layer of it, so that he cannot hear her speaking to him at all. Then she does the same for herself. They both roll themselves up in the blankets, covering their heads, and lie still.

The sun is high overhead, and the Jenu has come within sight of the four giants sent out to stop him. He opens his mouth, and a terrible sound, a Sound of Power, screams out from him. This sound strikes the man and the woman of the People like a blow, like Thunders, even though they are so far away and have their ears stopped up. It makes them sick, it makes them shake. Almost they do not survive it.

Then Jenu screams again. This time the sound is not so bad. And when he screams for the third time, it has become very faint. *Suel mu nutua'tikl.* They can hardly hear him at all.

Now Skun comes to them again. "You may get up now, and take the fat from your ears. There is no danger any longer. My hunters have killed this Jenu." He smiles. "Soon they will be coming home."

The two sons of Skun, and the other two hunters return and tell the whole camp of how they met and fought and defeated this Jenu. "It was a hard fight," they say.

"This fight is only the beginning," says Skun. "I have Seen death coming. I have seen a Kukwes coming. Soon I will again have need of warriors such as yourselves."

"Kukwes!" say all the hunters. "Kukwes. The Cannibal. The One Covered With Hair. The One Who Is Always Hungry. Kukwes."

"Kukwes is coming. After the passing of three nights, he will be here. I have Seen it," says Skun.

Once more the four giants go out to meet the enemy. Once more Skun tells the man and the woman of the People to protect themselves with fat. "This time you must wrap yourselves in two times as many blankets," he says to them. "The roaring of a Kukwes can also kill."

And so it happens. The first scream of that Kukwes makes their heads fill with pain. Their stomachs want to vomit. Almost it seems as if it will kill them. But then it is over, and the second scream is not as loud. The third scream is faint and far away, as the giants overcome Kukwes, and his Power drains away.

Skun comes to get them out of all those blankets.

As they are picking the tallow out of their ears, they see the four warriors returning. They are covered with blood. Enormous trees have been torn up by the roots and run through their arms and legs: Kukwes uses trees as his spears and arrows. These trees are still sticking into them. They have not had time to pull them out. Now they can sit down, and they pick these trees out of their legs as men of the People would pull out splinters.

"This has been a fearful battle," they tell Skun. And one of his sons is so exhausted and hurt that he falls dead just as he reaches the door of his father's wigwam.

Skun comes out. He sees his son lying dead before him, and he bends down to take his hand. "Why are you lying there, my son?" he asks him. "Why do you not get up and eat something?" And Skun's Power comes up in him; it passes through his hand into his son, and his son returns from being dead and stands up. Skun feeds him, and soon he is feeling much better.

Skun speaks to his visitors. "Now that these dangers are passed, are you not tired of remaining here with us? Perhaps there is something else you would like to be doing?"

"This is a wonderful place," says that man of the People. "And you have been very kind to us, but all our little children are at home, all by themselves, with nothing to eat, and we cannot help but worry about them."

"Very well," says Skun. "I will send you home tomorrow."

And in the morning, he has some of his giants carry their little canoe down to the sea. He packs it full of meat and furs for them, full of moose and beaver and otter. *"Tepa'tikw,"* he says to them. "The two of you get on." And then he calls a small dog and puts it on board the canoe with them. "This is one of my dogs," he says. "He will take you home. Each of you take a paddle, and send the canoe in whatever direction my little dog sits looking."

Now Skun speaks to his dog. He says, "Take good care of these People. Take them safely home." Skun speaks to that man of the People. He says, "You will be reminded of me once more, at the end of seven winters. Look to the southwest for me." *Toqo pusijik.* Then off they go. The man is sitting in the stern, paddling. The woman is sitting in the bow, paddling. The dog is sitting in the middle of the canoe, with his nose and ears pointing in the way they should go. The water is so smooth and calm, and the dog knows where their home lies, and it does not seem long to them before they come around a point of land and see their own wigwam.

The children spot them coming and run down to the shore, shouting and laughing. The dog is excited, too. He bounces up to the children and wags his tail and jumps a lot.

"This is a good dog," says that man to his wife and children. "I wonder if we are to keep him?" But that dog must return to his master. He must go back to Skun, and before they know he is gone, they see him far out to sea, racing back to Skun, jumping from one wave to another, just like he was running on ice. He does not need a canoe.

That man and his family keep on living in that little wigwam, but now they are doing much better. That man has acquired Power by visiting Skun. Now he is a good hunter. There is always plenty to eat. Many winters go past, and he has almost forgotten being lost in the fog.

But now the seventh winter passes, and this man begins to Dream. "I remember," he says when he wakes. "I begin to remember." He talks to his wife. "Skun is making me Dream," he tells her. "He said, 'Look for me after seven winters. Look for me toward the southwest.' And now I am Dreaming."

"So," says his wife. "What will happen?"

"I am Dreaming that I am about to change. Power is filling me in these Dreams."

"What are you to be?" asks his wife. "Are you becoming a *puoin?*"

"*E'e,*" says that man. "Yes. I am becoming a *puoin* or perhaps a *mi'kmwesu.*"

"What is a *mi'kmwesu?* Is it a *mn'tu?* Is it good or bad?"

"I am not sure," says the man. "I think it is like a human Person. It is not bad. Skun is doing this."

Now this man is Dreaming again. He is Dreaming about the southwest. A whale comes to him from this direction. It comes right into the shore to him, close by the wigwam, and

it begins to sing to him. And the sounds of this whale
singing are so beautiful that this man wishes to listen to
them forever. When he wakes up, he tells his wife about it.
"Something is coming. Something is getter closer."
This very day they see it. They are sitting outside the
wigwam, and out to sea, coming toward them from the
southwest, they see it. But it is not a whale. It does not sing
to them. It is a Shark Person, or a *puoin* Shape-Changer. It
is chasing all the little fish. They can see its back fin rising
above the surface of the water. Shark Person. The Deceiver.
Puksi-kluskapewit, the One Who Never Tells The Truth.

This Shark Person comes close to the shore. He looks at
them, but he does not sing. And after a while, he returns
back the way he has come, out of the southwest.

"This is bad," says that man to his wife. "Something bad
has happened."

"What shall we do?"

"We must wait and see," he says to her. "We must wait
and see."

And soon they do see. They see the little dog coming from
Skun, running over the surface of the water. The parents
and the children are very happy, and the dog seems happy
to see them too. He jumps up and down; he licks their faces.
He wags his tail. And this man of the People says to that
dog, "I will come to Skun. In three winters, I will come. And
I will always look toward the southwest."

The dog rises on his back legs, and he licks the hands of
that man. He licks his eyes. He licks his ears, and then he
returns to Skun, bouncing over the water.

Now those three winters have passed. That man of the
People gets into his canoe and goes in search of Skun. The
time has come to make his visit. And it is not hard for him
to find the way. Sooner than he can imagine, he sees the
three giant wigwams, standing on the shore. But all
except one of them are empty. The giants are gone.

Someone comes to the door of that wigwam. It is
Skun. All his sons and his kin-friends are dead.

"They are all dead, my little friend," he says
to that man. "Three winters ago. We were
attacked. Perhaps you saw the Deceiver?
That Shark Person? *Akaia,* that Puksi-
kluskapewit has killed all my
children." Skun gets food for that
man, and watches him eat it. "I
am glad to see you, little
brother," he says. "For I

am old now. Death is coming to me, and soon I will go to my own place. It is good that you have come, for I wish to give you something. I wish to give you the robes which my sons wore when they were alive. You must take them home with you. You must wear them, and then the Power which filled my sons will fill you."

"And when you wear them," says Skun, "and when you wear them, think of me."

This man of the People is greatly honoured. He thanks Skun. And when he leaves him, he takes with him the robes of his dead sons.

"Skun has given me these robes," he says to his wife. "They are much too big for me. They are made for giants. But I must put them on, and think of him. He was very kind to me."

So this man of the People takes off his own clothes. He washes himself, and then he puts on the robes of the sons of Skun. And as soon as he has put them on, he grows to fit them. He himself becomes a giant. Each time he puts them on, their Power fills him; their knowledge and their strength come to him.

And when he takes them off, he is a man of the People, and lives by the edge of the sea with his wife and children.

SAKKLO'PI'K

They are deep in the forest. Two old ones of the People are living there, on the edge of a large camp. They have two daughters, and these daughters are very shy and very beautiful. They won't come out where anyone can see them. They refuse to marry any man of the People.

The *saqmaw* of this band of the People has a son, a son who wishes a wife. So he asks his father to pay the two old ones a visit, in the evening.

"*E'e*," says his father. "I will do this."

It is a very pleasant visit. The old ones offer them food. They are all sitting around telling stories, smoking, playing games. But the two daughters are hiding from their visitors, hiding behind a woven screen on one side of the wigwam.

"My son wishes to marry," says the chief after a time. "He is a good hunter, he should have sons."

"Ah?" says the father of those two very shy girls. "Perhaps I may be able to tell you something in the morning." No more is said. After a while, the visitors leave.

"How do you feel about this?" the father asks his two daughters. They have been listening from behind their mat.

"Neither one of us wishes to marry," says Oldest Daughter.

"Very well," says their father, and in the morning he takes this news to the chief. The chief's son is very disappointed.

Living in this *meski'k wutan*, this large camp of the People, there is another young man. He is ugly. He is lazy, he can't do anything right. He is a great joker. This young man says to his friends, "I could get one of those girls, one of those beautiful shy girls, if I really wanted to." His friends are all laughing at him, and they decide to take him over there that very evening; make him try his luck.

"We will go right when they are eating," all the young men say, "and walk right in the door, before those girls have a chance to get up and hide. Then we will see about your boasting."

And this is what they are doing. They walk very quietly out of the camp, and listen. Yes, the old ones are eating with their two beautiful shy daughters. They can hear them talking.

Now these young men have suddenly appeared in the doorway. There is no time for the girls to hide. Each one gets to see their beautiful faces. The old ones invite them all in.

"Come and eat with us," says the father.

"No, no, we have already eaten."

"Come in and eat again," he insists, and they spend the evening with this family, eating and talking and smoking. Then they are going to play games. All the young men and the two girls must hide their faces, while the old ones throw the small bone ring in the fire ashes. They are going to play *Mimkwataqatijik,* "They Hide Things."

The first player takes a pointed stick and fishes about in the ashes. He finds nothing. Then one of the girls takes the stick, and goes looking for that ring. Nothing. Around and around the fire, they pass that stick, laughing. Finally one of them spears the bone ring, and wins the game. Then the old ones throw it back in the fire for another try.

All this time, that ugly young man says not one word about marrying, or women, or wives. And none of his friends says anything either. And now when it is late, and they are all going back to their own wigwams, all his friends are teasing him about how he has not won a wife, for all his joking.

So. Moons go past, and this young man, this ugly lazy young man, is walking out in the forest, away from the camp. He has been hunting with one of his friends, but they have gotten separated, so he is alone.

And now he sees a thing. It is a strange thing to see, out here in the forest. He sees an old woman. Her face is all wrinkled. Her shoulders are all bent over. But her hair is fastened up with many beautiful *sakklo'pi'k,* many wonderful ornamented hair-strings which tie up her hair and then trail their ends down over her shoulders, all the way down to her feet.

"Where are you going?" this old woman asks the young man.

"Nowhere in particular," he answers. "And you, *nukumi'*? Where have you come from, my grandmother?"

"I have not come far," says this old woman all draped with beautiful hair-strings. "But you, grandchild: it is said that you wish to marry, to marry one of those beautiful shy women, those daughters of the old ones living out on the edge of your camp."

"*Moqwe,*" he says. "No, I do not wish this." He is sorry he ever made that joke.

"But I can help you," says this old woman, peering up at him through all those *sakklo'pi'k.* "I can tell you how to make her love you, how to catch her for your wife. But you must tell me what you wish."

"What shall I do, my grandmother? For I would like this very much."

The old woman reaches up and removes one of her many hair-strings. "Take this. Carry it in your pouch, your medicine pouch. Carry it for a while, then watch out for a time to get close to her, and throw this *sakklo'pi* upon her back. But do not let her see you do this. Do not let her feel you do this. And do not tell anyone else about this at all."

"I shall do as you say, my grandmother," says the ugly young man. And he calls together his comrades, a few days later. He takes them once again to visit the old ones. They arrive right at dinner time. Those two shy girls are sitting with their parents around the fire, eating, when the visitors come in. There is not time for them to hide. But as they are all playing games after supper, there does come a time when that ugly young man can drop the *sakklo'pi* on the back of one of those beautiful girls. And soon after that, he and his friends say goodnight and return to their own wigwams.

Now it is morning. The sun has come from beneath the earth. That ugly young man is out walking in the forest, and he sees a thing. It is a strange thing to see deep within the forest. It is that young girl, that shy and beautiful young girl, on whose back he has dropped the hair-string. The Power of the hair-string has brought her to him.

"*Tami elien?*" she says to him. "Where are you going?"

"I am going hunting," he tells her. "But why do I find you out here alone in the forest? Where have you come from? Where are you going? Are you lost?"

"Oh, no," she says to him, bemused. "I am not lost."

"You should be at home," he says. "I will take you back to your parents, and tell them I found you out wandering in the woods. I will tell them you did not know the way home."

"Yes," says this girl to him. "Yes."

And so the ugly young man takes home the beautiful shy girl, and speaks with her parents. "I found her wandering in the forest, your daughter, and I have brought her home to you."

"Then she is your wife, if you wish," says the father, and the young man agrees. And a feast is celebrated where all the People recognize the marriage.

Some time later this young man is looking at his new wife. He smooths the hair back from her face. "Where did you get this pretty little hair-string?" he asks her.

"I found it in my *ntɨpunk,* my sleeping-place," she says to him, and the ugly young man just smiles.

Now the ugly young man is going to visit the chief's son. He wants to help him catch a wife. He wants him to have the old ones' other daughter, so that he and the chief's son will become *wijikɨtijik*—so they will be as close as brothers.

"My wife's sister is alone now," he says, looking at nothing in particular. "Now that her sister is living apart from their family. My wife's sister is left behind, with no one next to her to talk with in the night."

"It is not good to be alone," says the chief's son, looking at nothing in particular. "I have felt that way myself."

"My wife," says the ugly young man, "has a very beautiful hair-string. It came out of the forest. I have been thinking that her sister would like a hair-string such as that."

"When next you go into the forest," says the chief's son, "perhaps I will accompany you."

Now it is morning. The sun has come from beneath the earth, and these two young men are walking deeper into the forest, walking out to hunt, walking out to hunt *sakklo'pi'k.*

And then the chief's son is seeing something. It is a strange thing to see here, so deep within the forest. It is an old woman, all wrinkled up and bent over. She is sitting on a tree trunk, looking at him. And many beautiful hair-strings are tied from the roll of hair at the back of her head. There are so many of them, they almost cover her shoulders like a robe. They are hanging down almost to her feet. He greets her very politely.

"Nukumi'," he says. "My grandmother, where have you come from?"

"From not very far away," she replies. "And you, grand-child: are your eyes still following after the old ones' oldest daughter?"

"E'e," says the chief's son. "My eyes have sometimes been looking in that direction."

"Then take this *sakklo'pi,*" says the old woman. "Your brother here will tell you how to use it. Do not speak of anything you have seen. And grandchild—"

"What is it, my grandmother?" asks the chief's son.

"Have many sons," says this old woman, and she disappears.

Now the ugly young man instructs the chief's son. "This is what you must do," he says. And it is done. It is done, and when so many days have passed, the chief's son goes into the forest again. He is going hunting. This time he is hunting a wife.

He walks deeper into the forest, and he sees something. It is the oldest daughter of the old ones; she is following him.

"Where are you going?" asks Oldest Daughter.

"I am going hunting. But you, what are you doing here? Are you lost?"

"No," she says, gazing and gazing at him. "No, I am not lost."

"I will take you home to your parents," he says. "You cannot stay out here alone. I will tell them you were lost, and I have found you. For I have found you, have I not?"

"Yes," says Oldest Daughter. "You have found me."

It is a big marriage feast they are having, with much meat and fat to eat; with games and dancing to celebrate. The chief's son looks at his new wife. She is wearing the beautiful hair-string, the *sakklo'pi* which he dropped on her back. Its Power has called her to him. He smiles.

Now after this, that ugly young man and the chief's son were as close as brothers, *wijikitijik*. They are often together, and they hunt together as well.

One day they are sitting together. "If a man wanted to learn how to run very swiftly," says the chief's son to no one in particular, "there is a thing that could help him do this."

"A man who runs fast would be a better hunter," says the lazy young man, "and he could run away from his enemies so fast he would end up chasing *them*." He is still making jokes.

"Not many of the People know how to teach this," says the chief's son, looking up at the sky. "And perhaps not many can learn such a thing, either."

"Perhaps if someone would teach, someone would learn," says the ugly young man to his friend. And so the chief's son is showing him how to do it.

"You must gather feathers," he says. "You must wait for a day when the wind is blowing very fast. Let the feathers fly out into the wind; let them run before the wind. Then let yourself run after them. Soon you will be able to run fast. The feathers will pull you. The wind blowing will push you. Soon you will run faster. Soon you will be running right past those feathers. And at last you will find yourself running faster than the wind."

"Once you learn this," says the chief's son, "it will never go away from you."

The lazy young man collects feathers, and waits for a wind. Now the wind is rising and singing; he lets the feathers go, and he lets himself go after them. He lets himself go into the wind. And little by little, Power comes up in him, stronger and stronger, until he is running faster than a man can run, faster than feathers fly. He is running faster than the wind.

This time the chief's son and the ugly young man are having a smoke, out in the forest. The chief's son leans back against a tree and half-closes his eyes. "Many things are living in this forest," he says, to no one in particular. "Some of them are dangerous."

"E'e," says his wife's sister's husband, to no one in particular. "Some of them are very dangerous."

"Some things cannot be killed," says the chief's son, "and some things a man cannot escape from by running away, even if he can run very fast." He is watching his friend out of the corner of his eye. "If a man should meet one of those things...."

"... he can turn white and die of fright," says that ugly young man, still making jokes. He is lying on the ground, looking up at the sky. "But perhaps there might be something else he could do?"

"Not many of the People could teach something like this," says the chief's son. "And perhaps not many could learn it, either."

"If someone would teach, perhaps someone would learn."

And so the chief's son begins to teach Escaping to his friend. *Wijikitijik.* They are brothers.

"Find some old ragged clothes," he says, "the ugliest you can get, and put them on over your own clothes. Then you must go out looking for a fight. Provoke someone. Provoke someone until he attacks you, and when he has seized you, slip out of your rags and run away. If you can do this, then you will be able to escape from any man who may take hold of you. You will be able to escape from any animal which may leap upon you. You will be able to escape from any thing that lives in this forest.

"And once you have learned this," he tells him, "it will never leave you."

So. The ugly young man gets himself some really ugly clothes. He puts them on, and he goes looking for a fight. And he sees a man coming. *"Ya ya ya,"* he yells at him, until the man is crazy with anger, and attacks him to shut up his mouth, to stop all that *ya ya*. As soon as the other man's hands grab him, that ugly young man begins to wriggle out of his ugly clothes. Power comes up in him and he slips out of them just like an eel. He leaves them there, lying on the ground, and the man who has attacked him stomps up and down on them, believing he is killing his enemy. He beats up those clothes and leaves them for dead. And all this time the ugly young man is laughing at him, from some safe distance away.

One day the chief's son and the friend who helped him catch a wife are out paddling on the river. They are letting the canoe drift downstream, and the chief's son says, "If someone were to take a handful of moose hair, and roll it up between their thumb and first finger, they would learn something useful. If they were to take this hair and hold it into the wind, and let it loose to blow where it will, they would see something useful. They would be able to see any moose that is anywhere around, for a great distance. But perhaps this is not of any interest."

"If someone were to take the hair of other animals," says his friend, "and do likewise, perhaps he would see those kinds of animals?"

"Perhaps," says the chief's son. "But there are not many of the People who can learn such a thing."

"When someone teaches, someone listens," says the ugly young man, and he soon learns this lesson.

Now he is asking a question, one day while they are spearing salmon. "Fish," he says to the chief's son, "have no hair."

"That is true," says his friend as they thrust and jab their spears into the water. After a while, he speaks again, to no one in particular. "Fish have bones," he says, looking off into the distance. "If someone were to powder up their bones, and let their dust blow in the wind, who knows what he might see."

"Ah," says his friend, spearing a big salmon. "Here is a big one. I shall ask it if I may have its bones."

He takes salmon bones, he grinds them to a powder, and when the wind blows, he stands upon a rock by the river and lets the dust fly where it will. Now he has learned another lesson. Now he can see fish, and call them to him.

Moons go by, and this ugly young man is thinking. He is thinking and dreaming all the time. "I am Dreaming *putupaq*," he says to the chief's son. They are brothers. "All the time I am Dreaming of whales and of whale-songs."

"*E'e*," says the other man. "Whales live forever, unless they are killed." Then he smiles to himself, remembering, but that is all he says.

And so the ugly young man goes away to learn this lesson. He is going to do something. He is going to make something. He is going to take *putipewikan,* whale bone, and burn it. So. He burns whale bone, he crushes it up fine, until it is powder, and then he waits for the wind to change. He waits for the wind to blow out to sea. There is a rock-place, *kwiewey,* a point where rock runs way out into the sea. He waits there, out at the very end.

Now the wind is changing, it is blowing out to sea. He lifts his hand and lets some of the whale dust blow out on the wind. And at once he sees something: he sees a great number of whales, swimming far out on the ocean. So he blows dust toward them a second time, to call them in to him, and they come closer. Seven times this ugly young man blows that whale-bone dust, and then he sees the Person he has called, the Person who has come to him. It is an enormous whale, it is Putup, it is Whale Person.

Putup comes alongside the rock on which that ugly young man is standing, and he speaks to him.

"What is it that you want?" asks Putup.

"I have Dreamed you," says the man. "I want Power."

"*E'e,*" says Putup. "Put your hand into my mouth, under my tongue, and take it."

There is medicine under Whale Person's tongue, and now the man holds it.

"You have Power," says Putup. "You may accomplish whatever it is that you desire. This medicine defends you against sickness. It defends you against wild beasts and attacks of your enemies. This medicine makes you invulnerable."

Whale Person dives into the sea, and that ugly young man goes home again. And now in this camp of the People, life is very good. There are many animals in the forest, and they can be called right up to the doors of the wigwams, where they give themselves to be killed and eaten. No enemies can attack them, and they all have many children.

And when the old chief grows feeble, his son comes to the ugly young man. "Can he be made well and young again?" he asks.

"It is better not to do things like that," says his friend. "Let what is to come to him, come to him." And when death takes the old man, the chief's son speaks again.

"Perhaps a Powerful man should be chief," he says to his *wejusul,* his wife's sister's husband. "Perhaps you should do this, and not I."

"A Powerful man *is* chief," the ugly man replies. *Wijikitijik.* "And he has a brother to help him."

Kespi-a'tuksitkik.

NUJI-KESI-KNO'TASIT

A man and a woman are living in the forest. They have seven sons. They have seven sons, and the oldest is not good to the youngest of their sons. Oldest Son is hunting, and he does not give food to Youngest Son in the way that he should. He gives him all the hard tasks in the camp. He beats him. And he calls him only Nuji-Kesi-Kno'tasit, That One who takes the wrapping rags out of all the hunters' moccasins at the end of the day, That One who wrings out the water and sweat from the wrapping rags, and hangs them out to dry. For this is what Youngest Son must do for all the older brothers, the hunters, when they come in from the forest.

Youngest Son hates this duty which has been assigned to him, he hates his name, and the way Oldest Brother treats him. So he determines to run away. And secretly, he goes to his mother and speaks with her.

"My mother," says Youngest Son, "will you make something for me?"

"E'e," says his mother. "What do you need?"

"I want you to make me a bow," he says. "A tiny little bow and a tiny little arrow. And I want you to make me thirty pairs of moccasins."

So his mother does this, and Youngest Son waits until she has finished. Then he takes the bow and its one tiny arrow. He nocks the arrow and shoots, and as soon as it has left the bow, he is off and running after it. When he comes to the place where it has fallen, he picks it up and shoots it again, running as fast as he can to where it lands. He does this over and over until he is outrunning the arrow; he can catch it before it strikes the ground. His Power is coming up in him, and he runs faster and faster, faster than an arrow flies. And running this way, he is far away from home by the time night comes.

Night comes. The sun has gone beneath the earth. The father of Youngest Son comes home from hunting. He comes home with all six of his older sons. Oldest Son is angry. Where is Nuji-Kesi-Kno'tasit? He wants him to pull off his moccasins, and dry his foot wrappings.

"Where is that boy?" he says to his mother.

His mother just looks at him. "He has gone," she says, and she says no more. Oldest Son is furious, and wants to go out after him. He is going to bring him back and punish him.

Oldest Son waits until it is morning. The sun is coming up from beneath the earth when he leaves the wigwam, tracking his youngest brother. He is so angry that he tracks him for one hundred days. Every night he stops and rests until morning. Every morning he rises and goes on. But in all this time, all these hundred days, he has not even come to the place where his brother spent that first night. He has not seen any signs that his brother has stopped once to make a camp, to light a fire. And so Oldest Son gives up. He gives up and goes home.

Youngest Son is still running, still travelling. And now he meets someone. He meets an old man, walking along.

"*Tami elien?*" asks this old man. "Where have you come from and where are you going?"

"I have come a long distance," says Youngest Son. "And you, Old One? Where have you come from?"

"You say, my child, that you have come a long way," says this old man, "but I am telling you that your journey is nothing compared with mine; for I was a small boy like you are when I began it, and now I am old, and I assure you that I have not stopped once."

"I will try to go to the place from which you have come," says Youngest Son.

"You can never reach it," says the old man.

"Nevertheless," says Youngest Son. "I will try."

Youngest Son sees that this Old One's moccasins are worn out. He offers him one of the pairs of nice new moccasins which his mother had made for him. The Old One is pleased, and offers him something in return.

"I will do something for you," says the old man. "I am giving you something." It is a little box, a little birchbark box, with a cover tied down tight. "This will be a help to you in your travels."

Youngest Son thanks him. He puts the box in his medicine pouch, and keeps on going. After a while, he wonders what it has inside it. Youngest Son takes out his little birchbark box and opens it. He looks inside.

94

"Ai'e," says Youngest Son. "What is this I am seeing?" It is a tiny man, inside the box. It is a tiny man, dancing furiously. He is covered with sweat from all that dancing. And when Youngest Son takes the cover off the box and lets the light shine in, this tiny man stops dancing, he looks up, and speaks. "What is it that you want? What is required?"

"Mn'tu!" says Youngest Son. It is a *mn'tu,* taking the shape of a tiny man. A spirit-helper, a Person of Power, who can do anything that is asked of him.

Youngest Son looks down at him. "I wish," says Youngest Son, "I wish to be taken to the place from which that Old One came." And then he closes the cover of the box.

Darkness comes to Youngest Son. He faints and falls to the ground. And when he awakens, he sees a camp of the People close by, and he knows. He knows that this is the place from which the Old One started his journey.

Youngest Son walks into the camp. He is polite; he stops at the first wigwam he comes to and calls out greetings. An old woman invites him in, and offers him the seat of honour, up behind the fire. Youngest Son sits down, and as he does so, the old woman begins to cry.

"Why are you weeping, grandmother?" asks Youngest Son.

"Ah, grandchild," she says, "you young men all come here looking for wives, and our old chief will kill you by all the hard tests he sets for you, just as he has killed so many already."

"This chief has daughters?" asks Youngest Son. "Well, do not cry any more. We will see what we will see. He will not kill me, so stop your crying."

Now the news is all over the camp. A strange young man has come, come looking for one of the chief's daughters as a wife. The chief sends him a proud message, telling him to present himself at once.

"Moqwe," answers Youngest Son. "Tell him I say no. I will not come."

The next message the chief sends is not so commanding. "It is pleasant to have the sun shining into the wigwam early in the morning," this message says. "But a small something is in the way, and blocks my view of it. A man who removes this something, to let the sun shine on the camp, would be well received in that camp. He might find a seat beside one of my daughters."

The small thing which blocks that old chief's view of the sun is nothing but a high granite mountain. It keeps the sun from shining on the camp until it is late in the morning.

96

"Very well," says Youngest Son to the chief's messenger. He says it quietly, and then he sits back down beside the fire. He is waiting for evening to come.

Now it is night. The sun has gone beneath the earth. Youngest Son takes out his medicine pouch. He reaches inside. There is the little birchbark box, and when he takes the cover off, inside is *witapji'j*, his little friend, dancing away.

"Well?" says the *mn'tu*, stopping his dance and looking up. "What is it that you want?"

"I want that granite mountain levelled down flat," says Youngest Son, "and I want it done by morning."

"*E'e*," says the *mn'tu*, "*kisi-tla'teketes*. I will have it done by morning."

Youngest Son shuts the cover of the box. He lies down to sleep. And all through the night, there is the noise of many men working on the mountain, tearing it apart and throwing it down. When Youngest Son awakens, the mountain has been levelled.

The old chief wakes up. His face is hot. Sun is pouring in on him, pouring in through the door of the wigwam. He doesn't know where he is. Even when he shoves his head out the door, he doesn't recognize the place. Where is the mountain that once stood before his door? This old chief is astonished.

'This young man has Power,' thinks the old chief; 'I can use his Power to rid me of my enemies.'

"He shall be my daughter's husband," he says to all the People gathering around his wigwam, looking at the place that mountain used to be. "Go and call him. Tell him to come here to me."

Youngest Son comes to the old chief. "This sun is quite enjoyable," says the old chief. "It is good to feel it on our faces. But we cannot truly enjoy things of this nature while we are bothered by our neighbours."

"*E'e*," says Youngest Son.

The old chief tells him that in order to marry his daughter, he must lead an attack on a nearby camp, an enemy camp. He hopes to destroy both his enemies and Youngest Son, whose great Power is so uncomfortable to have around. So he makes this plan, and Youngest Son agrees to it.

"I will join you," says Youngest Son. "Call the warriors, and we will set out as soon as the sun has come from beneath the earth tomorrow."

That camp of the People prepares for war, and then lies down to sleep. But Youngest Son does not sleep. He does not sleep until he has first journeyed to the enemy camp, and told the *mn'tu* to slay all of them. Then he covers the birchbark box. He puts it back into his medicine pouch, and he lies down in the forest outside the camp to sleep.

All night long he hears the sounds of war. He hears the sounds of fighting, of women crying and children shrieking, of the wounded groaning and dying. These noises grow fainter and fainter, and after a while, all he hears is silence. A death silence.

Now it is morning. Youngest Son walks into that camp to see what the *mn'tu* has done. All the old chief's enemies are dead, from the oldest to the youngest. All the men are dead. The women are dead. The children are all dead. Youngest Son turns and walks back to the village.

He walks into the old chief's wigwam. "I have been over to the other camp," says Youngest Son. "It was very quiet there when I left."

The old chief sends men to investigate, and they find that it is just as Youngest Son has said. He has killed them all. There is no one left. So the old chief must fulfill his promise.

"What is your name?" he says to Youngest Son.

"Nuji-kesi-kno'tasit," says Youngest Son.

'What kind of name is that?' thinks the old chief, but he gives him one of his daughters for a wife. He gives him a wigwam of his own to live in, and he gives him a slave to do all the work. Youngest Son lives with the chief's daughter; he hunts with the men of the village.

But one day when he hunts, he leaves his medicine pouch behind, wrapped in his robes. He leaves it behind, and his slave finds it. Now this slave has been curious, very curious. What is the source of his master's Power? Is it in this medicine pouch? He opens the pouch, he sees the birchbark box and the *mn'tu* inside, and he is not stupid. This slave knows exactly what he has found.

When the *mn'tu* looks up, when the *mn'tu* asks what is required, this slave speaks to him. "Take me," he says, "take me and this wigwam and this woman. Take us away into the forest where no one can ever find us." Then he shuts the cover of the box, as darkness comes over him and he faints.

When he awakens, he and the wigwam and Youngest Son's woman are way, way, away, somewhere, deep within the forest. He is free. He is no

longer a slave. He takes
Youngest Son's woman, and
lives there, away from the camps
of the People. Youngest Son comes
home from hunting. He knows what
has happened. He does not have his
medicine pouch; he does not have his *mn'tu*
in a birchbark box. But Youngest Son has
something else. He has his tiny little bow and
its arrow. Youngest Son shoots his arrow, and
runs after it, faster than it can fly. It shows him the
way. He runs and he runs, and soon he has found his
wigwam, deep within the forest. He has found his slave
and his wife. He has found them, and he waits for night.

Now it is night. Youngest Son sees that the slave is
asleep, with the medicine pouch under his head. Quietly,
quietly he slips into the wigwam. Quietly, quietly he speaks
to his wife, lying by the side of his slave.

"Put your hand under his head," says Youngest Son to his
wife, "and pull out the medicine pouch." And when she has
done this, and when he has gotten out his *mn'tu* and
uncovered him, Youngest Son wishes to be taken back to
the camp, wigwam, wife, slave, himself, everything.

That slave wakes up. The sun is shining in the door of the
wigwam. The noises of the camp are coming from outside.
And there is Youngest Son, sitting, looking at him.

Youngest Son kills his slave. He flays him, he skins him,
and his wife makes that slave's skin into a door-blanket.

Youngest Son has shown his Power. And this Power is
making the old chief nervous. The old chief decides once
more to kill his daughter's husband. Now this old chief is a
puoin, and his spirit-helper is a *jipijka'm,* a Horned Serpent Person. He will use his spirit-helper to kill his daughter's husband.

One day this old chief calls Youngest Son to him. He says
to him quietly, "I would like you to bring me the head of a
jipijka'm for my dinner."

"*E'e,*" says Youngest Son, looking at him. "I will do this
thing."

Youngest Son speaks to his own *mn'tu,* the Dancer In The
Birchbark Box. "Bring me a *jipijka'm,*" he says to it. "Bring
it here to the village. Bring it alive."

Now the *mn'tu* is coming back to the camp, dragging a
jipijka'm. The Horned Serpent Person is bellowing and
thrashing its tail, and all the People are screaming and
running away, all except Youngest Son.

Youngest Son walks out to fight the *jipijka'm*. It is a terrible battle. The *jipijka'm* rages and roars, and Youngest Son grapples with it. He grapples with it and then he kills it. Youngest Son cuts off the head of that *jipijka'm* and drags it into the old chief's wigwam.

The old chief is weak and dying. He is bent over double. Youngest Son has killed his *tioml,* his spirit-helper, and his Power is draining away. Youngest Son walks up to him, where he is sitting behind the fire, and he pounds him on the head with that *jipijka'm* head. The old chief falls over and dies, and Youngest Son drops the *jipijka'm* head on his body and walks away.

MEDICINE BAG

Saq, saq, long ago. There is a man and a woman, with three children: two boys and a girl. This family is very poor, and the younger son is talking to his brother. He says to him that they should go travelling. Maybe they would find something better. Maybe they would find wives, if they went travelling.

"I do not wish to go," says the older brother. "But you go. Maybe you will find something. And I will tell you a thing, a thing that may help you. Make yourself a *pse'kmuti,* one of those large deerskin bags. And when you find a girl whom you want for your wife, put all sorts of pretty things into the *pse'kmuti.* Tell her you will let her go inside to see them all. Then tie this bag up tight and run away with her. That is the way to catch a wife."

"I will do this," says his younger brother, and he makes himself a *pse'kmuti* and starts off on his travels.

The first place he came to was a camp of the People where they were still making tools of stone, the way the Old Ones of the People did so long ago. They had nothing from the world outside there in that camp, that *sa'qewe'juey wutan.*

This young man asks to see the chief.

"We have no chief," they say to him, there in that camp. "We do not need one. We do not like strangers coming here. If you are looking for People like yourself, you must travel further on. You will come to a camp of them, but first you must go past a very large camp of People like us."

So this young man travelled on. He passes by the larger camp of the People, and stops to talk to one of the old men there. The men in that camp are all sitting around making stone arrows, and the old man says to him that they don't like all this new stuff, these new inventions, this metal for making arrows. They prefer their own ways. "We do not like the manners of other nations," says this old man. "But go further along. There you will find People like yourself."

After a while, this young man came to a deep broad river, which he crossed, and then to a lake. He goes around the lake and there he finds a camp of the People. All the People come running out to see the stranger, to touch him, to make him welcome. The young man asks for the chief's lodge, and they take him to it. "Where have you come from?" asks the chief. "Why are you here?"

"My father sent me," says the young man. "I have come a long distance, to pay you a friendly visit." All the People treat him kindly, as is due to a stranger paying a visit. They send him home with a young man his own age, and these two become friends. And all the young men and the young girls come to talk with him and look him over.

"There are many pretty girls here," this young man says to his new friend one day. "But the prettiest is that daughter of the chief's."

"E'e," says his friend. "You are looking at her, are you?"

Now this young man is going out and gathering pretty things to put in his *pse'kmuti*. He finds beautiful stones and pieces of mica, he finds flowers and berries and other strange and curious things. He puts them all in his bag, and then he asks his friend to help him.

"I want you to get into my sack, and when you come out, I want you to tell everyone how beautiful it is in there."

"E'e," says his friend. "I will do this for you."

Now all the young men and young women are together talking and joking, when the stranger says something. "This is a beautiful place," he says, "but it is even more beautiful inside my *pse'kmuti*." Of course they are now all curious, and wonder what he is talking about. And after much persuading, he finally agrees to let his friend, with whom he has been staying, crawl inside and have a look.

His friend comes back out again, after a while. He is shaking his head. "The things I have seen!" he says. "So beautiful ... so strange!" The young man smiles, and folds up his bag. Maybe later he will bring it out again, but not now.

He waits. He watches his chance, and when he sees the chief's daughter going off to gather firewood, he just happens to be standing in the path. They are alone, and he tells her something.

"You are as beautiful as the beautiful things I have seen

102

inside my *pse'kmuti*. You
should go inside and look, to
see these things for yourself."
This young girl is curious. He
has told her about all the rare and
strange things to be seen inside; he has
let them all have a glimpse of some of them:
the glittering rocks and mica, the sweet-
smelling flower petals. And so she agrees to
meet with him, out in the forest, if he will let her
step into the bag and see all those things for herself.

"If I should let you do this," says that clever young
man, "you must keep very quiet. Walk forward slowly,
inside the bag. At first it will be dark. But keep silent and
still, no matter what happens, and then you will begin to
see."

"I will do this," says that young girl, the chief's daughter.
So she goes with him, and when they are away from all the
People, he opens the bag and lets her walk into it. And as
soon as she is inside, he ties the top up tight, throws her up
over his shoulder, and begins to run.

He runs as fast as he can and as far as he can, and when
she finally begins to suspect and cry out, she is so far away
that no one of her People can see or hear her. No one can
save her. And she cannot find her way home again.

The young man lets her out of the bag, and she begins to
weep. She knows what has happened, she knows she
cannot get home again, and her parents will be sorrowful.
They will think she has drowned in the lake. They will
think she has starved in the forest.

"Stop your crying and come with me," says the young
man. "I have promised to show you strange and beautiful
things, and I will. I have caught you; you are my wife now.
Stop your crying, and I will show you a *sa'qewe'juey wutan*,
a camp of the Old People. They are still making stone
arrows there."

She has no choice; she has to follow him. He shows her the
two camps of the Old People, and then he takes her to the
small camp of People near where his own family is living.
They stay there for several winters, and then he takes her
home. He takes her home to his own family, and they do not
recognize him. "It is I," he says to his older brother, "your
younger brother."

His parents are glad to see him, and they are very wel-
coming to his wife. A short time later, this young man dies,
and his brother takes the chief's daughter for his bride. The
pse'kmuti has caught him a wife too.

MI'KMWESU

In the time of the Old Ones, there is a large camp of the People. Many People are living there with their chief. One of them is an orphan, a young man. He lives with his grandmother, and he hunts with the other men, but he is awkward. He is ugly and clumsy and everyone laughs at him.

Now this young man is out hunting with the other men, but he lags behind them. He is always lagging behind. And this time a storm comes up and catches him. The wind is blowing and the rain is pouring down on him, and he gets lost.

He is going to give up and die out there, lost, when he sees a thing. It is a strange thing to see, out there deep within the forest. He sees a man smiling at him.

"You are lost," says this man. "Why don't you come home with me and eat and talk?" And this strange man helps him back to his wigwam. Then they are sitting all night around the fire, talking and smoking and eating. This wigwam is full of smoked and dried food, full of cakes of tallow and bags of marrow. This wigwam is full of the furs of otters, beavers, moose and martens, foxes, minks and muskrats, all stuffed in behind the poles of the wigwam all around.

Finally these two men sleep, and in the morning, when he wakes up, the ugly young man is given presents by his host. "Take this back with you," says the strange man who has found him lost in the forest. He gives him such a load of meat and furs that the poor boy cannot even lift it.

"I will come with you and carry this," says the man, and he hoists it easily upon his back. Off they go, walking through the forest, until they come to a place where they can see that camp of the People in the distance.

"I cannot go any further than this," says the man, laying down his load. "But if at any time you need me, come out

104

here and I will find you." Then that man leaves, and the orphan walks down into his own camp to tell his grandmother he has returned with meat.

The People all come running out to see him. And then he learns a thing: he learns that he has been missing, lost, for a whole year, during that one night he spent in the wigwam with the stranger. Everyone has thought he has been drowned, or starved. Everyone has thought him to be dead.

He knows then. He knows he has been spending the night with a Mi'kmwesu.

"Where have you been?" they all are asking.

"I have been hunting," he tells them. "I left my catch back there."

So all the People go out to help him bring it in. They are astonished at the size of it. No one can lift that load, so they break it up into many smaller loads and take it back to his wigwam.

Now this young man is living with his grandmother, there in his wigwam, and one morning he says to her, "*Nukumi', nuku-wloqi-mittukwey.* Let us go and make an evening visit, Grandmother." At once she knows what he has been thinking of. He wishes a wife, and he wants her to make inquiries for him.

"*Nuji'j,*" says his grandmother, "whom shall I ask?"

"Pay a visit to the chief's wigwam," says the ugly young man.

So his grandmother makes herself ready, and when it is evening, she goes over there and enters. She speaks with the chief. "*Saqmaw,*" says this old woman, "my grandson and I are weary of living alone. There are only two of us. I am tiring now. I am growing old and feeble, and I cannot take care of the wigwam and my grandson as is required." That is all she says, but the chief understands why she has come.

"*Moqwe,*" he tells her. "Your grandson is ugly and lazy, and you are poor. I cannot help you." He refuses to give away his daughter, and the old woman can do nothing. She goes back to her wigwam and repeats to her grandson what this chief has said.

He is very cool about it; he does not get hot and angry. It does not drive him mad. He says only, "*Ejela'tu'kw,* we can do nothing. It is not our fault." And he sits looking into the fire.

But in the morning he goes out of the camp, to the place where the stranger had left him. And there is the Mi'kmwesu, waiting for him. He is smiling. The young man goes home with him, and on the way, they kill a moose. They kill a moose and the stranger cuts that moose in half. One half he picks up and drapes over his shoulder, then he gestures toward his friend. "Pick it up," he says, smiling. So the young man tries. And to his surprise, he is able to carry it. He walks through the forest carrying half a moose on his shoulders.

That evening, in the camp of the stranger, he hears beautiful music. His strange friend can play the *pipuk-waqn,* the alder-wood flute. He takes it out of his robes and the sounds he makes are like birds singing, like whales crying. *"Nitap,"* says the stranger, *"netawi-pipuk-wen?* My friend, can you play a flute like this one?"

"Moqwe," says the ugly one. "I cannot." So the Mi'kmwesu takes the flute and places it in his hands. He puts his fingers in the proper places, and presses the flute against his lips. "Play," says the Mi'kmwesu, and the young man plays. He plays as beautifully as his strange friend can play, and he is delighted.

This time he spends two nights at the wigwam of his friend, and when the time has come to return to his own camp, he is given pres- ents as before. This time he is strong enough to carry them himself: his friend has given him Power. He has given him strength and music. He has taken away his ugliness, and made him a Mi'kmwesu. That ugly young man, now beauti- ful, lifts his enormous pile of furs and meat, and returns to his camp of the People. "Where have you been?" they all are asking him. "You have been miss- ing for two years, for two winters. And what has hap- pened to you? Your face! It is so handsome!" The new Mi'kmwesu just smiles.

His grandmother is very glad to see him. The whole camp of the People is trying to fit into her wigwam, exclaiming over her grandson, and the mountain of meat and furs he has brought back with him.

Now it is evening. This young man brings out his flute and begins to play. The beautiful sounds float past the ears of the People and all the young girls begin to put on their finest clothes and to paint beautiful designs on their faces. They begin to drift past the wigwam where that young man is playing his flute. Eventually they become brave enough to go inside. But he will not look at any of them. He turns his back to the door, and sits playing his flute to the wall.

Someone is pulling back the door-blanket. Someone is coming in. It is the chief. He wishes to speak to the old grandmother. He is making her an evening visit. He now is willing for one of his daughters to come over to her wigwam and live as her grandson's wife.

"*Moqwe,*" says the young man, the Mi'kmwesu, "we have no need to trouble you, to think of you. We have no need of any service you might do us."

Now several days have gone past, and this young man speaks to his grandmother. He wants her to make an evening visit herself.

"*Nuji'j,*" says his grandmother, "*tami li-etes?* Where shall I go?"

"Go to that poor little wigwam on the other side of the camp, where those two girls are living. Those two girls without father or mother. Go there."

So his grandmother makes a visit to the little wigwam. She goes in and slowly lowers herself to sit by the fire. The two girls are polite to her. Grandmother looks at one of them. "Will you come and live with us?" she asks her. "With my grandson and me?"

This girl is quiet. She is polite. She says, "If you and your grandson both desire it, then I will come."

"*E'e,*" says the grandmother. "This will be a good thing for all of us."

And she takes that girl home with her this very night, to stay with them as her grandson's wife.

When the other girls in that camp of the People hear what has happened, they are furious. They want to kill that girl. But her husband is watching out for her. He takes her, he takes her sister, he takes his grandmother, and they all move deep into the forest, away from that camp of the People.

Kespi-a'tuksitkik.

107

KLUSKAP AND
MI'KMWESU

Now in a large camp of the People, two young men are
setting out. They are going on a journey, a journey to find
one of them a wife. One is going to find a wife. One is going
to help him, to be his companion and his friend.

These two young men come to a place, in their journey. It
is an island, the island where Kluskap is living. He lives
there with his Old Grandmother, and with Little Marten.
When the young men come into his wigwam, he welcomes
them, and Old Grandmother begins to make them something to eat.

She takes an old beaver skin and scrapes a bit from it; she
puts these scrapings into her cooking pot. The two young
men are watching her, puzzled. This is a strange meal. And
when it is cooked, Old Grandmother puts the stuff into a
bowl, a tiny little bowl, and passes it to them.

The two young men begin to eat. The bowl is never empty.
The more they eat, the more there is in that bowl. They eat
until they are full. And when night comes, they all lie down
to sleep, there in the wigwam of Kluskap.

One of these young men has eaten too much. He was very
hungry. The little bowl has fooled him, and his stomach
gets too full. He is lying next to Kluskap, his head at
Kluskap's feet, and his stomach is full of cramps. Before he
can go outside, all this food begins giving him bad diar-
rhoea, and he soils himself.

"Get up, little brother," says Kluskap. "Come outside."
Kluskap takes that young man down to the river and strips
off his clothes. He washes him, he gives him new clothes,
clean clothes, he combs his hair.

Kluskap combs this young man's hair, and then he ties it
up with a *sakklo'pi,* a hair-string, a hair-string of Power.
This hair-string changes that young man, changes him into
a Mi'kmwesu. Kluskap has given him Power.

Now Kluskap gives him something else; he gives him a tiny flute and teaches him how to play it. They are creating music in the night. The sounds float over the camp where everyone else lies sleeping.

"Can you sing, little brother?" says Kluskap.

"*Moqwe*," says that young man, that Mi'kmwesu. "I cannot."

"Follow my voice," says Kluskap. "Sing with me. Come. Open your voice and do it." So they are both singing. The young man, the Mi'kmwesu, discovers his voice. It is a deep voice, and strong. He can sing with ease. And the sound of their singing floats over that camp, where everyone else lies sleeping.

Now it is morning. And in the light of day, the new Mi'kmwesu asks Kluskap to lend him a canoe. "We have a long way to go," he says. "And that way is filled with dangers."

"I will lend it to you, if you promise to bring it back to me. For never yet have I lent it, without having to go and fetch it home again."

"I will bring it, I will fetch it home to you, when the time comes," says the Mi'kmwesu. And he and his friend go down to the shore to find it. There is no canoe there. They see nothing but a little island, a small rocky island. Where is the *kwitn*, the canoe?

"This island is my canoe," says Kluskap. "You may take it for your journey."

The island is very easy to sail, to paddle. The two young men are steering straight out to sea. They see something. It is land, another island, rising up out of the sea. When they reach it, they take the canoe into the woods and hide it there. Then they go walking, walking in search of People.

Here is a large camp, a *meski'k wutan*. A *saqmaw* lives here, with his beautiful daughter. He has killed many times, killed young men who have come seeking his daughter as a wife. He gives them tasks to do, impossible tasks. Either they die trying to accomplish these works, or he kills them for their failures.

But now the two strangers are invited in, asked to come up to the guests' seats behind the fire. The Mi'kmwesu is speaking for his friend. "*Siwi-nkutukwa'lukwet*," that is what he says. "My friend is tired of living alone."

"*E'e*," says that chief, that *saqmaw*. "There is, however, a small thing that requires doing first. If my daughter's husband were to bring in the head of a *jipijka'm*, that would be a pleasing thing to me."

"This thing will be done by morning," say the two young men, and they leave, to spend the night in another wigwam. And some time in the night, the Mi'kmwesu wakes. He wakes and goes out into the darkness. He is going to hunt *jipijka'm.* He tracks *jipijka'm,* he finds the hole in the ground where that Horned Serpent Person lives. The Mi'kmwesu puts a log in front of this hole, and he begins to dance. He dances the *nskowaqn,* calling that *jipijka'm* up. Calling him up out of his hole.

Something is coming. Something is making a noise. It is *jipijka'm,* coming up from under the earth. His head comes out of the hole first, and as it passes over the log, the Mi'kmwesu strikes. With a single blow of his axe, he cuts the head from Horned Serpent Person. He takes this head, he takes it by one shining yellow horn and carries it back to the wigwam. He places it by the side of his sleeping friend, and then he wakes him up.

"Here," he says, "take this over to your wife's father."

"*Ai'e,*" says the old *saqmaw,* "this time I shall lose my child. But first, there is something I should like to see."

"What thing is this?" they ask him.

"I should like to see my daughter's husband coasting downhill on a hand-sled."

Now close to this camp is a high mountain. The sides are very steep and rocky. Two sleds are taken out there. The young man and his friend, his Mi'kmwesu friend, will ride one sled. The other sled will take two *puoinaq* of the People, the old *saqmaw*'s People. These four all climb up the mountain together, but the two *puoinaq* let the other two start first. They are expecting them to fall; they are expecting them to fall off their sleds. Then they will ride over them and crush them.

The race begins. The sleds are flying, they speed like the wind. The young man loses his balance, he falls from the sled, but his Mi'kmwesu friend catches at his clothes and pulls him back on board. He slows the sled, pretending to adjust their weight, and the two *puoinaq* sail right past.

Instantly the Mi'kmwesu sends his sled off again, steering straight for a bump. Up soars his sled into the air, flying off that bump, over the heads of the two *puoinaq.* The Mi'kmwesu is shouting and singing, his voice comes out of him like thunder. His sled roars down the mountain to the foot, but it doesn't stop there. It tears on, crashing through the old *saqmaw*'s wigwam, ripping out both the walls.

The old man jumps up in terror. "I have lost my daughter this time," he says. His Power has met its match.

But there are still some games and races to be done, to celebrate the wedding. The bridegroom must race one of the *puoinaq*. His friend gives him his pipe to hold; he lends him his Power this way. The two racers begin to run, slowly and quietly at first, so that they may talk together. "Who are you?" asks the bridegroom. "What are you?" The *puoin* speaks. "I am Wikatisk," he says, "I am the Northern Lights. Who and what are you?"

"I am Wasoqotesk," says the young man, telling his Power-shape. "I am Chain-Lightning." And off they go, running, running.

By the middle of the day, when the sun is overhead, Chain-Lightning returns. He has run all around the earth. Northern Lights does not come home until dark, panting. Chain-Lightning has won, and the old chief says, "I have certainly lost my daughter."

Now the bridegroom must dive, dive with one of the *puoinaq*. "Who and What are you?" he asks.

"I am Jikmui'j," says that one. "I am a Sea-Duck. Who and What are you?"

"Kwimu," says the bridegroom. "I am Loon." And down they go, diving to the bottom of the water. After many long minutes, the Sea-Duck comes up, gasping. The Loon stays down for hours.

"I have lost," moans the *saqmaw,* "I have lost my daughter. Now I am satisfied. You may take her and go. But first we will celebrate this wedding feast. We will dance. All of us will dance."

The dancing-ground is near the chief's wigwam. It is a cleared space, smooth, the earth is beaten down, so that many men may dance there. And when all is ready, the Mi'kmwesu jumps onto the dancing-ground first. If there is Power hidden there, he will deal with it. He will unwind it. Round and round the circle he is dancing. He dances, he beats his feet down onto the earth. He slams his feet down, and with every step they sink into the earth, deeper and deeper. The Mi'kmwesu is dancing within the earth, sinking down and down until at last they can only see his head as he spins around this circle, this dancing-ground. Everyone sees his Power. And when he stops, that is the end of the dancing. He has torn that dancing-ground all up.

Now at last the young girl, the chief's daughter, is given to her husband, and he and his friend help her into Kluskap's canoe. They are going home, *pusijik.* But still something is feeling wrong. They can smell it. The old chief has sent *puoinaq* to follow them, to kill the two men, and to bring his

111

daughter home. The surface of the sea is smooth, but up ahead, clouds are coming. Black clouds, terrible clouds, coming to kill them. The *puoinaq* have called the winds.

"Hold the canoe steady," says the Mi'kmwesu. He stands up, he fills himself with air. His Power comes up in him, and he begins to breathe out. A great wind rushes from him to meet the storm which is coming. The Mi'kmwesu's windstorm beats back the storm which the *puoinaq* have raised, and defeats it. Now the sea is calming down again, *ewipniaq*.

The two friends and the captured bride journey on through the sea, sailing in the *kwitn* of Kluskap. And then they are seeing something. It is a dark thing, sticking up out of the water. It is a beaver's tail. They know what it is. It is a *puoin* Shape-Changer. He has taken the form of a beaver to fool them, and as they pass, he will smash the canoe with his tail.

So Mi'kmwesu steers that canoe straight for the beaver, and just as they are passing it, he cries out, "I am a great hunter of beavers. Many of them have I killed!" As he cries out, he strikes down with his axe. He cuts the tail from the body, and leaves that Shape-Changer floating dead in the water.

They have crossed the bay, and now they are going around a point of land, *kwiewey*. Kluskap's canoe is close to the shore, and on this point of land, they see a thing. It is another *puoin*, another Shape-Changer. It is Apukjilui'j, Skunk Person. He intends to slay them with his terrible smell, and stands with his tail pointed right at them, ready to shoot.

Mi'kmwesu stands up in the canoe. He has a small spear, whittled from a stick, and he throws it. Straight at Apukjilui'j it flies. Skunk Person gives two or three small kicks and dies. The Mi'kmwesu steps ashore. He cuts a pole; he impales Apukjilui'j on that pole, and shoves one end into the ground.

"*Likjo'jine'n,*" he says to the body, the body of Apukjilui'j. "Point your arse in that direction."

Finally their dangers are all over. They see the camp of Kluskap in the distance. He is waiting for them on the shore.

"Well, my friends," says Kluskap, "I see you have brought back my *kwitn.*"

"*E'e,*" say those two young men. "We have indeed brought it back."

"And have you done well on your journey?"

112

They tell him all that has happened. Kluskap already knows these things; he has been Seeing them, he has been watching over them, helping them. And after he feasts them, he sends them home. But first he speaks to the Mi'kmwesu.

"If you ever need me, think of me, and I will come."

KWIMU

Saq, saq, in the time of the Old Ones, there is a camp back in the forest, by the shores of a big lake. And further off from that camp, deeper into the forest along the lake edge, a poor family is living. This family has two children; the older is a boy, the younger is a girl. And these two children are always going down to the lake side, fishing.

"Can you tell what kind of fish I am catching?" the boy asks the girl one day.

"E'e," she says, "you have caught a trout. Of course I know what a trout looks like."

After a while she catches a fish. "Do you know what kind of fish this one is?" she says to her brother.

"It's just another trout," he tells her.

"Moqwe, moqwe," says that little girl. "It is not a trout. It is a *taqu'naw,* a rainbow trout. So I have beaten you, my older brother."

These two children go on fishing all along the shore, and then they begin to hear something. It is a Kwimu Person, a Loon, calling and calling in the distance. And the sound of his calling makes that little girl so lonely that she asks her older brother if he will take her home.

So. They take their fish and go back to the wigwam, and their mother cooks those trout for them to eat. And now all the time those children are staying very close together. They build a little house to play in, and they sit in there, talking and talking, but nobody can understand what they are saying. They look very serious, talking like that. All the People think that they are strange.

Now one day the boy says to his sister, "I am going to make you something. I am going to make you some clothes. And then we will see what happens."

He makes her a robe of leaves: red leaves and yellow leaves, red leaves and orange leaves. He puts many sizes

115

and colours of leaves into this robe, and then he wraps his sister up in it, and takes her down to the shore.

"Walk up and down here, my younger sister," he says to her. "I am going to hide further up the bank."

"What is going to happen?" she asks him, holding her leaf-robe around her.

"Watch and see."

That little girl is walking up and down the lake shore, wearing a robe of red and yellow leaves, when she begins to hear something. It is Kwimu, calling and calling in the distance. And then Kwimu is coming closer, he is calling from close by. Finally she sees him, looking at her red leaves.

She speaks to him politely. "*Nikskami'j*, my Grandfather. Where have you come from?"

"From nowhere in particular," comes the voice of the Loon.

Kwimu has spoken to her. She runs to find her brother, and he comes back down to the lake shore with her. He hides himself behind her, while Kwimu is speaking to them.

"What is it that you wish?" asks Kwimu.

"We do not want anything," say that little boy and his sister.

But Kwimu is talking to them. He is talking to them about Power; he is giving them lessons in it. And afterwards, that girl is lonely whenever she hears the Loon calling. She sits all by herself, thinking. Power is growing in her. Kwimu has been talking to her.

Kwimu talks to her all the time.

Now it is morning. The sun has come from beneath the earth, and that girl goes down to the lake. Kwimu is waiting for her.

"Death is coming," says the Loon.

"Kukwes is coming," says Kwimu.

Kukwes. Cannibal Giant.

"What shall we do?" the young girl says to Kwimu.

"You must leave this place. Tell your father. Tell your mother. Tell your brother. Take down the wigwam and go. Kukwes is coming; he will eat this whole camp. I have Seen it. You must take everything and go away around the other side of the lake. And when you hear the Kukwes screaming, come out into the water."

So this girl goes home and tells her family what Kwimu has said. "Kukwes is coming. We must go quickly, around the lake."

116

"If Kwimu has said this, it must be true," says her father. "Get up. We must go at once."

This family begins to pack up their possessions, and to remove the bark cover from their wigwam. From further down the lake the People in the big camp are watching them. "Where are you going?" they ask, wandering over. "Why are you leaving?" the *saqmaw* wants to know.

"Kukwes is coming," says the father of those two children. "We are going to be attacked, and the whole camp destroyed."

"Who told you this? How do you know?"

"The Loon has said so, to my child."

"*Ya*," says that chief. "The Loon, *ya*. The Loon is not very much, and your child is nothing." And he refuses the warning.

But that family is ready, and they leave that camp of the People, walking away as fast as they can, walking deeper into the wild forest, along the edge of the lake. For a long time they are walking, until they hear Kwimu calling. When he has called three times, there they stop, and set up their wigwam, close to the shore.

Now it is morning. Kwimu calls to the children, and they go down to the lake to speak with him.

"Death is coming," says the Loon.

"Kukwes is coming. In the evening you will hear him. At the first yell, you must all wade out into the water. You must not delay."

And in the early part of the night, they hear the first terrible scream of Kukwes, and the awful shrieks of the People they have left behind. They can hear wigwams crashing to the ground and catching fire from the hearths. Men are shouting and women crying for their children, and all through it they hear the terrible screams of Kukwes as he slays.

They wade further and further out into the darkness of the lake, until only their eyes are showing above the water. Not until morning, when the sun has come from beneath the earth, and everything is silent, silent back in the direction from which they had come, do they dare to come out of the water. The father and the boy leave the two women at their wigwam, and creep, creep through the woods back toward their old camp.

Everyone is dead. They are all lying there, dead. Some of them have been gnawed on, and some of them have been eaten. Kukwes has done this.

The man and his son creep away from that place and run

as fast as they can back to their new camp. They lived there for a long time, and Kukwes did not find them.

Now all the time Kwimu is talking to the boy and the girl, teaching them, giving them lessons in the use of Power. He shows the boy how to run as fast as the wind. He shows him how to walk on the water, as if it were dry land. And finally he shows him how to travel through the very air itself: he shows him how to fly.

The boy can hunt the land.

The boy can hunt the water.

The boy can hunt the air.

And so they are living well. They have plenty to eat. And Kwimu says to that boy, "If you ever need me, call. Call me and I will come to you."

Always Kwimu is talking to that girl. Kwimu. Loon Person. Sometimes she sees him in his Loon shape, sometimes he appears to her as a man. And one day he tells her that he wants her. He wants her to be his wife.

"This lake is my country," he says to her. "And should you choose to live with me, it will give you everything you wish, everything your heart asks for."

"*Moqwe,*" says this girl. "I think I do not wish to marry." But she goes home and speaks with her mother about it.

"Kwimu," says her mother. "He would be a good husband. He would never be unkind to you. Loon Persons never quarrel with their wives. And he has Power. He has been talking with you for a long time now, the whole time you have been growing up."

And so that girl walks back down to the lake. He is standing there, waiting for her. She goes to him, within the lake.

Now she is Kwimue'skw, Loon Wife. Loon Woman. Sometimes she comes back to the wigwam for a while, then she returns to him. But Kwimu never leaves the water's edge.

One day when she comes up to the wigwam from the lake, she is carrying something. "He has given me this," she tells her mother. "He has given me this to play with." It is a large speckled egg, very beautiful. This girl is smiling. "What shall I do with it?"

"Put it in this medicine bag, this bag full of feathers," says her mother. "Put it in carefully." This girl is very protective of it, waiting for her baby to be born.

One day Kwimu speaks to his wife. "Danger is coming," he says to her. "I have Seen it. Men are coming, and if they see me they will hunt me."

"You must go behind the rock that sticks up from the middle of the lake," says Loon Woman, his wife. "Hide there until they are gone. I will go up on land and see what they are about."

This girl goes up to talk to her mother, and when it is morning, they see a canoe coming. There are two men in it, who pay them a friendly visit. "We did not know there were People here," say those two men. "You must be lonely. Come over the water to our camp and pay us a visit."

In the night, Kwimu talks to his wife. "It would be dangerous for you to go there," he tells her. "Your parents may go. Your brother may go. But you should stay here."

She smiles at him. In the morning she tells those men that she is pregnant, and will not make the journey to visit their camp. But after a while, her mother and her father decide to go down there. Her brother will go with them.

Kwimu has been teaching her brother. Her brother has Power. And after a while, in that camp of the People they are visiting, the People begin to whisper about her brother. He does everything too well. He hunts better than their young men. He fishes better. He catches birds more often than they do. And he can run so fast! He beats them at all their games. These People decide to poison him.

"Let's kill him," they say to each other. "Tomorrow night, when we are eating together."

But the night before, Kwimu calls to this young man while he is dreaming. "Death is coming," says the Loon. "Run away from it." So he quietly wakes his parents, takes them down to the lake, and paddles away so silently that no one can even hear the water drops as they fall from his paddle.

But those People now know where this family is living. Kwimu tells them, "Come away from here. Come up to the farthest end of the lake, where they cannot find you."

The young man sets out with his sister, leaving the parents behind to follow later. But those men of the People find them first. They kill the old man and the old woman. Kwimu tells their children what has happened, and they stay up there, way up at the farthest end of the lake. They will not go back, they will stay hidden from the People.

One day Kwimu is talking to his wife and her brother. "I will stay with you for seven years," he says. "Then I must return to the place of the Kwimu'k, to my own place. But until then, I will always help you. I will watch over you." And this he does. Several times he gives them warning, and they move away from danger. They move away from death.

And when the seven years are up, he says to them that the time of parting has come. Kwimu disappears from them. He has gone to the place of the Loons.

Three days later, his wife is walking beside the lake shore, mourning him. In the distance, she hears a Loon calling, and she feels a terrible loneliness. But then she sees a thing. It is a Loon Person swimming underwater, coming toward her. And as he breaks this surface, it is a man leaping from the water. It is Kwimu. It is her husband.

"I could not remain away from you," he says. "I could not stop thinking of you. And so I have come back, even from the place of the Loons."

That girl is very glad to see him. Her brother is glad to see him.

Now it is morning. Something is coming across the lake. Three Loon Persons, swimming toward them. These are Kwimu's brothers, come for a visit.

"We have come to see whether you are happy, living here," they say to him. "And we see that you surely are." And after a few days, these Loon Persons went back to the place of the Loons, leaving Kwimu behind with Kwimue'skw and her brother, to stay with them beside that beautiful lake which was Kwimu's own.

"This lake belongs to me," says Kwimu to his wife. "And if you live with me, it will give you all that your heart might wish."

TIA'M AND TIA'MI'SKW

Na meski'k wutan qospemk. There is a large camp of the People on the edge of a lake. And at the far end of the camp lives Tia'm.

Tia'm. His spirit-helper, his *tioml,* it is the Moose. He has the Power of Moose.

Tia'm. He has the Power to do another thing: he has the Power to make himself invisible.

Tia'm is living with his sister, in the wigwam at the far end of the camp. No one can see him. One day Tia'm says, "I will marry. I will marry the first woman who can see me."

In this camp by the lake are living many young women. All of them are trying to see Tia'm. He has the Power.

The young women go to visit his sister. She made them all welcome, whenever they came. And when the sun began to go beneath the earth, in the evening, the time when the hunters come home, she would rise. She would say to them, "Let us walk along the shores of the lake."

The sister of Tia'm had Power. Always she could see her brother, and when he came out of the forest, walking toward the camp, she is saying to the other women, "Can you see my brother?"

Al-tluejik, "E'e": some said yes.

Al-tluejik, "Moqwe": some said no.

The sister of Tia'm would look at the ones who thought they saw him, and at the ones who wanted others to think that they did. "Ah," she would say, "and can you tell me, *koqoey wiskopuksi'j?* Of what is his shoulder-strap made?"

And all those women, those women who wanted Tia'm, they begin to guess. They guess all the things from which a hunter's shoulder-strap is usually made: "A strip of raw-hide." "A withe." And the moment they spoke, Tia'm's sister knows. She knows that they are not seeing him.

"Very well," she says, "And now let us return to the wigwam."

The women all go back with her, and this is what she is telling them:

"Come in," she says to them, to all of them. "Come in and sit on my side of the wigwam." They must not cross to the hunter's side; they must stay on the women's side.

And when Tia'm comes in, these women cannot see him. He throws down his burden, his catch: they see it. He takes off his moccasins for his sister to hang up to dry: they see them. But they do not see Tia'm.

"Help me cook the supper," says the sister of Tia'm to all these women, one by one as they came to visit her wigwam. And all these women are helping to cook and eat. They are hoping that they will see Tia'm as they eat his food. They eat and they drink, but their eyes cannot find him. Sometimes they spend the night on the women's side, watching, looking, yet still they are not seeing Tia'm. In the morning they leave, they go back to their wigwams. Others come to take their place. But no one sees Tia'm except his sister.

Now in this camp, there is another man of the People. His wife is dead. He has three daughters. Oldest Daughter is taking her mother's place; she is running the household. Middle Daughter helps her. But Youngest Daughter is weak and often she is getting sick. Her oldest sister is unkind to her: she kicks her, she beats her, she is taking a red-hot stick from the fire to burn her. She burns the face and hands of her youngest sister, she burns her on her legs and chest. And when the father comes home, Oldest Daughter says, "That child is careless. She plays near the fire. Can I help it if she burns herself? I am doing all the work, and I cannot be watching her all the time."

Youngest Daughter is so covered with burn scars that everyone is calling her Wjikii'skw, the Girl Who Is Covered With Scabs.

Middle Daughter is kinder than Oldest Daughter; sometimes she speaks up for Wjikii'skw, but she does not tell their father what is happening.

Now it is the day when Oldest Daughter and Middle Daughter decide to go to the wigwam of Tia'm. They put on their finest painted clothes, and together they make a visit to the sister of Tia'm. She invites them to spend the afternoon.

Evening is coming. The sun is going beneath the earth. "Come," says the sister of Tia'm, "let us walk beside the lake, and wait for my brother's return."

Tia'm is coming, he is walking from the shadows of the forest, carrying his game. His sister can see him, in the last light of the day, coming out of the trees. "Can you see my brother?" she says to Oldest Daughter and Middle Daughter. "Do you see Tia'm yet?"

"I see him," said Oldest Daughter.

"I do not see him," said Middle Daughter.

"Ah," says his sister to Oldest Daughter. "And can you see his shoulder-strap? Can you tell me of what it is made?"

"Yes," Oldest Daughter is saying, "I can see it; it is made of rawhide."

"Very well," said Tia'm's sister. "Let us go back to the camp and wait for him."

Tia'm comes into the wigwam. They see the robe move, the robe that covers the door. They see the great load of moose meat he carries; they see it when he drops it. They see his moccasins, when he takes them off. But him they do not see, even through the whole night which they spend with his sister, lying together on the women's side. And in the morning, they return to the wigwam of their father.

Now once more evening has come, and the father of these three girls is coming home. With him he is bringing shells, handfuls of shells, the small beautiful shells which women make into beads, the shells called *witpeskul.* "Here are some gifts for my daughters," he says.

All the next day they are making them into beads and *napawijik:* stringing them up and sewing them to their clothes.

And that day Wjikii'skw is getting a pair of her father's old moccasins and soaking them to make the leather supple again. "Please," she says to her sisters, "please may I have some of the pretty little shell beads? May I have a few of each kind, to put them on my moccasins?"

"Don't give her any," says Oldest Daughter to Middle Daughter. "She is nothing but a pest, a lying little pest."

"Oh, no," says Middle Daughter. "The poor little thing, let her have some. Just a few. Some of each." And Middle Daughter gives Wjikii'skw a small amount of beads.

Wjikii'skw is sewing them to her father's huge old moccasins.

Now Wjikii'skw goes into the forest. She is looking for a white birch tree, with smooth white bark, white like the skin of an animal before tanning, and when she finds one, she cuts it. She cuts it with her little knife and peels it off the tree. And with this bark she makes herself a costume.

She makes a bark dress. She sews it up with spruce root. She makes bark sleeves, one for each arm. She makes bark leggings and a cap of bark. She sews them all up as neatly as she can, and then she draws lines and designs on the white bark, in the same way her sisters have painted their soft leather clothing, and embroidered it with quills from the porcupine, or with moose hair dyed many colours.

Wjikii'skw puts on her new bark clothes. She pulls on her father's big old moccasins which come up almost to her knees, and she sets out to visit the sister of Tia'm, in her wigwam at the far edge of the camp.

"Come back here! Come back at once!" screams Oldest Daughter.

"Wjikii'skw!" calls Middle Daughter.

The whole camp of the People comes out to see what the noise is. All the men and boys are shouting at Wjikii'skw as she stumbles in her big shoes through the camp. "Shame, shame," they yell at her. But Wjikii'skw is brave. She walks on. And finally she comes to the door of the wigwam of Tia'm.

Her face and her body are covered with sores and scabs. Her hair is singed off, her dress is nothing but bark and roots and charcoal lines, her moccasins come up to her knees.

"Come in," says the sister of Tia'm. "Come in and welcome."

Now the sun is going beneath the earth. Now the two women leave the wigwam of Tia'm to walk beside the lake. And now Tia'm himself is coming, coming from beneath the long shadows of the forest, walking toward his sister, and toward Wjikii'skw.

"Do you see my brother?"

"*E'e,* yes, I see him."

"Of what is his shoulder-strap made? Can you tell me?"

"Yes. It is the *walqwan,* the rainbow. He wears the rainbow on his shoulders."

"Ah," says Tia'm's sister. "You have truly seen him. Let us hurry to the wigwam and make things ready for him."

The sister of Tia'm has Power. She takes the clothing, the bark clothing from Wjikii'skw and she washes her. And as she is washing her, all her scabs and sores and hurts are washed away. Her skin is being made smooth and beautiful.

Then the sister of Tia'm opens her bark box and brings from it the wedding clothes which she has made for the woman who would be her brother's wife. Wjikii'skw puts it on, and then her new sister-in-law begins to comb her hair.

Wjikii'skw was sad. "I have no hair to comb; on my head there is no hair. What will she find to comb?"

But the sister of Tia'm has Power. And as she combs, hair springs forth from the head of Wjikii'skw, black and long and beautiful; dark like a river, hanging almost to the ground.

"Now," says the sister of Tia'm, "you must cross over to the men's side, to my brother's side of the wigwam, and take the wife's seat, next to the door."

Tia'm is coming in. He is laughing. "So," he says, "we'ju'lkwiss, she has found us, has she?"

Elajl, "E'e." Wjikii'skw says to him, "Yes."

And so he takes her for his wife.

It is night. The father of Wjikii'skw has come home from hunting. He throws down his load of meat for Oldest Daughter to butcher. He takes off his moccasins for Middle Daughter to hang up to dry, and he is lighting his pipe while his dinner is cooking. But where is Wjikii'skw?

He looks around the wigwam. "Where is Youngest Daughter?" he says to her sisters.

"We do not know," they tell him. "We saw her. She was going away. We called to her to come back, but she would not. She would not listen to us." They said nothing about her visit to the sister of Tia'm.

"Ah," says their father. He begins to eat.

Now it is morning. The sun has come from beneath the earth. The father of Wjikii'skw rises, he leaves his wigwam, he goes in search of his daughter. All through the camp he goes, looking, until he comes to the wigwam of Tia'm. He calls out and enters.

But he does not recognize the beautiful young woman sitting next to the sister of Tia'm. He does not know her until she speaks, telling him all that has happened. The father of Wjikii'skw is glad for her. "Good," he says to her, "this is good. Remain here and be a useful wife to your husband. Help his sister in the care of his wigwam."

When he returns to his own wigwam, he sits and lights his pipe. After a while he speaks:

"Youngest Daughter has seen Tia'm," he says. "She sits beside him as his wife. Even now I have seen them. I

have seen Tia'm: he is tall, he is strong. I have seen
Youngest Daughter: she is beautiful, her hair is a dark
river. May they have many children."
Oldest Daughter says nothing. Middle Daughter smiles.

▲

Now comes a long time of happiness for Tia'm and his
wife and sister. Hunting is good, he brings home many fat
kills. His wife and his sister butcher the meat, cut up the
flesh into little strips, and dry it. He brings home many fine
skins: his wife and his sister tan them, smoke them and sew
them into clothing for the family. And Youngest Daughter,
the girl once called Wjikii'skw, Tia'm's wife, she gives birth
to a son.

Now this little boy is growing up, he is walking and
running about, playing outside the wigwam. He is the son
of Tia'm.

Tia'm: his *tioml* is the moose. He has the Power of Moose,
he takes the shape of Moose, he is Moose Person.

It is in the morning. Tia'm has gone into the forest; he is
hunting. His son is playing. Tia'm's sister says to his wife:
"You see that moose's leg-bone, lying here in the wigwam?
You must be very careful with it, while Tia'm is out on the
hunt. Do not let the child play with it; do not let the child
break it. Only when his father has safely returned—then
he may break this bone and eat the marrow."

"*E'e,*" said the wife of Tia'm. "I will do this."

Once more it is morning. Tia'm has gone out to hunt. His
sister and his wife are busy: they are cutting up meat, they
are stringing meat, they are hanging it up to smoke. They
are so busy, they forget to watch the little boy.

The women are working outside. The child is in the
wigwam, playing. His father has made him a little club.
"Smack," he says, "smack, smack. I have killed you. Bang,
smack." He is hitting everything with his little club, and
eventually, there is the moose's leg-bone, lying there
in front of him. He raises the club over his head, he
brings it down. The leg-bone splinters. Bone
chips fly up into the air. Red marrow is leaking
from that bone, slowly leaking onto the floor
of the wigwam. The boy touches the bone.

Deep in the forest, his father stag-
gers under his load of moose meat.

Tia'm's sister runs into the
wigwam. She sees the broken
bone, lying on the ground.
"*Akaia,*" she cries, and

begins to weep, calling to her sister-in-law to come. "Tie up the baby in his carrier, quickly, quickly. Tie him up and come; my brother lies in the forest, his leg broken. For see, the leg-bone lies here, smashed."

Tia'm's wife takes the little boy on her back in his carrier, and sets off into the forest with Tia'm's sister. They travel a long journey, a hard journey, following the signs of his passing, going the way he went. And finally, these two women are seeing Tia'm. He lies by a load of moose meat. His leg is broken.

Tia'm speaks to his wife: "Take my son. Go to your father's wigwam. I can no longer hunt. I can no longer care for the two of you. You must live with your father now."

"Akaia, akaia!" His wife mourns for him, but she obeys. She takes the little boy and begins her journey out of the forest.

"Now, my sister," says Tia'm. "It is time. Go with my wife as far as our wigwam. Bring the axe from the wigwam. Bring the kettle. Return to me here."

Twice the sister of Tia'm makes that long journey through the forest: she goes out to fetch the kettle and the axe, she brings them back as Tia'm has commanded. And she finds him still lying there, by the back-load of meat.

"So," says Tia'm, when he sees his sister coming. "You are here. You are here, and I am going to tell you what you must do for me. You must take this axe and kill me with it."

"Moqwe," says his sister, weeping. "No, I cannot kill you."

"My sister," says Tia'm, "if you love me, take this axe and kill me with it. Cut off my head."

"Your leg is broken," says his sister, "I know this, but it will heal. I will splint it for you. You will heal, and hunt again."

Tia'm looks at her. "You do not understand. My Power has left me. It is my time to die. It is my time, and if you kill me, it will save me pain, for it will allow me to pass my Power on to you, so that I may still protect you. You must do this, and you must do it exactly as I shall tell you."

Tia'm's sister takes up the axe. Tears are running down her face.

"Now," says her brother. "Strike me, and when I fall, I will be in my tia'm shape, my moose shape. Skin the body, gut it, dry and preserve the meat. Skin my head: take the skin off whole, and make it into a medicine bag. Keep this with you: your tioml will be the tia'm. The Power of the Moose will protect you. Keep it always. Do not let another touch it: the Power will turn on you if you do."

Tia'm straightens his back. He looks around at the forest, the sky—one last time he gazes at it. Then he turns to his sister and says, "Strike!"

She hits him hard and clean. Tia'm falls, and at her feet lies the body of a moose.

She guts the body, she cuts off the head. Now she is dragging it away from the shores of the lake, away from the spilled blood and the entrails, dragging it deeper into the forest where no one can see the work that she must do.

It is getting dark. The sun is going beneath the earth. This woman lights a fire and begins to cut up the flesh of this moose to dry and preserve, as her brother had told her. For two days and nights she works. She boils the fat and pours it out to set in hard white cakes. She cracks the bones, she crushes them up and boils them to get the marrow out; she pours the marrow into a dried bladder to save it. And she skins the head, she tans the skin, she makes it into a medicine bag.

When all this is done, she travels further into the forest, she builds herself a wigwam, and she hangs within it all the cut up strips of meat, so that it may cure in the smoke of the wigwam fire. Now it is night, the third night, and she can sleep.

The medicine bag which holds the Power of Tia'm is protecting her: she wakes to hear a noise. It is morning, the sun has come from beneath the earth, and outside there is a noise of Something Coming Through The Forest.

What is it?

It is Kukwes. It is Cannibal Giant Person, taking the shape of a huge man. He is coming into her wigwam.

The sister of Tia'm rises. She greets Kukwes respectfully; she addresses him as Older Brother, and invites him to seat himself by the fire.

Kukwes is looking up, he is seeing all that meat hanging in the smoke. He praises her: "You have smoked a good supply of meat here, Younger Sister." His face is looking hungry.

So the sister of Tia'm feeds him on this flesh that once was her brother. Half of it she gives to him, flesh and fat and marrow. She hangs her kettle over the fire, and when the meat is cooked, she serves it to him on a sheet of birchbark. She brings a wooden dish full of fat and marrow to him. Kukwes is pleased. He does not eat her. Instead, full of meat, he lies down to sleep. Tia'm's sister sits there, watching him, holding her medicine bag.

Now Kukwes is waking up. He gives her some advice.

"This is a good place you have chosen, Younger Sister," he says to her. "A good place. You should stay here. There is no other place to go to in this forest, no place with other humans. The People are far away from you now; you could not reach a camp of People now. Between you and the closest place where the People sleep are two *jipijka'maq,* two Horned Serpent Persons. They are as big as mountains, one on either side of the path. You cannot go around them. You cannot climb over them. You cannot possibly pass between them. Better you stay here, Younger Sister."

Now Kukwes is leaving. Tia'm's sister gives him the other half of the meat, the fat, the marrow. Enough for one more Kukwes meal.

Her medicine bag is watching over her. She knows what to do. As soon as Kukwes is out of sight, she leaves her wigwam. She leaves everything but her medicine bag, and she goes as fast as she can, getting away from Kukwes.

The medicine bag is in her hands. "Run," it tells her. "Escape." It pulls her on the right path through the forest, getting away from Kukwes.

All day she runs, she runs like a moose, like *tia'm.* She has the medicine bag, the bag made of the skin of the head of Tia'm. She has the Power of Moose, she is Tia'mi'skw, and she runs.

Now the sun is going under the earth, and its last light shows her that she is coming to two mountains. These mountains are the biggest mountains she has ever seen. She cannot go over them, she cannot go around them. And behind her lies Kukwes, Cannibal Giant Person, The One Who Is Always Hungry.

The sun is sinking now, and it is shining between the two dark mountains. The sister of Tia'm holds her medicine bag close to her, and she Sees that Kukwes is right. These are two enormous Horned Serpent Persons, taking the shapes of mountains. She cannot walk between them. She cannot follow the sun's light, the path it has shown her.

But the Power of Tia'm is very great. She will take this path, holding her medicine bag in her hand. And when she comes into the shadow of these two mountains, these two Serpents, she Sees.... *e'e,* she Sees that they are sleeping. The bag has saved her. The Horned Serpent Persons sleep and dream. They do not notice the woman who passes between them, following the sun as it journeys to sink beneath the earth.

The medicine bag is in her hands. "Run," it tells her. "Escape." It pulls her on the right path, getting away from Horned Serpent Persons.

130

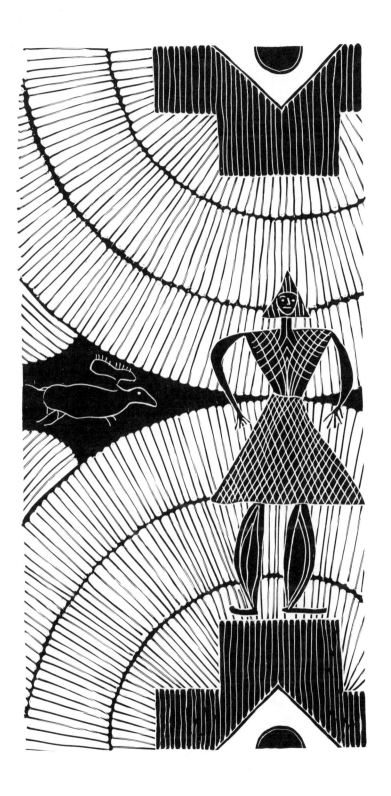

The sun has gone beneath the earth now, but the sister of Tia'm runs on through the night.

Now it is morning. The sun has come from beneath the earth. This woman running like a moose sees the sea before her. And on a point of land, *kwiewey,* stretching out into the water, there is a *meski'k wutan,* a large camp of the People, *pikwelkl wikuoml,* with many wigwams.

At last she can rest. She goes to the first wigwam she comes to, out on the edge of the camp. It is a small little wigwam. She calls out greetings and enters, and there she spends the night.

In the morning, she goes out into the camp, she visits the People, she plays *waltes* with them. They can see she has Power. In the evening she returns to the same small wigwam.

Two old women are living here: one of them is kind, she is polite. The other one is a wicked old woman, a Dog Woman, Lmu'ji'juij. She is tricky. She is crafty. She has Power, and that night, while she is pretending to be asleep, she is watching the sister of Tia'm out of one wrinkled red old eye.

Tia'm's sister is lying down to sleep. She tucks the medicine bag into the fir boughs of the wigwam floor, thinking that no one can see her, that she is safe. But Old Dog Woman is looking from under her hair, she is watching Tia'm's sister. Now she knows where her Power is hidden.

In the morning, the sister of Tia'm wakes up. The sun has come from beneath the earth, and she goes out of the wigwam, leaving the medicine bag hidden in the fir boughs. Carefully, carefully, Old Dog Woman crawls over to her visitor's sleeping-place. Carefully, carefully, she feels around in the fir boughs until she grasps the medicine bag. She pulls it out from under the bedcovers.

And as she pulls it out, she realizes that she has her hand in the hair of a living man! And this man is a warrior, a *kinap* ready for fighting. He is painted the red of blood, the red of war. His arms are bound round and round with his leather bands. He rages to his feet, screaming the war cries that kill.

Power is loose, and it kills Lmu'ji'juij. She lies dead at his feet. Power rages in him. He slays the other old woman, and then he rushes out of the wigwam.

Power is loose: the killing frenzy is on him, and he cuts down everyone in that camp of the People, that *meski'k wutan.* His sister sees him. She recognizes him.

"Tia'm!" she shrieks. "*Njiknam*. My younger brother!"
"*Punajimi,*" he snarls at her from his Power-shape.
"Leave me alone, stop talking to me. Why did you not take
care of me? If you had looked after the medicine bag, we
would always have been together. We would always have
shared together. You would have been safe. But now—"
Power roars in him. He screams with it, killing his sister.

PLAWEJ

Two men are living and hunting together; they have a wigwam deep in the forest beside a lake. One of them is Plawej. One of them is Wijɨk. They are as close as brothers, those two men.

Now it is winter, and Plawej is walking along the shores of the lake, looking out over the ice, when he sees something. He sees three women sitting out on the ice there, combing and braiding their hair. Very very slowly, Plawej creeps up on them. He wants to see if he can grab one or two of them.

But these women are too quick for Plawej. They see him coming, and they jump down through a hole in the ice and disappear under the water.

Plawej is cunning. He is patient. For many days he waits, until he sees them out there on the ice again, unbraiding their long hair and combing it, then braiding it up once more. Plawej gets fir boughs; he makes a blind and hides behind it, as he creeps across the ice on his stomach. This time he gets very close before they see him and dive under the ice.

He has gotten so close that one of those women is startled. As she is diving into the water, she drops her *sakklo'pi,* her beautiful hair-string. Plawej picks it up. He looks at it. "Ah," says Plawej, and he takes that hair-string home.

He ties it down tight to the place which is his place, the place where he sits and sleeps in the wigwam. He has caught one of those women after all.

It is not long before she appears, looking for her hair-string. Into the wigwam she comes, and sits down beside him, and there she remains.

Now it is morning, and Plawej is going out to hunt. Wijɨk has been away all this time, hunting in another part of the

134

forest, so he goes out alone. Around evening, Wijɨk comes home first, and seeing a strange woman in the wigwam, he goes and sits beside her. But then Plawej comes in and tells him what has happened.

"I have caught a wife," he says. "She is mine, and you, my brother, are sitting in my place." And Wijɨk moves back to his own part of the wigwam. He is not angry. And so they all continue living together in that wigwam beside the frozen lake.

Now those two men are going off together to hunt. They must go deep into the forest, many days into the forest. It is winter, and game is scarce. Plawej speaks to his wife. He tells her always to block up the door at night. "Do not let anyone in," he says, "do not let in even your father, your mother or any of your kin-friends. For if you do, you will be slain. Remember my words, and do as I have told you." Then he leaves for the hunt.

So this woman blocks up the door when night comes. She builds up the fire and lies down to sleep. But at midnight, she begins to hear something. Someone is calling to her, outside the door. Someone is asking to be let in.

"*Panta'tekewi,*" calls that voice. It sounds like one of her cousins. Several of her kin-friends seem to be out there. "*Panta'tekewi,*" call their voices. "Open the door for me." Now she seems to hear the voice of her brother calling to her. "My sister, open the door. It is cold out here. Wake up, and open the door."

This woman hides her head under her sleeping-robes. But she is worried. What if it really is her brother? Now she is hearing her mother crying out to her, "*Tu's,* my daughter, open the door for me. *Lo'q kewji.* Indeed, I am cold."

That woman crawls deeper under the covers and puts her hands over her ears. But at last she hears the voice of her old father. He is crying out to her. "*Tu's, tu's,* open the door. *Panta'tekewi.*"

Her heart crumbles within her, she cannot refuse him. She gets up and unblocks the door.

Something is moving the door-blanket. Something is coming in. It is not her father. It is not her mother, or any of her kin-friends.

They are Shape-Changers. They are *puoinaq.* They take that woman away, and when they have finished with her, they kill her.

Now Wijɨk has come home from hunting. He gets back to camp right before Plawej, and he smells something feeling wrong. Someone has taken the wife of Plawej. Wijɨk sets out to track them. He tracks them and he finds them, but they are more Powerful than he, and they kill Wijĭk.

When Plawej gets home, the smell of something feeling wrong is very strong in that camp. Where is his wife? Where is his friend? Plawej must Look; he must call up his Power and See what has happened.

He takes a *waltes* bowl, and he fills it half-full with water. This he places at the back part of the wigwam, across the fire from the door, the place of honour. Then he lies down on his face and sleeps. And when he wakes, the bowl is full of blood.

Now he knows. He knows that they are both dead. He knows how they died, and he will have revenge. He will seek out the Shape-Changers and kill them all. Plawej gathers up his weapons. He takes his bow, and his arrows in their quiver. He takes his war club and his axe; he takes his spear.

All through the day he is tracking, tracking, following those Shape-Changers. He looks at everything he sees, searching for something unusual. And then he finds it: here is a cliff, a cliff of solid stone, but there is also a man's knee. This knee is sticking right out of that rock. It is a Shape-Changer, trying to hide. But he has forgotten his knee. Plawej takes his axe and chops that knee off; he leaves that Shape-Changer trapped inside the rock forever.

Now he is seeing another thing. Further on along the face of the cliff, there is a foot sticking out of the rock wall. He chops it off, and traps another one within the stone. "I have killed two of you," says Plawej. "But soon I will have killed you all."

Plawej sees something crawling along on the ground. It is a tiny little squirrel, half-dead, exhausted. He picks it up and tucks it inside his robe. "You must help me fight today, my brave little squirrel. And when I tap you on the back, you must give birth to your children."

Up ahead of them is a lake, and this lake is full of geese, full of *senumkwaq*. But these are Shape-Changers, taking the forms of geese so that Plawej will pass them by.

Plawej knows. He does not pass them by. Instead he shoots them; he kills them all with his arrows, he ties them all together by their heads and slings them over his shoulder. Then he keeps on walking.

Now he has come to a wigwam, and he goes in. A Shape-Changer is there, taking the form of a man of the People. But he does not welcome Plawej as a man of the People would. He does not say, "*Ketaqamu'kwa'l,* come up to the best seat, the seat behind the fire." He sits sullenly cooking.

When the food is done, he cuts some and holds it out to his guest, but when Plawej reaches out for it, this Shape-Changer jerks the food away from him. "I would rather give this to my dog," he says, insulting him. Twice he does this. And he asks Plawej if he has had any adventures that day or seen anybody.

"*E'e,*" says Plawej. "I found a man's knee sticking out of the cliff, and I cut it off. I found a man's foot sticking out of a cliff, and I cut it off. I found a lot of Senumkwaq swimming, and I shot them all. Their bodies are lying just outside your wigwam. Step outside and see." These two men go outside. The Shape-Changer sees the bodies of his friends lying there and turns to Plawej. "Very well," the Shape-Changer says. "Our dogs must fight. They must kill."

"Bring out your dog," says Plawej, "your *lmu'j,* and I will bring out my own, *nitap.*"

This Shape-Changer calls his dog, but it is not a dog, it is a huge savage *waisis,* it is a beast.

Plawej calls his dog, but it is not a dog, it is a small tired pregnant squirrel. He puts it down carefully before the fire, and his squirrel begins to grow. It moves and stretches and shakes itself, growing, and it grows until it is almost the size of the *waisis* which it must fight.

"Kill!" say the two men to their animals, and the fight begins. The squirrel and the *waisis* bite and claw and grapple with each other, and when it looks as if the *waisis* is winning, Plawej steps forward. He taps his squirrel on the back, and immediately she gives birth to two young ones. Even as they are born they are growing, larger and larger, to bite and claw and rend the *waisis.*

"Call off your dog," begs the Shape-Changer. "Do not let it kill the *waisis*. It is not my *waisis,* it is my grandmother's, and she will mourn it."

But Plawej doesn't listen. He lets his squirrel and her children kill the *waisis,* and when its body lies upon the ground, he smiles. The *waisis* is another Shape-Changer.

Now his enemy turns to Plawej. "Come with me," he says. "Come with me in my canoe."

"E'e," says Plawej.

They send the canoe out into the middle of the river. The current is strong here, and it takes hold of the canoe. Soon they are in the rapids, and heading for a high cliff. The water dashes against it in great roaring sprays. There is a small hole in this cliff and through it the water pours, taking the canoe with it.

Now Plawej discovers that he is alone, rushing through the darkness under the cliff. The Shape-Changer has jumped out at the last minute, in some form that could get him away from the river. Furiously he uses his paddle, steadying the canoe as it drives on through the dark.

At last the water comes out from beneath that cliff. It calms into a smooth flat sheet. There is almost no current at all. Plawej paddles quietly along. He has seen smoke rising in the air up ahead.

There before him is a cave. Smoke is coming from it, and as Plawej stands outside the door, he hears talking. It is that Shape-Changer, talking to his grandmother.

"He has killed your *waisis,* your friend, your favourite," says that Shape-Changer. "But do not grieve. I have killed him."

"If only he were still alive," says the old woman, "I would roast him alive. I would."

"But he is not alive. I have sent him where he will never see daylight again."

Plawej steps into the cave. He looks at them. "But I am alive," says Plawej. "So roast me. *Paqsipkoqsui.* Roast me to death."

The old woman glares at him as he seats himself. She is a Matues, a Porcupine Woman, and she takes that shape, with all her quills rising up. She calls up the fire, she piles on the bark. Heaps and armfuls of dried hemlock bark, that is what she throws on the fire. She throws it on until the cave walls begin to melt, but Plawej says nothing. He smiles and sits there, waiting until they have burnt up all their fuel.

Now it is his turn. He gathers up fuel and builds up the fire. And as it begins to burn, he shuts up the door of the cave. He can hear them calling out for mercy, there inside. The roof and the walls of that cave are turning red hot with his fire. By and by, the noises stop. The rock cools down. The fire ceases to burn. Those thieving, killing Shape-Changers are all dead.

Plawej walks away.

KITPUSIAQNAW

In the days of the Old Ones, there were giants in the forest. They were fierce. They were cruel. They were Kukwesk.

Kukwesk. The Cannibal Giant Persons.

Kukwesk. Covered With Hair, the Ones Who Are Always Hungry.

The Kukwesk have Power, Power to catch, to kill and eat the People. There is a family of them, an old man of the Kukwesk, his old woman, and their son. The old man is too old to hunt much any more, so it is the business of his son to go out every day, tracking People. He tracks them to their camps, he kills them and guts them and brings them home to his father.

He hauls their bodies home on his *tepaqna'skw*, his broad-bottomed sled. His mother cooks the flesh, and as long as the supply lasts, they are content, sitting about in the wigwam, eating and talking and amusing themselves just like any other *mimajuinu'k*, any other living Persons.

Now it is a time when the son is out hunting. He is tracking People, and he finds one. But this one is a young woman, a beautiful young woman. He sees her. He sees her face and he wants her. He cannot kill her. He cannot tell his father where she is. He follows her back to her wigwam, and lies hidden in the brush all day long, watching her.

This young woman is the only child of her parents. They are getting old now, and she is doing most of the work for them. They need a hunter to bring them food. Their daughter needs a husband to hunt for them, and this young man of the Kukwesk decides that this hunter shall be himself.

He rises from the brush and walks into their wigwam.

"I have followed your daughter in from the forest," he tells them. "I wish to have her for my wife."

"We are old," says her father. "She feeds us. If she left us, we would soon die."

140

"I will hunt for you," says the young man. "I will bring you moose and caribou and bear to eat. I will bring you seal and walrus. I will bring you beaver and otter to make your clothes. But there is a thing I must tell you: I am of the Kukwesk."

"Ah," says that girl's father.

"I will never tell my own father where to find you," says this young man. "I will never lead him here; I will conceal your wigwam from him."

"Very well," says that girl's father. How can he say otherwise?

The son of the Kukwesk Persons returns home. He will speak with his mother about this.

"Did you find anything in the forest, my son?" asks his father.

"*Moqwe,*" says his son. "I made no kills today." He says nothing about the girl, and his father does not guess it.

The next day this young man sets out to track People; and when he has found some, he returns home with the news to his father. His father brings out the sled. He will go and make the kill himself. And after he is gone, the young man begins to talk to his mother. He sits next to her, and his face is sad.

"What is troubling you, my son?" asks his mother. "Your face is sad. You have been silent ever since you returned home."

The young man sighs. "I am thinking," he says. "I am thinking of taking a wife." He looks at his mother. "I have seen a young woman of the People, and I want her. She is living out in the forest with her two old parents, as I live here with my mother and father. Her father has given his consent, but she is a woman of the People, and I am of the Kukwesk. And I am afraid that my father will not permit it. I am afraid he may want to kill and eat my wife."

"I will speak to him," promises his mother. "When he returns from the hunt and has eaten, I will speak to him."

"Will you treat her kindly?" asks the young man. "And if he refuses to let me have her, will you help me hide her from him? For I will have her, whatever he says."

"I will speak to him," says his mother.

Now that old Kukwes has come home. He has eaten. He is lying by the fire, and his wife is talking to him.

"Our son wishes to marry," she says. "He wants a woman of the People."

"Very well," says the old man. And then he adds, "Tell him not to let me see her. He must not bring her here. He must make a place for her where I cannot see or smell her."

142

In the morning, this Kukwese'skw, this Kukwes Woman, she tells her son what the old man has said. And he goes off to bring his new wife home. But he does not bring her to the wigwam of his parents. That first night he hides her close by. His mother helps him hide her. And for the next two days, he is working hard. He is building a stone wigwam, for his wife of the People to live in. When it is done, he brings her to it, and they live there together. And now all the time he is hunting. He is hunting animals for his wife's parents, but for his own parents, he is hunting People.

Now it is spring. His wife gives birth. She has a son, and he grows up strong and is running around the camp playing. He and his mother eat the flesh of animals, but his father must eat the food of the Kukwesk Persons. He keeps his food hanging in their wigwam, that stone wigwam. He keeps it in the stomach and intestines of a bear. No one must touch it.

His wife must teach their son about it. "You must not touch your father's food," she says to him. "You must not shoot at it with your little bow, your little arrows."

Now several winters have gone past. This woman is about to give birth to a second child. Her husband is out hunting, and her little boy is playing in the wigwam with his arrows. He is shooting at the walls. Several times his arrow strikes close to the bear's stomach and intestines, the stomach which contains his father's food.

"Be careful, my son," says his mother. "Do not shoot so close to the bear's stomach. Do not strike your father's food."

But that little boy does not listen. He nocks another arrow. He pulls back the bowstring and lets it fly, that arrow. And that arrow pierces the bear's stomach, the container which holds his father's food.

Oil slowly begins to drip out of that sack, that bear's stomach.

"Akaia," moans the boy's mother. She rises and puts a birchbark bowl under the sack, to catch the drip, to save the oil.

Out in the forest, the man of the Kukwesk knows what has happened. His Power is draining away, draining away from him with every drop of oil leaking out of the bear's stomach. He is tiring, he is faint. When he finally reaches his wigwam, he has no appetite. He cannot eat. He blames his wife, but he doesn't say much to her. He just lies down and sleeps.

Now it is morning. This young man of the Kukwesk throws back his sleeping-robes. He gets up and goes out the door. He walks over to the wigwam of his parents, and he says something.

He says, "Father, you may have my wife for food."

And then he walks off into the forest.

"*E'e,*" says his father. "I will do that."

The old Kukwes has an iron cane. He slays with it. So he takes his iron cane and his *tepaqna'skw* and goes walking over to the stone wigwam, the place where his son's wife and his son's son are just waking up.

The little boy sees him coming first. He is frightened. He runs to his mother. "*Kiju',*" he screams. "Mother! *Kukwes wejkuiet!* A giant is coming!"

"Do not be afraid," she says to him. "That is your grandfather." And when Kukwes enters the stone wigwam, she greets him respectfully. She invites him up to the seat behind the fire. And Kukwes sits down. He sits down, and he thrusts the end of his iron cane into the fire. He wants it to be red-hot.

After a while he speaks to his son's wife. "You should look over yourself," he says. "I see lice crawling on you."

So the woman unwraps her robes. *Nutkmalsit.* She begins hunting lice and killing them. And while she is distracted and not looking up, the old Kukwes takes his cane from the fire. The end is so hot, it glows red.

"*Kiju',*" screams the little boy. "*Kaqsɨsk!* He burns you!"

The woman looks up, but Kukwes has put his cane back in the fire. The woman sees nothing to be frightened of, and she again begins hunting lice and killing them.

Now the old Kukwes waits. He waits with the patience of a hunter until the little boy is playing with something, and the woman is not looking. He waits, and then he kills. He shoves the red-hot iron into her and holds her until she dies. Then he guts her and butchers her, and throws her body on his sled, to take it home to eat. He guts her as if she were an animal, and he throws her unborn child into the spring of water nearby.

All of this he does in front of the little boy her son, and then off he goes, dragging his load of flesh, leaving the child behind, weeping.

Now the young man of the Kukwesk comes home. His son tells him what has happened, still weeping. "Kukwes came. Kukwes killed my mother and cut her up and took her away."

"Do not cry," says his father, rocking him until he falls asleep. "Do not cry."

His unborn child, cut from its mother, is floating in the water of the spring. Mikjikj is holding him up. Mikjikj,

Turtle Person, holds up the unborn child, Kitpusiaqnaw, the Unborn Cut From Its Mother.

Now after a while, the woman's husband sends her son down to the spring to get some water. And there he sees something. He sees his brother, a tiny little boy, laughing at him from the water.

Now the older boy's heart is happy. He laughs back. "My brother," he says, "come out and play with me. My younger brother, come out."

And so the child unborn comes out of the spring and plays all day with his brother. But when the sound of their father coming home out of the forest reaches them, the child Kitpusiaqnaw goes back into the water.

The older boy asks his father to make him two little bows, to make him two little arrows. And the next day he takes them down to the spring, to play with his younger brother. At first they play outside, near the spring. But then they go into the wigwam, the stone wigwam. They are making messes, throwing things around, playing like boys play. But when they hear their father coming, Kitpusiaqnaw takes the two bows and smashes them. He breaks them and then he runs. He goes back to the spring and jumps in.

"What is all this mess in the wigwam?" says the father of those two boys. "What has been going on here, my son? Has someone been playing here with you today?"

"I have been playing with my younger brother, my younger brother who was thrown into the spring," says his son.

"What?" says his father. He is amazed.

"I cannot get him to stay in the wigwam. He is wild. When he hears you coming, he jumps back into the water. But I have been thinking. I am thinking of a way to make him tame."

"Tell me," says his father. "Tell me, and we will do it."

"We should get all kinds of pretty feathers, all kinds of birds' tails, all different colours. All different sizes. Then I will hold him, and you can try to give them to him to play with."

"Very well," says his father, and he begins to collect birds' tails. When he has gotten lots of them, he hides outside the wigwam until his older son can lure his younger son into the camp. Three times Kitpusiaqnaw comes to the wigwam without being caught. But at last his father hears his brother calling from inside the wigwam, the stone wigwam. He rushes in, and there is the older boy holding the young one, who is struggling to get away. He sits down in the doorway, blocking it, and his younger son begins to cry.

"E'e," breathes the father. Very quietly he reaches out to them. He is holding out a pretty tail, a bird's tail with beautiful feathers. Kitpusiaqnaw seizes it and throws it into the fire. Slowly the father pulls out another tail from his medicine pouch. He holds it out. Kitpusiaqnaw throws that one into the fire. He throws them all into the fire, one by one, still crying, still struggling to break away from his brother and return to the water. At last his father holds out the tail-feathers from the Heron, Tm'kwaliknej. And Kitpusiaqnaw laughs. He takes the tail and plays with it. After that, he lives there in the wigwam with them, with his older brother and his Kukwes father. His father loves him. He has given him his heart. He brings him all sorts of nice little things to play with.

Every day Kitpusiaqnaw is growing. He has Power. He is growing very fast, faster than a boy of the People would grow. He asks his father to make him a bow, but he is now so strong that the bow his father makes breaks when he bends it back. So he has to make one for himself. It is ten times as strong as any bow a man of the People could bend.

Every day he is speaking with his brother. "Our father gave our mother to our grandfather to kill," says his brother. And one day, Kitpusiaqnaw says to his brother in return, "Come with me." They go into the forest to gather birchbark. They gather birchbark, many loads of birchbark, and they take it into the stone wigwam and shred it up. They shred it up; they scatter it around. Then Kitpusiaqnaw gets a stone from the spring. He gets a stone from the spring where he was thrown, unborn, cut from his mother. It is a smooth flat stone. This stone is very heavy.

That night their father comes home tired with a heavy bundle of food. He eats, and then he takes a little stretch. He sees the heaps and shreds of bark.

"You boys are going to set this place on fire," says their father. "You better be careful with the bark."

"We are playing, *Ta'ta,*" says the older boy.

Kitpusiaqnaw stares at his father. "You had better look over yourself," he says to him, using the words the old Kukwes had spoken to their mother. "I see something crawling on you."

Their father takes off his robe, and *nutkmalsit,* he begins to hunt lice. He is combing out his hair and picking the lice

146

out of it, throwing them
into the fire, and it is making
him sleepy. Soon he is lying
down, asleep. Soon he sleeps deep.
"Now!" says Kitpusiaqnaw to his
older brother. "Come! *Tua'tinej*. Let us
go out." Kitpusiaqnaw runs three times
around the wigwam. He sets fire to the heaps
of birchbark, and then the two boys slip outside.
They fasten the door. They close it up tight, they
put that heavy stone against it, the stone Kitpusiaqnaw got from the spring. The door is sealed tight.
When their father wakes up, the inside of the wigwam
is full of fire. It is raging, it is blazing all around him. *"Aqq
kjiknam, na mimatua'luk!"* he cries. He is calling to his
older son, telling him to save his younger brother. He calls
out to him, and then he begins to scream. The fire is eating
him, burning him. Still he calls to the older boy to save the
younger one. But after a long time, the sounds die away.

Kitpusiaqnaw and his brother sit outside the wigwam,
listening, until the very last crying stops. The fire is so hot,
the whole wigwam burns. And when it is done, they take his
bones. They gather them up from the ashes and take them
outside.

Kitpusiaqnaw takes his father's bones and puts them
between two stones. The bottom stone is the door-stone, the
stone he got from the spring. He grinds his father's bones
on that stone. When they are powder, he makes a wish. He
throws a handful of that powder up into the air. The powder
from the big bones he turns into flies. The powder from the
smaller bones, he turns into mosquitos. The powder from
the tiniest bones he turns into sandflies. And because he
ground them on the door-stone, all those flies and mosquitos come into the wigwams of the People through the door.

Their father is dust blowing. There is nothing left of him
but flies.

"Now," says Kitpusiaqnaw. "Let us go to visit our grandfather."

His brother goes with him. He does not know what will
happen, but he follows Kitpusiaqnaw. They are walking
over to their grandfather's wigwam, and they pass a pretty
little birch tree. It is white and smooth. The bark is very
beautiful. Kitpusiaqnaw takes a handful of fir boughs.
"Look at this bark," he says to his brother. "It is so smooth
and white." He whips it with the fir twigs, and the needles
leave little marks on the birchbark, marks that are still

there, on every white birch. These are the *susu'n,* the little lines on birchbark. That is how they came to be there.

Kitpusiaqnaw and his brother are still walking. They see a moose and kill it. They do not gut it, they do not dress it. They are leaving it there for their grandfather.

Kitpusiaqnaw is standing in front of the Kukwesk wigwam, the place where his grandparents live. "Grandfather," he calls. "Come out. My older brother and I have killed a moose for you."

Their grandfather comes out. He gets his sled and goes with them to fetch the moose. "Build a fire," he tells them. "I will skin this moose and butcher it." They are butchering and roasting meat, standing it up on sticks before the fire to cook, then turning it around to the other side, when one side is done.

When they are all full of meat, Kitpusiaqnaw looks at his grandfather. "You should look over yourself," he tells him. "I can see something crawling on you. *Nutkmalsi!* Hunt your lice!"

"*E'e,*" says his grandfather. He takes off his robe and begins to pick off his lice. Soon he is asleep.

"Come," says Kitpusiaqnaw to his older brother. "Help me with this." He takes the *wtelkui,* the membrane from the moose abdomen, the membrane which covers the moose intestines, and he stretches it over the old Kukwes's face. He is on one side, his brother is on the other side, holding it down over his face. Then Kitpusiaqnaw does a thing. He sets the fat which clings to the *wtelkui* on fire.

Old Kukwes, their grandfather, he burns and screams and smothers under the burning fat, the burning skin. And when he is dead, Kitpusiaqnaw cuts out his liver. He roasts his grandfather's liver on the fire, then he throws it on the heap of moose meat, lying packed there on the sled.

"Come," says Kitpusiaqnaw. "Let us go to find our grandmother. I have something special for her to eat."

Now they are at the Kukwesk wigwam. "Grandmother," says Kitpusiaqnaw, "come out. Here is meat."

His grandmother unloads the meat and brings it into the wigwam. Kitpusiaqnaw tosses the liver to her. "Here," he says, "I have roasted this for you. Eat it."

His grandmother eats the liver. She knows. She looks at her grandson. "My poor old man," she says. "Still, he had a very sweet liver."

"You ate my mother," says Kitpusiaqnaw. "Now you can eat the one who killed her." And he takes his axe and strikes his grandmother dead. He leaves her lying there. He and his brother lie down to sleep, and in the morning, they go away from that Kukwesk wigwam.

"Where are we going now?" asks the older brother.

"We are going to kill all the Kukwesk," says Kitpusiaqnaw. "All of them. All."

These two brothers are walking until they come to a lake. Now they are thirsty. But the lake is dry. The rivers are dry. All the streams of this country are dry. Aplɨkimu has done this. Aplɨkimu, the Bullfrog Person. He knows they are coming. He knows they are coming, and he fears them. He wishes to kill them. So he calls all the waters of the country into his wigwam. He stores them in buckets of birchbark; he hangs them up in his wigwam, all the waters of that country.

Kitpusiaqnaw and his brother see a small wigwam, on the edge of a camp. It is the wigwam of Muini'skw and her grandson, Marten. Kitpusiaqnaw goes inside. He and his brother are thirsty. They ask Muini'skw for a drink.

"Go over to the wigwam of the *saqmaw*," she says to Little Marten. "Tell him that strangers have come. Ask him to give us some water."

"Where is all your water?" asks Kitpusiaqnaw. "Your lakes are dry."

"Bullfrog has taken it," says Muini'skw. "He has all the water there in his wigwam, and if any of the People want to drink, they must give a woman to Bullfrog."

Little Marten is speaking to Aplɨkimu. "Give us some water for our guests."

"What guests? You want this water for yourselves. What strangers? Where have they come from? You are going to drink this water."

"*Moqwe*," says Little Marten. "This water is for the strangers sitting in our wigwam."

Aplɨkimu gives him as much water as he can carry in a mussel shell. He is so thirsty that all the way home he is sticking his finger into that water and licking it. When he comes into the wigwam, the mussel shell is only half-full.

"Is this all he sends?" says Kitpusiaqnaw, throwing it out of the wigwam in a rage. "Go back and tell him to send more."

This time the mussel shell comes back with dirty water in it.

But as Kitpusiaqnaw is about to throw it out in disgust, Muini'skw asks him to give it to her grandson. "Little Marten is so thirsty," she says. "Let him have that dirty water."

"He may have it," says Kitpusiaqnaw. "I will go and see this Bullfrog myself."

When he enters the big wigwam of the *saqmaw,* there is Bullfrog, Aplïkimu, sitting with all his women. Aplïkimu is selling water to all the People, who are dying of thirst. He is selling it for women.

Aplïkimu sits at the back of the wigwam, and all his women are busy skinning a bear. When some of them grow tired, others take their place, skinning this bear. It is a huge bear.

Kitpusiaqnaw watches them for a moment. "Let me skin this bear," he says, and he rips the entire skin off whole, with just one jerk of his arm. Then he seizes Aplïkimu and smashes him across his knee. He breaks Bullfrog's back in three places, and he kills him.

Kitpusiaqnaw throws the body outside the wigwam. "You must leave this place," he says to all those women. "You must leave the wigwam quickly." And he takes up a club. He takes up a club and he smashes all the birchbark containers of water. Then all the rivers and streams, all the brooks and ponds and lakes of that country come pouring out of the wigwam of Aplïkimu, pouring out to fill up all the dry lake beds and stream beds, so that the water runs free for all the People.

Kitpusiaqnaw goes back to the wigwam of Muini'skw. Very quietly he says to her, "You can now hang up as much water to dry as you choose."

"No need to dry water," says Muini'skw, "when there is such an abundance of it fresh."

Ever since Kitpusiaqnaw broke the back of Aplïkimu, all those Bullfrog Persons have had crumpled backs.

Now it is evening. The sun has gone beneath the earth. Kitpusiaqnaw asks Muini'skw to make something for him. He wants her to make him a tiny little canoe, a *kwitnu'j.* While she is making it, he is hard at work. He is making a bow. He forms it from a small fir bough, and he strings it with a single hair.

Now it is morning. The sun has come from beneath the earth, and Kitpusiaqnaw and his brother must leave. They go down to the shore, and there is the tiny canoe, only now it is large enough to hold both of them. They get into it and start off on their journey, their journey to kill the Kukwesk. Now they are seeing one. There

150

is a Kukwes standing on the river bank. He is holding a large fishing spear above his head. He looks like he is fishing, but he is getting ready to kill and eat anyone who should come down the river. Kitpusiaqnaw brings out his tiny little bow, and his one tiny little arrow. His Power comes up in him, and he shoots. The little arrow strikes Kukwes.

Kukwes leaps across the river to the other side, and there he falls dead.

Now Kitpusiaqnaw is further down the river. He sees a fish weir, a Kukwes fish weir. He tears it to pieces, and goes on his way. Soon the Kukwes comes down to check his weir, and finds it destroyed. He is in a terrible rage, and he goes home to scream at his wife and his children, at all the people in his family.

"The weir is destroyed," he screams. "You were not watching it. You were not watching it, my wife, and now it is gone." He kills his wife for failing to watch the weir.

"My weir is gone," he screams. "You were not watching it, my children, my sons and my son's wife." And he kills them all for failing to watch the weir.

"It was my weir," he says to himself. "It was my weir and I did not watch it either. It is my fault that the weir has been destroyed." And he kills himself as well.

So Kitpusiaqnaw has avenged himself on all the Kukwesk. They are all dead.

Kitpusiaqnaw and his brother are going on down the river. They stop at the den of the Porcupine People. Porcupine's wife is there, and she builds a fire for them so hot that Kitpusiaqnaw's brother dies of the heat.

"I'm so cold in here," says Kitpusiaqnaw, and he wraps his bearskin around himself. Soon the heat is too much for Porcupine Woman, and she dies. Kitpusiaqnaw revives his brother, and the two of them are going on down the river. They see a porpoise and kill it; they haul the body into the canoe. Now they have come to a pond. There are many geese on this pond and they all rise up and beat their wings and begin to cry out. These geese are Kluskap's dogs. They tell him when anyone is coming. But Kitpusiaqnaw holds up his hand and says to them, "Be quiet!" And those geese don't make any more sounds. They cannot.

Kluskap is surprised. Someone has silenced his geese. He comes out of his wigwam and sees Kitpusiaqnaw and his brother setting up their wigwam nearby. Kluskap smiles. He invites them to come eat with him, and his grandmother gives them plenty of meat and fat. Kluskap Sees Kitpusiaqnaw; he Sees that he has Power. He wants to play with him. So when the two guests are leaving, he says, "The sky is red, we shall have a cold night."

Kitpusiaqnaw knows. He knows Kluskap will call up the cold.

"Get that porpoise," he says to his brother, "and cut it up to heat, so we can get the oil. I am going to look for fuel." All night long they are going to sit up to keep that fire going. And they keep pouring on the porpoise oil, to make it burn hotter. But Kluskap has called up the cold so fiercely that at midnight, the fire freezes, and Kitpusiaqnaw's brother is frozen too.

Kitpusiaqnaw cannot be killed by the cold. *Wapk eksitpu'k,* in the morning, when it is light, he calls up his brother, he calls him to life. "Get up," he says, and his brother springs to his feet.

Kluskap smiles. He invites the two young men on a beaver hunt. "I am ready," says Kitpusiaqnaw. They go deep into the forest, until they come to a lake. Kluskap looks around. "Here are traces of beavers," he says. But the only beaver they kill is one very small little one. Kluskap gives it to the brother of Kitpusiaqnaw, who ties it to his garter to carry home.

When they come back to the two wigwams, Kitpusiaqnaw says to Kluskap, "The sky is red this evening; I think the night will be bitter and cold." Now Kluskap must fight the cold, he must show his Power. He sends his nephew Apistane'wj out to gather fuel, and he builds a big fire. But by midnight the fire has frozen, and Apistanew'j and Old Grandmother are dead. They are stiff with ice. In the morning, Kluskap must say to them, *"Nukumi', mn'ja'si!* Grandmother, get up!" The Old Grandmother gets up and begins to cook for him.

"Apistane'wj, mn'ja'si!" Apistane'wj jumps up and goes out to bring in some wood for the fire.

The morning is bright and Kitpusiaqnaw is out on the river in his canoe. Soon the river runs out into the sea, and the water is smooth like oil. He and his brother are chasing loons, hunting them, following them when they dive and forcing them back underwater until they tire and can be caught.

Kitpusiaqnaw and his brother are hunting whales. They kill one and bring it home to Old Grandmother. They tell her how to cut it up and dry the meat. She builds a flake. She cuts up the meat, slices it up fine, and lays it out on the flake to dry. It takes her two days and two nights to finish drying that whale.

Now Kitpusiaqnaw and his brother journey on. They leave their canoe and go off into the woods. That little tiny beaver skin is still hanging on Older Brother's garter, and now it begins to grow heavier and heavier. It grows so big it breaks the lashing and falls down to the ground. Older Brother twists a sapling into a withy, he ties it around his waist, and he fastens that beaver skin to it.

Now the beaver skin has grown so large that it is breaking down trees as Older Brother makes a path through the forest. Older Brother cannot go any further. He must stay and trade with this enormous beaver skin that Kluskap has given him.

Kitpusiaqnaw travels on. He comes to two camps where Skunk Woman is living. She has daughters, Skunk Woman, Apukjilui'skw. When Kitpusiaqnaw comes into her wigwam, she says to him, "Come up to the back of the wigwam, my daughter's husband." So he stays there with one of her daughters, and in the morning, she says to him, Skunk Woman, "We'll go to the island to get eggs."

They are on the island, gathering eggs, when Skunk Woman says to Kitpusiaqnaw, "There are more eggs, further in from the shore. I want you to go get them." So off he goes to get those eggs, and Skunk Woman takes the canoe. She paddles away and leaves him there on that island to die.

Kitpusiaqnaw comes back to the shore. There is no canoe. So he calls the Gull Persons, and asks them to take him home. When Skunk Woman beaches her canoe and steps out, there is Kitpusiaqnaw waiting for her.

Skunk Woman says nothing; she looks at Kitpusiaqnaw. When it is dark, she speaks to him. "Tonight you must sleep with me," she says. "It is the custom." She is going to kill him another way. She is going to pull the sleeping-robes over his face and smother him with her odour.

"Very well," says Kitpusiaqnaw. But he cuts holes in all the sleeping-robes, little round holes, one in each robe, as she pulls them over his face. He breathes through them when she calls up her Power and releases her odour, and he lives through the night.

Skunk Woman will try one more time. There is a deep hole, a hole where she throws all her daughters' husbands to kill them, and into this hole she throws Kitpusiaqnaw. At the bottom of this hole, a Turtle Person is sitting, waiting to kill Kitpusiaqnaw. But while he is looking around for his knife, Kitpusiaqnaw climbs out. Skunk Woman cannot kill him.

Kitpusiaqnaw finds his brother and they travel on. They are walking three days toward the north, where it is very cold. And now they are seeing something. They see a Person walking with his legs all bent, going from side to side.

"Look at That One," they say to each other. "Doesn't he look bad?"

"Where are you coming from?" says Kitpusiaqnaw.

"I have been to my brother's," says the Person.

Kitpusiaqnaw kills him with his axe. "We will use him for a door," he says to his older brother. And the two of them went walking on. Kitpusiaqnaw is carrying the body on his back.

Now they are seeing something else. It is an old man, an old woman. It is a young girl, their daughter.

The old woman speaks to the girl. "Your brother Malu'jiekn does not come back. Go and look for him."

"Perhaps this is the one you are looking for," says Kitpusiaqnaw, and he throws the body down in front of them.

That girl cries out. She sticks out her tongue. Snakes and frogs begin to come out of the faces of these strangers, trying to frighten Kitpusiaqnaw.

"I won't keep you here," says the old man to Kitpusiaqnaw, and Kitpusiaqnaw says to his brother, "It is too cold here, we had better leave." So they go away from that place. They find their canoe and paddle to an island. Here there is a camp of the People. Here they are living for many years. Kitpusiaqnaw's brother grows so old he turns into stone. And then Kitpusiaqnaw himself, he turns into a stone.

And that is the last told about him, about Kitpusiaqnaw.

MISKWEKEPU'J

Saq, saq, long ago, in one of the camps of the Old Ones, lives Muini'skw, Bear Woman, and her grandson Apistane'wj, the Little Marten. Someone else is living with them, another grandson of Muini'skw.

Miskwekepu'j is his name. He can play the *pipukwaqn,* the alder-wood pipe. Miskwekepu'j has Power. He is a *puoin,* a shaman. He has the Power of calling animals. And so whenever men go hunting, the best part of the catch is given to Miskwekepu'j.

This makes one woman cross. She says to her man, "The next time you come home with meat, I am not giving any to that boy, that Miskwekepu'j."

Miskwekepu'j has Power. He hears what she says. His is the Power of the herds of caribou, and the families of moose. And so he keeps those animals away from the hunters. He makes the animals stay away. And such is his anger at that woman, that he says to his Grandmother, Muini'skw, Bear Woman: "Let us go away from here, into the forest."

Grandmother Bear Woman says, "What shall we take with us?"

"Only a little cooking pot, and a little moose-hide tent."

Miskwekepu'j himself takes his bag of *jipijka'm* bones, horned serpent bones; and snake bones, and all kinds of bones. *All kinds of bones,* that's what he takes. Miskwekepu'j has Power. He has the Power of all those bones.

He calls the moose: "Come right up to my door."

Next day there is a moose right outside his tent, and he kills it. Grandmother Bear Woman cuts up the meat. Soon all the people follow Miskwekepu'j, to camp near him again. Because Miskwekepu'j has Power. He has the Power of the Moose and the Caribou.

But this Power also frightens people. One day the band goes in canoes to an island. Miskwekepu'j goes too. And the

people leave Miskwe-
kepu'j, they leave him there
on that island. They take all the
canoes away.

Miskwekepu'j stays on the island for
a year. He has Power. A year is nothing
to him. And after one year, he calls the
Whale.

"Grandfather," he says, "Put me back on the
shore where I was before." Whale comes in close to
the shore. Miskwekepu'j is standing there, with his
bow, with his arrows, with his tobacco pipe in his
mouth. Whale comes in so close he sticks on the bottom,
and then Whale begins to cry.

Miskwekepu'j says, "Don't cry, Grandfather. We will get
off by and by." He refills his pipe with tobacco, and lights it.
He gives it to Whale to smoke. When Whale is done, Miskwekepu'j takes his bow and his arrows, he puts them
under Whale, and he shoves him off into deeper water.

Whale is very grateful. *"Nuji'j,"* he says. "Grandchild.
Come and sit on my back." Miskwekepu'j sits on the whale's
back, and Whale carries him home to his own shore.
Miskwekepu'j gets off and wades to land. Whale says,
"Farewell, Grandchild."

So now Miskwekepu'j is walking to the camp of his
Grandmother Bear Woman and Little Marten. No one is
there.

Miskwekepu'j has Power. He puts his finger into the
ashes of the campfire and asks them, "How long have they
been gone?" The ashes tell him, "One year." So he walks, it
grows dark, he finds the ashes of another camp.

"How long have they been gone?"

"Twenty-four days."

Miskwekepu'j walks on. Again he comes to a camp; again
he asks the ashes to speak.

"They have been gone for seven days."

Seven days ahead of him is walking Chief Antawesk,
Yellow Woodpecker, and his wife Niskwa'ji'j, wearing her
white beads. Niskwa'ji'j, Brown Bird With White Around
Her Neck. Their little baby is in a carrier on the mother's
back. Lagging behind comes Grandmother, Muin'i'skw,
Bear Woman and Little Marten.

It is winter. The day is cold. Grandmother is carrying
Marten on her back, too. He faces back the way they had
come, and by and by, he sees his brother, Miskwekepu'j.

Marten calls out: *"Anjija! Anjija! Nemi'k.* I see him!"

156

"Be quiet," says the old Bear Woman. "You will never see your brother again. These people left him behind, on the far side of the island."

But Marten keeps calling, and finally his grandmother throws him down in the snow. "I told you to be quiet."

And Miskwekepu'j comes. He overtakes them. He says, "Grandmother, leave my younger brother, *njiknam,* leave him alone. I am here."

Miskwekepu'j begins to question Muini'skw: "Grandmother, how are you living? Who hunts for you? Who keeps you?"

"Antawesk." The Bear Woman spits out his name. "Poor Little Marten. Antawesk makes him fetch the water, wherever we are. He has to melt it from the snow. Antawesk makes him do it over and over. He must have the clean water. If the water isn't clean, he throws it into the face of your younger brother. 'Get clean water!' he says."

Miskwekepu'j has Power. He tells Marten, "Take the water dish. Fill it up with dirty water and piss in it. Carry it to this chief. I will be next to you. He cannot see me."

So Apistane'wj, Little Marten, he takes the dirty water into Antawesk. This chief says, *"Ekse! Ekse!* I can't drink this!" Then Marten throws the filthy water into this chief's face. Antawesk stands up. Marten calls out for Miskwekepu'j: *"Nsi's, nsi's,* my elder brother, come!"

Antawesk says to Marten: "Where is your shoulder-blade?"

"Not in my backside," says Marten, "but in my back." And Miskwekepu'j appears.

"I have come myself," says Miskwekepu'j to this chief. "We shall fight." Now Antawesk was afraid. He would not fight. So Miskwekepu'j says to Marten, "Take the baby. Take the baby and throw her into the fire." So Marten takes the child of Antawesk and throws her into the flames. "Burn her up," says Miskwekepu'j to Little Marten.

Now this chief was mad, this Antawesk. "I will fight," he says. So they build ice-shelters, to fight behind. Antawesk takes his bow. He takes his arrows. But Miskwekepu'j has Power. And in the morning, he kills them all. He kills Antawesk. He kills Niskwa'ji'j. He kills this chief, and he kills all his people.

And then only three are left: Marten, Grandmother Bear Woman, and Miskwekepu'j. Miskwekepu'j has Power.

THE THUNDERS AND MOSQUITO

The Thunders are talking to Klmuej, talking to Mosquito. The Kaqtukwaq are saying, "Where do you get all this blood that tastes so good? We are good hunters, but we can never find any."

Klmuej, Mosquito Person, he is clever. He thinks, "If I tell them about the People, they will kill them all. There will be nothing left for me to eat." So he says to them, "Do you see that forest down below us? That big forest? I peck there, at the trees. That is where I get this blood."

Kaqtukwaq, the Thunders, they say, "We will have some of it, then." And they bring up the clouds, boil up the clouds. They bring up the lightning, *wasoqotesk*. They say, "Let's do it. Clap your wings and shoot."

The first thing those Thunders hit is a big rock, a granite rock. "That's not right," say those Thunders to each other. "There is no blood in granite. Do it again. Hit that *kuow*. Hit that big pine tree."

The Thunders clap their wings and boom out over the forest. They hit the pine tree, and tear it up from top to bottom. "But where is the blood, the blood Klmuej eats, the blood that tastes so good?"

The Thunders go looking for Mosquito. "You lied to us," they say. "There is no blood in trees."

"Try that little tree over there," says Klmuej. "You are being too hasty."

A little animal was sitting under that tree, a porcupine. The Thunders clap their wings and strike down the little tree and that porcupine sitting under it. "Here is some blood," they say, drinking it up. "But it does not taste the same. It isn't good, like that blood Mosquito drinks."

Once more they go looking for Klmuej. "That blood is not the same," the Thunders say to him. "We still think that you are lying."

"If I tell them the truth," thinks Mosquito, "they will surely kill all the People, the way they're feeling right now."

He hums his little whiny song. "Try the brook," he suggests to them. "The brook that runs through the forest down below."

So once more, the Thunders call up their clouds, they call up lightning, they clap their wings and strike the brook. This time they kill three or four fish.

"Well," say the Thunders, tasting fish. "Those are queer things to get blood out of."

"Try the ocean," says Klmuej. "Try some of those big fish. Plenty of them in the ocean."

Kaqtukwaq strikes the ocean, and kills a porpoise.

"Wrong kind of fish," sings Klmuej, Mosquito Person, right into the ears of the Thunders. "Wrong kind of fish."

"Wrong kind of answer," roars Kaqtukwaq, and turns Mosquito into a hail-stone. But still they do not find any blood that tastes as good as the blood Mosquito Person drinks.

Even today it is only once in a while that the Thunders manage to strike anyone of the People.

MUINI'SKW AND PKMK

In the time of hunting the moose, there was a very old woman, a Bear Woman, Muini'skw. The People called her "our grandmother." She could hardly move, she was so old and blind. And Muini'skw was living with Pkmk, Fisher Person.

Pkmk is a good hunter. He kills many moose, he is a strong hunter, and he kills often. But Pkmk gives Muini'skw the leanest, stringiest meat from his kills. He keeps the juiciest, fattest meat for himself.

Muini'skw is thinking to herself, she is thinking, 'Why is Pkmk making all that noise, every time he eats? His jaws are really slapping together, he is making all those sucking and chewing and licking noises. He is making Fat-Eating Noises.'

And one day Muini'skw asks Wowkwis, the little Fox boy, she asks him for a knife. "Wowkwis, can you get me some kind of knife?"

"What do you want a knife for, my grandmother?" he asks her.

"Well, *nuji'j*," she says. "I will tell you. My nails are all worn down short, and I want a knife to cut my cakes of tobacco with. You bring me a good sharp knife, grandchild, and I will always be very good to you."

So Wowkwis brings a knife to Muini'skw, a good sharp knife, and she hides it away.

Now Pkmk is coming home from hunting. He has killed a moose. And as he sits inside by the fire, stripping off his moccasins, he says to Muin'iskw, "Did you have a good dinner today, my grandmother? I suppose you are very hungry?"

"Hold your tongue," says Muini'skw. "You know I cannot see. It is always very hard meat you are bringing me, but never mind. Someday, *you* will see."

"I will see what?" says Pkmk.

"You will see what you will see," says Muini'skw, and settles back into her corner of the wigwam.

"Now, grandmother," says Pkmk. "I will tell you why that meat is so hard. That is a bull moose. They are always hard and lean this time of year. If it had been a cow moose, now, that would have been nice fat meat. You'll see. If I get a cow moose, then we'll have a fine time."

The whole time he is talking, she can hear him slurping and chewing and smacking his lips over something. She doesn't say any more, but the next morning, when Pkmk goes out to hunt again, Muini'skw pulls out her sharp knife, her very sharp knife.

"Maybe," she says to herself, "maybe if I cut across my eye, maybe I could see a little."

The mother of Wowkwis is worrying about Muini'skw. She tells her little boy to go over and check up on his grandmother. "Maybe her fire has gone out," says Fox Woman. "Put some sticks on it for her. Get her a little more wood."

"E'e," says Wowkwis, and off he goes to the wigwam where Muini'skw is sitting, staring sightless down at her knife.

"No, child," she tells him when he comes in, "I don't want you at all. You better go home. I am going to do a great work here. All night long I have been Dreaming. I didn't sleep last night at all. You better go back to your mother now."

And when Wowkwis is gone, Muini'skw takes her knife and she begins to cut across her eye. First she makes a little tiny slit. She can see a little bit of light. So she cuts deeper, and cuts clean across, and now she can see everything! She cuts her other eye.

The first thing she sees with her two new eyes is a huge pile of nice fat meat, way over in the corner on the men's side of the wigwam.

"Ah," says Muini'skw. "So that is what you have been doing. That is how you have been treating me. Putting all the fat in the corner for yourself, and giving me the very worst meat."

Now after this Muini'skw no longer lives with Pkmk. She finds herself a nice big Bear husband, a strong able husband. He can catch anything: moose, fish, cranberries, blueberries. All the things that Bear Persons like to eat most. He is Muin. He can outdo any of the other Persons, hunting. Muini'skw can eat fat all the time.

THE NAMES OF STARS

The stars all have names, up in the sky. The Old Ones teach us how to speak of them. On dark nights, they point them out to us. They say, "That star is the Bear, and these nearby are the Bear's Den." They are naming five tens of stars for us. They are naming ten tens of stars for us.

They show us the three Hunters of the People, fishing up there with their fishing lines of stars. These three Hunters are trying to catch Makwis, the Fish-Hawk Star. And then we watching see that they have caught him, and are pulling him up into the sky for us to look at.

Those seven stars right up there are the Bear's Den, "Hahjalquelch," and that red star is Jipjawej, a robin.

The North Star is Kisiku Kloqoej, the Old Man Star. He is the One Who Seldom Blinks. And the Morning Star is "Oakladabun," the Last One Made. When we see him, we know that soon all the stars will fade as the sun comes from beneath the earth.

These are things the Old Ones are telling us, pointing upwards in the darkness. "All the Stars have names," they say. "All the Stars have names."

THE WORLD ABOVE THE EARTH

THE WORLD ABOVE THE SKY

KLUSKAP

Kluskap is a great *mn'tu*. He has Power. But there is a greater *mn'tu*. And That One is Kji-kinap, the greatest of the *mn'tu'k*. Kji-kinap made Kluskap. Kji-kinap made the world.

Kji-kinap is making the world. He makes the world and then he takes a rest, lying on the ground, looking around to see what he has done. And there on the ground is a stone image. It looks like a man. Kji-kinap speaks to it.

"What are you doing here?" he asks it, but there is no reply.

A second time he speaks to it: "What are you doing here?" But the image says nothing.

"What are you doing here?" says Kji-kinap for the third time, but that stone which looks like a man makes no sound.

So Kji-kinap does a thing. He breathes into the image; he blows his breath into the image's mouth, and the stone man becomes alive.

Kji-kinap says to the man, "Sit up," and this man sits up.

Kji-kinap says to the man, "Stand up," and this man stands up.

Kji-kinap says to the man, "Walk," and he walks; "Stop," says Kji-kinap, and this man stops.

Kji-kinap names this man Kluskap, Liar, The Cunning One, and gives him work to do. He tells him to take his bow, and with it to clean out all the muddy-running waters. He tells him to take his bow, and with it to clear a passage so that all those waters may run down to the sea.

Now after Kluskap has worked for one day, he returns to his wigwam to rest. And right before sundown, he sees a thing. He sees a young woman walking toward him, coming along the same path which he himself had travelled. She comes right up to the door of the wigwam and stands there.

"What are you doing here?" asks Kluskap.

"I am come to help you," says the woman. "I am clever. I am young."

Now it is morning, and the sun has come from beneath the earth. Kluskap and this young woman are working hard all day, cleaning out the riverbeds so that all that muddy water can run down to the sea. And when they return to the wigwam in the evening, they can see a thing. It is a young man, walking toward them over that path they have both travelled.

Kluskap speaks to him. "Come in. What are you doing here?"

"I have come to help you," says the young man. "I am young. I am clever."

Kluskap then says, "Where have you come from?"

"I have come from the Sky World," says this young man.

The next day all three of them work together, and they clean out the riverbeds and all that muddy water runs away into the sea.

"Now," says Kluskap to the woman, "here we have trees, but no buds and no leaves and no flowers. I want you to put leaves on all these trees. On the hackmatack, fir, spruce and pine, I want you to put needles. On the other trees, I want leaves. Put burrs on the trees as well. These burrs are filled with seeds, and so there will be young trees. And in all these trees there should be birds, who will sing for you."

"I have left all my pets, my birds, behind in the Sky World," says the woman. "I would be glad if there were some way we could get them."

So Kluskap calls Kulu, the Great Bird. He sends him up to the Sky World to fetch the little birds down, all the birds. And each bird brought its songs with it from the Sky World. These songs filled up the forest with music. And each bird had his own song, from the littlest bird to the biggest bird.

Now Kluskap speaks to the young man. "We need animals here," he says.

"I will call Kulu," says the man. "I will send him up to the Sky World to fetch animals."

Now all of the People know that the stars have names. And when that young man sends Kulu up into the Sky World, he tells him the names of the Star Persons that he wants brought back down to the Earth World. Kulu fetches all those stars, and they become animals on the Earth World. But animals were first stars, living up in the sky.

The work that this man and this woman had done suited Kluskap. He thinks that they have done well. "I am going to marry you together," he tells them. "You will live together and have children, and they will have children. Go and make yourselves a wigwam. The man can go out into the forest and hunt animals. The woman can cook them."

This is what he told them. And that is how the People know that their grandparents came from the Sky World, to help Kluskap when the Earth World was new.

KI'KWA'JU AND SKUSI'SKWAQ

Deep within the forest, Tia'm is living.
Deep within the forest, Apistane'wj is living.
These two hunters live near each other. Tia'm has his grandmother taking care of his camp. Marten has his grandmother looking after him. But Marten is lazy. Always he waits until Tia'm kills fresh meat, then he goes to pay him a visit.

One day Tia'm goes out to hunt, and he kills a bear. And when the sun is about to go under the earth, he comes back to his camp, carrying a back-load of bear meat.

This time, Tia'm does not want to share his meat with Apistane'wj, but he needs to borrow his kettle to cook it in. So he sends his grandmother over to ask for it, and he tells her not to speak about the bear. "Tell him you will put water in it," says Tia'm.

So his grandmother goes to Marten's camp to ask for the kettle. Now Apistane'wj, Marten, he has Power. He can smell something feeling wrong about what this old woman is saying. So he waits, and when she has finished with the pot, and she brings it back empty, he is ready.

When she comes into the wigwam, with the kettle all nice and clean and empty, Marten jumps up! And there is the kettle, half-full of bear's meat, cooked and ready for him to eat.

"*E'e,*" says Tia'm, when his grandmother tells him this. "It is his Power. He has called it up. Very well," he says, "tell him he can come with me tomorrow, to bring this bear in, and we will share it as we have always done."

So these two hunters bring the bear home, and they continue to live together in the same camp, and to be friends.

Now it is a good day to walk within the forest, and Marten is out, looking around. He comes to a lake, a little lake

168

hidden behind trees, deep in the forest. And what does he see there? He sees young women, many young women. They are all washing themselves in that lake, and their clothes are lying up on the bank, keeping dry.

"*E'e*," says Marten. "Now I am going to catch myself a wife."

Slowly, slowly, he crawls down to the edge of the lake, where the clothes are, and he reaches out and grabs the prettiest, from the nicest girl there. He grabs her clothes, and he runs away.

Well, this girl is scared. This girl is angry. She has to get her clothes back. So she wades up out of the lake as fast as she can, she climbs up the bank, and she begins to run after Apistane'wj.

She calls to him. "Give me back my things!" But Marten pays no attention. He just runs as fast as he can, back to his wigwam, with this girl following him all the way. And when she runs up to his door opening, Marten is ready.

Marten has Power. He takes a tiny stick, and he hits her with it. He hits her head with it, and she is stunned. She falls like a dead woman right at his feet. And after that she has to stay with him as his wife.

Now Tia'm has been out hunting all day, and when he comes back to camp, he sees a strange woman bringing wood into the wigwam of Apistane'wj.

"What is this?" he asks his friend Marten.

"Today I have caught a woman," says Apistane'wj.

"How did you do this?" says Tia'm.

"Ah," says Marten. "Would you like a woman too?"

So Apistane'wj takes Tia'm away from their camp, deeper into the forest, and there he shows him the small lake, the hidden lake, the lake where the young women come to wash themselves.

"You must hide," says Marten. "You must watch." And he tells him what to do to catch a wife.

Poor Tia'm. He hides. He watches. He sees the women come, and chooses one. But when he has stolen the clothes of the one he wants, when she has chased after him all the way back to his wigwam, he takes up a big stick and hits her. Wham! He hits her too hard, and she falls down dead at his feet.

"Why didn't you TELL me about this?" he says to Apistane'wj. "Now what good is she, lying here dead?"

"I told you," says Marten. "You just didn't do it right."

So. One morning Marten decides he needs another woman, another wife, and off he goes, walking deeper into the woods, until he comes to that little lake, that hidden lake where the women wash themselves.

And Tia'm is right behind him, stalking him, hiding, waiting to see how Apistane'wj will catch a woman.

He hides. He watches. And then he knows. He knows how it is done, and he catches a woman for himself.

Tia'm and Apistane'wj and the three women are all living in this camp. The two grandmothers are still living there too. And several moons are passing. But then the husbands begin to quarrel.

"You have two women," says Tia'm. "I have only one."

There is no peace in that camp any more, and so the two wives of Apistane'wj decide to leave.

E'e, in the morning, when the men have gone out to hunt, these two women just walk off deeper into the forest, and disappear from that camp.

They are happy, these two women. They are Skusi'skwaq, Weasel Women, and their skins are very white, like every Weasel Person's fur is, in the wintertime. And these two Skuski'skwaq are sisters. Older Sister has Power. She takes them deep into the forest, and there she builds them a shelter-camp. Younger Sister makes a small fire.

Now it is night. The sun has gone beneath the earth, and those two sisters, those two Weasels, are lying there looking up at the stars. Older Sister says to Younger Sister, "Those are Persons, up in the Sky World. Look at their eyes, shining up there."

Younger Sister says, "Which one would you like to have for your husband, lying with you in the morning? One with big eyes, or one with little eyes?"

Older Sister says, "I choose that one there, the shiniest and brightest."

Younger Sister says, "Oh, that one. That one is ugly."

"So," says Older Sister. "So then. Which one would you have?"

"I will have that little star there, the little red one."

And then these two Weasel Women fall asleep, looking toward the east, where their two stars are hunting across the night.

Now it is morning. Younger Sister stretches under her furs; she is waking up. Her foot touches something.

"Be careful!" cries a little
squeaking voice. "You have
upset the bark dish of *ne-
pi'jekwati*, the medicine for my
eyes." Younger Sister sits up. Who
has spoken? By her side is a little small
old man, with a wrinkled face and sore red
eyes. It is that small red Star Person. She
has called him to be her husband, by talking in
the night. She has called the Star With Sore Eyes.

Now Older Sister begins to wake up. She moves a
little, under her sleeping-robes. "Watch out, woman,"
says a man's voice. It is a deep strong voice. "You have
upset the bark dish with my *sikwan*, my red ochre." Older
Sister rolls over and sits up. Lying there next to her is a
man, a tall man, a strong man. His face is painted with red
ochre. It is her Star Husband, whom she has called to her
by her talking in the night. She has called the Star With
Shining Eyes. So these two Weasel Women are caught
again, and they must be the wives of Stars.

"I have nothing to give you to eat," says Older Sister.

"We will not eat until we have come home from hunting,"
says her husband. "You can gather wood and tend the fire,
and prepare for our return. But there is one thing you must
not do."

"*E'e,*" says Younger Daughter's Husband, the Star With
Sore Eyes. "There is one thing you must not do. You must
not move that flat rock which lies before the wigwam. You
must not move it; you must not lift it."

"Very well," says Older Daughter. "We will cook for you
on your return."

Now many days go by. The Weasel Women go out to look
for *sipeknk,* the ground-nuts, wild potatoes. They are digging them up, they are going to cook them. And Younger
Daughter is talking again.

"I wonder what is under that flat stone?"

"You leave that flat stone alone," says Older Sister.

But Younger Sister keeps talking about it, and soon she
has talked herself right up to it, and soon she has talked her
hands right on it, and then she is lifting it up.

She lifts up the stone, and she looks under it.

"What is there?" asks Older Sister.

Younger Sister screams.

"Where are we?" shrieks Younger Sister. "Where are we,
my Older Sister?"

171

Older Sister pushes her aside, and looks under the stone, looks to see what is making her little Weasel Sister yell so. And she sees: they are in the World Above The Sky. They are standing on top of the sky. The stone is covering a hole in it, and through this hole she can see down, down, down to the earth below, to the forest, to the little shelter camp she built the night the two of them lay talking together about the eyes of stars.

Older Sister bursts into tears. Younger Sister bursts into tears. These two Weasel Women weep until their eyes are red with crying.

Way out in the forest of the World Above The Sky, the Star Husbands are hunting. And they begin to know something feeling wrong. They begin to feel their wives crying. "We had better go back," says the Star Husband With Shining Eyes. "They must have lifted the stone," says the Star With Sore Eyes. "Listen to them crying."

It is almost evening when those Star Persons come out of the forest. Their Weasel Wives are trying to cook, trying to pretend that nothing has happened.

But Star Persons have Power, and they know. "What has troubled you today?" they are asking their wives. "What have you been crying about?"

"Nothing is wrong," says Younger Sister. "We have not been crying."

"Ah," says the husband of Older Sister. "I think you have been looking through the hole in the sky. I think you have been lifting the stone, and looking down at your world. And I think that you are lonely, and want to return to it."

Older Sister looks up at her Star Husband. She cannot say anything. She looks at him, and tears start to come out of her eyes.

"Very well," he says to her. "You may go back to the earth world."

The old Star With Sore Eyes tells them, "Tonight, Weasel Women, you must sleep close together. You must keep your fur robes over your heads. And in the morning, when the sun comes from beneath the earth, you must lie very still. Do not take the robes from over your heads, do not open your eyes. First you will hear the chickadee calling. Keep your eyes shut. Next you will here Apalpaqmej, Red Squirrel Person, you will hear him singing. Do not open your eyes. After a long time, you will hear Atu'tuej, Striped Squirrel. He will sing, and then you may open your eyes."

"If you do as we have told you," says the tall Star

Husband, "you will find yourselves back in your shelter-camp, the place you were lying that night you invited us to come and be your husbands."

So these two Weasel Women lie down together and cover their heads with sleeping-robes. The night passes, and in the morning, they hear the chickadee. Younger Sister, always impatient, wants to leap up, but Older Sister forces her to lie still. "Wait! Wait until we hear Atu'tuej," she says.

After a long while, they hear something singing. What is it? It is Apalpaqmej, Red Squirrel. And that foolish Younger Sister, that silly Weasel Woman, she jumps at the noise, and throws off the covers. And then she begins to squeal.

"Where are we, my Older Sister?"

Older Sister sighs and opens her eyes. The sun has come from beneath the earth, and these Weasel Women are back in their own world. But they have opened their eyes too soon on the way down, and now they are stuck in the top of a tall, tall pine tree, a *kuow* tree. There are no branches in this tree, except a few at the very top, and these two women cannot get down.

"What shall we do?" cries Younger Sister. "How shall we get down?"

"Have patience," says Older Sister. "Have patience and wait. Someone will come." Older Sister has Power. "Someone will come and get us down from this Tree With No Branches."

And soon someone is coming. It is Ki'kwa'ju, Wolverine Person, and he is passing by under the tree. The Weasel Women call down to him, "Help. Help, Uncle, help! Please get us down out of this tree." Wolverine laughs at them and walks on.

By and by comes Muin, Bear Person. "Help," cry the two sisters. Bear looks up at them. "I haven't got time to help you, you silly Weasels," he says. "Come down the way you got up there. You must have gotten up there somehow."

Older Sister sighs.

Now Tia'm is walking beneath them. Tia'm, Moose Person. *"Nsi's minen,"* they call. "Oh, our older brother! *Apkwa'lin aqq nisa'lin.* Untie us, let us down." Moose walks on, snorting.

"Please come up this tree and get us down," says Older Sister. "Do you need a wife? Here are two nice Weasel Women."

"I took a wife in the autumn," says Tia'm. "I do not need another."

"I took a wife in the early spring," says a Marten Person to them. "I do not need another."

Now what is this they see? Someone else is coming. It is Ki'kwa'ju, Wolverine, coming back. He has decided to come back and tease them. "I will come up and get you," he calls.

Ki'kwa'ju begins to climb, and soon he reaches these Weasel Women. He grabs Younger Sister and begins to carry her back down the tree trunk. But Older Sister has Power. She knows that Wolverine means mischief. She knows he will try to trick them. So she snatches off Younger Sister's hair-string, her *sakklo'pi,* and she takes off her own hair-string, and then Older Sister ties them both all around the branches of this pine tree. She ties them in very complicated knots, all tangled up.

And when Wolverine comes back up the tree and is carrying her down, she tells him, "Oh, I have lost my hair-string. Oh, I see both of them up in the tree. Please can you get them for me? Do not cut them, do not snap our *sakklo'pi'k.* Please can you untangle them and bring them down?"

And Ki'kwa'ju is fooled. He agrees to go back for the *sakklo'pi'k.* "You must be building the wigwam, while I am gone," he shouts to them. "I am going to have you both for my wives."

Older Sister has other ideas.

While Ki'kwa'ju is up the tree, working hard to undo all those cunning knots, she is setting up the wigwam. And into it she brings a number of things. A porcupine. A handful of the sharp chips from where one of the People has been making a stone tool. She brings wasps' nests, and thornbushes. And then she waits.

Now it is getting dark, and she hears Wolverine coming down the tree at last. Older Sister puts damp leaves onto the fire, and the fire begins to fill the wigwam with smoke. The two Weasel Women leave that wigwam, and go off into the dark. But Older Sister has touched some things inside there with Power, to make a little surprise for Ki'kwa'ju.

Here comes Ki'kwa'ju. He can smell the smoke, and he is thinking about food cooking. He is thinking about Weasel Women. He pushes back the door-blanket, and goes into the wigwam. Inside it is dark and smoky. He cannot see very well, but he can hear something, someone. It is the porcupine speaking. "Come here," it says to Wolverine.

Wolverine rushes to grab her, thinking it is one of the Weasel Women. On the way, he cuts his feet all up on those sharp stone chips. A voice encourages him. *"Nmiska'li,"* it invites. "Go to my older sister. *Nmiska'li! Nmiska'li!"* Wolverine lunges, and he grabs the dead porcupine.

"Ai'a!" yells Ki'kwa'ju. "What is this? Your sister has too many pins in her back. I will have you instead." He hears the wasps buzzing. He thinks it is Younger Sister laughing at him. "I'm going to get you," he says to her, "and when I do, I'm going to...."

But what is this he hears? It is another voice, encouraging him. "Go on," it says, "go to my younger sister over there. *Nkwe'jka'li.*" Wolverine jumps on Younger Sister, he pins her down with his body, but it is the wasps' nest he is tearing at, and all the wasps come out and cover him, stinging. "Who would marry you women?" screams Ki'kwa'ju. "No matter what kind of husband you might get, he could never stand the smoke in here." And Wolverine charges out of the wigwam, falling into the thorn brambles on the way.

Ki'kwa'ju wants revenge. He goes after the Weasel Women. He is going to tear them to pieces.

All this time Older Sister and Younger Sister have been running away, running down the path as fast as they can go, getting away from Wolverine. They run until they come to a river. This river is big, and they cannot get across it.

"What shall we do?" asks Younger Sister, panting. "Ki'kwa'ju is coming after us."

"I can feel him," says Older Sister. "But look! Someone is here with us."

It is Tm'kwaliknej, Heron Person. Heron is fishing in that river, and the two Weasel Women call out to him.

"Uncle, Uncle," they beg, "please put us over the river. Wolverine is chasing us, and we must get across the water."

Heron has a very sore neck. He does not want two Weasel Women to use it for a bridge. *"Moqwe,"* he croaks. But Older Sister has Power. She begins to speak to Heron, praising his beauty. "What beautiful robes you wear, my Uncle," she says. "I have never seen such smooth feathers."

"And my legs?" asks Heron Person, admiring them in the water. "Are they not straight and beautiful?"

"Pekikato'p jo'." His legs are indeed wonderful. Older Sister and Younger Sister both agree about that. And his neck! It is the straightest and most well-made neck they have ever seen.

So Tm'kwaliknej bends his neck. "Perhaps you would like to try how strong it is," he invites the Weasel Women. Older Sister thanks him most politely, and they run across his neck to the other side.

Ki'kwa'ju has come to the river bank, tracking them. He knows they have crossed to the other side, and he goes up and down the bank looking for a shallow spot, a fording place, when he sees Heron Person, fishing in the river.

"You!" says Wolverine. He is insolent, he is angry. He is not taking the time to be polite."Come here," he commands Tm'kwaliknej. "I need to cross this river."

"My neck is sore," says Heron Person.

"No wonder," says Ki'kwa'ju, "it is so straight and fine ... as straight as this!" And he bends a stick back and forth, back and forth, until he has crumpled it completely.

Tm'kwaliknej gives him a look. "But my feathers?" he asks. "Aren't they nice? So smooth and fine?"

"Smooth and fine indeed, and so covered with dust and mildew," says the irritated Wolverine. "And your legs. Yes, of course, your legs. So straight and beautifully pointed too, in that peculiar sort of way they have ..." He cannot resist tormenting Heron.

"Very well," says Heron Person, and he bends his neck. "Please do not jiggle me, or trod heavily."

"E'e," says Wolverine, and he rushes over his neck. Halfway across he stops to stomp up and down and jeer. But Heron is ready for him, and he throws him, he throws him right off and right into that river.

And then Tm'kwaliknej, Heron Person, he calls up his Power and a roaring, roiling torrent of water comes pouring down that river. It catches up Ki'kwa'ju and carries him away.

"I wish to land at Kaje'liknuj," screams Wolverine, as the water boils up his nose, as the water fills his mouth. And his Power gives him his wish. At Kaje'liknuj, this water throws him up out of itself, it throws him against the rocks there. This water kills him, and leaves him there to dry.

So now those two Weasel Women are safe from him. They walk quickly on through the forest, trying to find their way to the sea. It is very dark now, very dark when they come to a camp.

A single wigwam is there, outlined against the night sky.

It sits empty, there by the sea. Older Sister hesitates, and then she goes inside. It will be a good place to spend the night.

The floor of this wigwam is lined with fir boughs. There is sand in the centre, all around the fire pit. And on the far side of the fire pit, in the seat of honour, are three bones: one in the middle, and one on either side.

And a Voice says to them, *"Pjila'si.* Come up to the seat by the fire."

Older Sister has Power. "The bones are speaking," she says to Younger Sister. "The bones are speaking."

"That is stupid," says her sister. "I hear nothing."

Older Sister has Power. And she begins to feel afraid. There is old Power here; she can feel it. She speaks to Younger Sister: "Do not meddle with anything you see. Leave it all alone. We will sleep here, but that is all."

E'e, that Younger Sister! She never is paying attention. She crawls about, restless, while her sister is lighting the fire. She goes outside. And there is a bone there, the neck-bone of an animal. Moose Neck-bone. And as she looks at it, she sees that it looks rather like a face. It has a nose. It has two eyes.

But does Younger Sister let it be? Does she treat it respectfully?

Moqwe. No. No. Younger Sister pisses on this bone.

Her sister comes bursting out the door. "WHAT have you done?" she hisses. And then she sighs. Older Sister pulls Younger Sister inside, and tells her to go to sleep.

It is very quiet and very dark inside that wigwam.

Then they hear a Voice. It is the neck-bone, *jimijkikwej.* "That girl has been very stupid," it says. "I complain against her. I complain. Though it is dark, I see her. Though it is night, I smell her. Though it is silent, I hear her. And I will come."

Younger sister is rigid with fright. "Hide me, hide me," she whispers to Older Sister. "Hide me by your Power. Hide me under the fir boughs on the floor."

Older Sister sighs. "Why do you not *listen* to me? I told you the bones were speaking. I told you these things were *puoinoti.* I told you to leave them alone. There is a Person out there, and you are being hunted."

"Hide me!" says Younger Sister, gripping her by the arm. "Hide me under the fir boughs."

"HIDE ME UNDER THE FIR BOUGHS," says the Thing Outside The Door. And then it laughs. It is not a nice way that it laughs.

"Hide me inside the door-posts," whispers Younger Sister. "He won't look there."

"DOOR-POSTS, DOOR-POSTS, DOOR-POSTS," sneers the Person Outside.

"Put out the fire," suggests Younger Sister, in a whisper as small as a bird's breath. "Put out the fire, and bury me under the ashes. Light a little fire on top."

"A LITTLE FIRE ON TOP!"

Younger Sister is terrified. "Hide me under your *kni'sikn*," she begs with her lips right up to her sister's ear.

"UNDER YOUR *KNI'SIKN*," mocks the Person Outside The Door.

But Older Sister takes Younger Sister and makes her very very small. She calls up her Power and makes her into a tiny little Weasel Woman, and this she tucks up into her *wni'sikn*, the large roll of her hair which she has tied up at the back of her head. And then she waits for morning.

Now the sun has come from beneath the earth. And the door-blanket is moving. The Person who had taken the shape of a neck-bone, a moose's neck-bone, is coming in. And Older Sister sees him.

It is Sinama'ju. It is the Person Who Sucks Blood. Older Sister sees him. But what does Sinama'ju see? He sees a man, sitting at the back of the fire.

"Where are those two women?" growls Sinama'ju.

The man just looks at him. "There are no women here," he says. "It is as you see. I am alone."

"I smell a woman on you."

"*E'e*," agrees this man. "It is my wife you smell. I slept with her last night."

Sinama'ju is angry. Sinama'ju is hungry. He thirsts. "If," he says, "there are no women here, still I must have blood. I will have your blood. I will suck it from you."

"You may do that," agrees the man, still not moving, "if first you can suck this white stone dry."

So Sinama'ju, Blood Drinker, Blood Sucker, he calls up his Power. He bends his mouth to the white quartz, and he begins to suck. He cannot do it. The more he tries to suck it dry, the more this stone is draining him. And so he has to go away hungry.

Now the man rises. He leaves the wigwam, he walks away from the shore and into the forest, and then he begins to run. This man is Older Sister, and she carries Younger Sister safe, tucked into her *wni'sikn*, under her knot of hair.

Now she has reached the river. Heron is there, and once more he bends his neck to her, and she crosses over.

"Sinama'ju is on the other bank," she tells him. "Do not let him over."

So Heron Person, Tm'kwaliknej, he spreads his wings and leaves that river. There is no bridge for Sinama'ju, pacing up and down the other side. Older Sister looks at him, she looks right into his eyes. And then slowly, slowly, she changes shape. She changes into her Weasel Woman shape. And slowly, slowly, she takes down her roll of hair, looking into the eyes of Sinama'ju. She takes down her hair, and she pulls Younger Sister from it. Younger Sister takes her Weasel Woman shape. And then those two Skuski'skwaq turn their backs on Sinama'ju and walk away.

▲

Ki'kwa'ju's body is lying on the rocks at Kaje'liknuj, rotting. Two little boys are watching it. They are going to shoot sea-ducks with their little bows, with their small arrows.

The younger one says, "I shall shoot that thing. Watch!" He pulls back his bowstring and fires.

"*Kokja!*" says the body of Ki'kwa'ju.

"What made you shoot that old man?" asks the older boy. They run up to the body. It looks like an old man now.

"See," says the older boy, "it is a dead man. His eyes are full of maggots."

"Oh, that's only a little dirt in my eye," says the body of Wolverine.

The younger boy says, "Look at his mouth. Look at his nose. They are full of maggots, *kulpatkijk.*"

"*Wja'laq,*" says Wolverine. "Nothing but snot."

This boy is peering at his ears. "And his ears are full of maggots, too; they are crawling with them."

"*Nokikamjik,*" says Wolverine. "That is nothing. That is only ear wax." And Ki'kwa'ju jumps up. He jumps up and shakes all those maggots off, and his body begins to change until those two little boys are looking at a strong young man. He is whole. He is Ki'kwa'ju.

"Those look like good bows you have," he says to these two little boys. "Let me try them." And Wolverine takes the older boy's bow and bends it back and forth until he breaks it.

"Hm," says Wolverine, "This bow was weak. Look, I have snapped it. Let me try the other." And he takes the bow from the younger boy. This time he draws the string back until he snaps the bow and the bowstring. Wolverine has Power. He smiles. "This one was weak as well. But do not

179

worry. My wigwam is not far from here. I will give you two
of my bows in their place."

He points down the river. "Can you hear that sound,
where all those children are playing, further down the
river? That is where my wigwam is. You may go down there
and get my bows for yourselves." He shows them a point of
land sticking out into the water. He tells them to go around
it, and they will find his home. He makes them hear the
sounds of children, shouting and laughing. And so those
two little boys leave Ki'kwa'ju, and start walking away
down the river.

"What are your names?" shouts Wolverine after them.

"I am of the Kulu," says the older boy. "And he is a Kulu
Person as well."

Kulu. Giant Bird Person. Big enough to carry many men
on his back. Wolverine looks about him for their wigwam.
It must be close by.

"E'e," says Wolverine. "I see it." He is hungry, that
Ki'kwa'ju. He wants fat and meat. So up he goes to the door
of this wigwam, taking the shape of a Kulu Person. He
wants to fool the mother of those two boys into feeding him.

But this Kului'skw, this Kulu Woman, she is feeling
something wrong about him. She knows he is not a Kulu
Person, even though he wears that shape.

"I am, I am!" says Wolverine, trying to convince her. And
he begins to sing a song that Kulu children sing when they
are very small.

> *Akukeapi'l*
> A seal-skin strap.
> *Wetkisnapi'l*
> A shoulder-strap.

But Kului'skw does not believe him. And she will not feed
him. He is trying to deceive her. So that Wolverine picks up
an axe, and he kills her. He kills Kului'skw, and then he
helps himself to her food. He eats up all her moose meat. He
eats up all her moose fat and marrow. And then he sets the
kettle boiling.

Ki'kwa'ju cuts off the head of Kului'skw, and puts it in the
pot to cook. And then he goes away.

When those two little boys come home and find this, they
know at once who has done it. They go after Wolverine to
kill him. But Wolverine has Power. He has broken their
bows, and all they can do is to snatch off his gloves, and then
they return to their wigwam.

These two little boys are angry. They call their uncle, Ka'qaquj. They call Crow Person. "Wolverine has killed our mother. Wolverine has broken our bows. Wolverine has eaten all the food in the wigwam."

Ka'qaquj goes after Wolverine. But Wolverine has Power. Ka'qaquj can only manage to snatch off his hat; he cannot catch him. He cannot stop him. He cannot kill him.

"Thank you," says Wolverine as he runs, "You have helped me. I was getting quite warm, and now I feel better."

Those two little boys are angry. Ka'qaquj is angry. They call their Uncle Kji-ka'qaquj. Kji-ka'qaquj, Raven Person. Kji-ka'qaquj flies after Wolverine. But Wolverine has Power. Raven only manages to strip the coat off Wolverine as he is running. He cannot stop him. He cannot kill him.

"That feels good," says Wolverine, still running. "I have been wishing for my younger brother to come and remove my coat. All this work is making me hot."

Those two little boys are angry. Ka'qaquj their uncle is angry. Kji-ka'qaquj their other uncle is angry. They want that joking Wolverine dead. And so they call upon Kulu, the Great Bird Person.

And Kulu hears them. His wings make a great noise coming, and when his shadow sweeps across the wigwam as he lands, the whole day grows dark. Kulu is standing before them. "I will kill that Wolverine," he says. "I will catch him running." And then he leaps into his Kulu shape and up into the air he goes again, flying.

And he gets him. Kulu catches Wolverine as he runs. He sinks his claws into him, and lifts him right off the ground. And then he beats and beats with his wings, carrying Wolverine up and up, up into the World Above The Earth. Wolverine is singing:

What are they saying, grandchild?
They are saying,
"High up, where you are going with That One."

Always Wolverine is making jokes, even about himself. "Higher, higher," he screams to Kulu. "I want to go higher."

And that is where Kulu takes him: right up to the world above the earth. And there he sets him down on a cliff.

Ki'kwa'ju. Wolverine Person. He looks down over that cliff edge, and he sees the Earth World way down below. The forest looks smooth and flat and green down there below, like a wigwam floor covered with fir boughs. Wolverine begins to sing.

Kmitkinuek
Telaptmanek
Staqe'j kisi nqasikel
Yoqwe'ken
Yoqwe'kenu
Staqe'j nkuteymusqun

That is what he is singing.

Our homeland, it looks to me
Now looks to me like it has been left behind
Yoqwe'ken, Yoqwe'kenu,
It looks to me like the sky.

He feels the shadow of Kulu, he feels it even before it sweeps down on him, and the claws bite again into his body. Kulu lifts Wolverine off the cliffs of the sky, and throws him down.

And the whole time Wolverine is falling, he is still making jokes. "A race, a race, let's have a race," he yells up to the Kulu flying above him. And he begins to beat his arms and flaps them up and down like wings. "Whoosh, whoosh," yells Wolverine, making the noise of wings flapping.

But now he is coming faster and faster nearer to the earth. He sees the rocks below, and he quietens. He calls up all his Power for one last shout: "LET MY BACKBONE BE PRESERVED!" bellows this Wolverine, as the earth rushes up to him. And then he hits. He smashes against the rocks, and his whole body is crushed. There are pieces of Wolverine all over, flesh and blood and bones. But in the middle of all this sits his backbone. And it is intact.

Now Wolverine has fallen from the Sky World to the earth and been killed. But he has fallen close to his home, *Esaqwese'kati Nmitkik.* And his younger brother is nearby, walking about. He sees Wolverine's backbone, and he recognizes it.

"What's this?" asks Wolverine's younger brother. "Whatever are you doing?"

And when he has spoken, he hears a Voice. It is coming from that backbone, and it is calling all the parts of Wolverine's body back together again.

Nulukun ba ho! My thigh, come here!
Npitnokom ba ho! My arm, come here!

This is Wolverine singing. He sings, "My head, come," and it comes to him and reforms itself around his backbone. He sings, "My brain, come," and his brain goes inside his head. He calls his belly, and his guts to come into his belly again. He calls for his eyes to enter their sockets. *"Ntinin, ba ho!"* sings Wolverine. "My body, come together." And it does.

Ki'kwa'ju, Wolverine Person, he stands up. He looks at his younger brother and grins. "Let us go walking about in the forest together," says Wolverine to his brother, "and see what we may see." And these two Ki'kwa'ju'k start off on their travels, going toward a mountain in the distance. A long time they are travelling, and slowly, slowly, that mountain is growing larger before them.

Now they are climbing it, climbing to the top. And at the top, a huge boulder is resting, right on the very edge of the drop. Wolverine looks at it. "I could push that over," he says. "Get some sticks. We will have some fun." And those two Wolverines jam the ends of sticks under that rock and shove. They shove and they heave until they roll that giant boulder right off the face of the mountain they have been climbing so long.

Off it goes, roaring down the mountain, and off they go right after it, screaming and whooping and challenging the rock to a race. Finally, the rock comes to the bottom. It rolls a little bit further on the flat land, and then it rolls to a stop. And Wolverine and his little brother go racing past it, yelling, "We have won! We have beaten you!"

Those two Wolverines walk away from the mountain. They walk until it is night. The sun has gone beneath the earth, and it is time to rest. So Ki'kwa'ju kills a muskrat, and Younger Brother guts it and prepares it to cook over the fire. He is putting it on a stick to roast, and hanging it over the flames, when he begins to notice something feeling wrong. What is it?

The hair stands up on his neck. He is cold. He is hearing something. What is it?

Way back in the forest, on the trail they have been walking, there is a Noise. It is a Noise Of Grinding. It is a Noise Of Crushing. It is that Person they had wakened on the mountain. It is that Person they had challenged to a race. That Rock Person has finished its rest, and now it is coming to finish the run.

Ki'kwa'ju leaps to his feet. He can see tree-tops tumbling to the ground as that big old rock rolls over them. *"Ai'e,"* says Wolverine, "I don't think we will eat that muskrat tonight. It looks too old and stringy. Perhaps we will go for a walk instead." And he begins to run as fast as he can. Younger Brother is right behind him. Now the Noise is roaring like the Thunders. Now the Noise is coming like an avalanche down a mountainside. It is breaking down the forest; it is making itself a road. It is coming after Ki'kwa'ju. Ki'kwa'ju runs as fast as he can. But it is not fast enough. He runs uphill. The rock runs uphill too. The rock runs even *faster* uphill. The rock runs so fast it runs right over Wolverine, and grinds him to a powder. "LET MY BACKBONE BE PRESERVED!" screams Wolverine. "LET MY BCKK …" The rock silences him. It rolls on a little bit, and then it comes to a halt. Rock Person has won the race.

Younger Brother picks himself up off the ground and brushes the leaves and dirt away. He has thrown himself out of the path of that rock. He is alive. "*E'e,*" says Younger Brother. "Where is Ki'kwa'ju?" He limps up to the top of the hill, and there he sees the rock sitting still. And there he sees the backbone of Ki'kwa'ju, sitting just as still.

Younger Brother looks at it. He is hungry. He is remembering his muskrat cooking. "*Koqoey wejismuktmin?* Why are you lying there for?" he asks it.

And he hears a Voice. This Voice is calling up the parts of Wolverine's body: "*Nulukun, ba ho!* My leg, come! *Ntinin, ba ho!* My body, come back together!" And when Ki'kwa'ju has called himself back to wholeness, when he is standing up and shaking himself and feeling everything to make sure it works, he looks all around.

"What *have* I been doing?" asks Wolverine.

"You have been racing a rock," says his younger brother. "The Rock Person won."

"Ah," says Ki'kwa'ju, "you think so? We shall see." And then Ki'kwa'ju goes over to that rock. He builds fires all around it. He heats it and he beats it with stones, until he has cracked it all to pieces and ground those pieces to a powder.

Now Wolverine is taking all that powder and throwing it up into the air. "I have beaten you," he says to the rock. But the rock powder turns itself into blackflies, *jipjunji'j,* and ever since, those blackflies have been biting the People in a very spiteful fashion. They are getting their revenge, because Wolverine ground that Person to powder.

185

▲

Those two Weasel Women are spending the night in a little shelter-camp under the trees. And now it is morning. The sun has come from beneath the earth. Older Sister says, "We will walk on down this river until we come to the sea. There we will be sure to find some of the People." Older Sister has Power.

After they are walking for a while, they see a young man of the People. He is on the other side of the river. Younger Sister calls out to him. She asks him to help them pass over the river so that they may come to the camps of the People. "We will be your wives," she says to him, "if you will help us."

This man of the People stretches out his bow, so that they may cross the river on it as a bridge. But when they reach the other side he tells them he has no need of wives. There are plenty of women in his wigwam, looking after him. So the two Skuski'skwaq must keep walking on down that side of the river.

Now Older Sister sees two men in a canoe, out on the water. "Will you take us in?" she calls out to them. "We want to find a camp of the People."

This is the canoe of two of the Sea-Bird Persons. One of them is Kwimu. One of them is Makwis. And as they all paddle down the river together, Loon begins to admire the white white skin of those two Weasel Women, and the white furs of their robes.

"I am Kwimu," he says to them. "I live with the *Wikem* in the lands of the Awialkesk, the Very Beautiful Sea-Duck Persons. I am one of them."

"Do not believe him," says Makwis. "He is trying to ensnare you. Wait until we get to the camp. Then you will see what you will see." And soon the river goes around a point of land sticking out into the water, and there is the camp of the Awialkesk. These two men beach the canoe, and those two Weasel Women get out.

The Awialkesk are all excited. Two strange women have come. Their skins are white and beautiful. Their robes are white fur, beautifully decorated. "Will you marry?" ask the Awialkesk. And, "Yes," say the Weasel Women. Two Awialkesk chiefs take them into their wigwams as their wives, and prepare to celebrate the wedding feast.

There is meat to eat. There is meat and fat and marrow to eat. And they are wrestling and running races at that feast. The Awialkesk race on foot and in their canoes. Kwimu is angry that he did not get at least one of those

Weasel Women. So he overturns his canoe during the race, and calls out to the young girls of the Awialkesk to come out and save him before he drowns. He will have one of them instead.

"Do not listen to him," says Makwis. "He is safe. The water will not hurt him. He is trying to ensnare you."

So no one comes to Kwimu. And after a while he gives up and swims in to land.

Those two Weasel Women stay there. They are wed to the Awialkesk now.

▲

Ki'kwa'ju and his brother have been walking on through the forest. And they see up ahead a camp of the People. Wolverine decides to trick them. He wants a little excitement. But first he must take care of his younger brother.

Wolverine finds a nice hole for his brother away under a hollow stump. He fills it up with bird down, nice and soft and warm. He fills it up with dried meat, so that his brother will have food while Wolverine is away in the camp of the People. "Stay here until I come for you," says Wolverine.

Now Ki'kwa'ju is changing his shape. He makes himself into a beautiful young woman. He makes himself into a young woman whose clothes are beautiful, whose clothes are covered with painted designs and ornaments. And then this young woman walks into that camp of the People and asks for the hospitality of the chief.

She is invited into the wigwam. Inside are sitting the old chief, his wife, his son, his three daughters. All of them are sitting in there, and they are wondering about the beautiful stranger.

The chief's son is looking at her face and thinking about getting married. He asks his parents to come to some arrangement with her.

"Yes," says this Beautiful Woman Wolverine, "if you will treat me kindly. I am a stranger and perhaps we will have different customs."

"We will respect your customs," says the old chief.

"Very well," says Wolverine. "I will tell you what they are. When our women marry, they do not sleep next to their husbands for three moons. They stay on the women's side."

"You may do this," says the old chief. And so the wedding feast is celebrated. Beautiful Woman Wolverine is married to the chief's son, but he gets to sleep with the three daughters.

Wolverine has Power. He keeps his Beautiful Woman shape strong, but still the People are feeling something wrong. "Is this really a woman?" they begin to whisper to each other. "Is she fooling him? Is this why she will not sleep next to her husband?"

So Beautiful Woman Wolverine goes over to the men's side, and lies next to her husband. The People build them a wigwam of their own. And then the whispering stops, because Wolverine says that soon there will be a baby in that wigwam.

Now the men are going out to hunt. And this young husband of Wolverine returns to camp to say he has killed. He has killed a cow moose, and he wants his wife to come out with him and dress it: gut it and butcher it and help to bring it home.

So Beautiful Woman Wolverine goes with him. Now this cow moose has two calves inside her. Wolverine takes one of them. He hides it. He hides it under his dress, and when he returns to camp, he dries it and stashes it off somewhere, for later on. Later on, he will need this dead dried baby moose.

Wolverine's younger brother is still in his hole underneath the hollow stump. But now he is getting hungry. Now he is getting lonely. He wants his brother. He wants Wolverine. And he begins to cry and yell and scream for him.

Back in the camps of the People, they are hearing this noise. It is a Noise Of Loneliness. It is a Noise Of Hunger. They cannot understand what it is saying, but it is frightening them. They call out Beautiful Woman Wolverine. Perhaps she can tell them what it is saying.

"E'e," says Wolverine. "I know that sound. I know that noise. It is the Noise Of Famine, it is the Noise Of Starving. This is Eula'qmuejit coming. He must not come here. His visits bring death. He has visited my own village until nothing was left." Beautiful Woman Wolverine turns to the People. "I have seen this Eula'qmuejit before. I can speak his language. Do you wish me to go out to him? He must not come into the camp. Eula'qmuejit brings death."

"Go out to him," say the People. "Can you drive him away?"

"Yes," says Beautiful Woman Wolverine. "You must give me a well-dressed moose-hide, the hide of a yearling moose.

You must give me *qamu,* fat. Much fat. Then I can stop the
noise this Eula'qmuejit is making. Then I can chase him
off."

So all the People gather up fat, hard white cakes of fat.
And the chief's wife brings a moose-hide, a well-dressed
robe from a yearling moose, just the size to fit Wolverine's
younger brother. Then Wolverine takes these things and
goes off into the forest, running. *"E'e, jowea, lmie!"* Beautiful Woman Wolverine is screaming. "Yes, *jowea,* go away!
Go back to where you came from!"

"What is that word *jowea?*" the People ask each other.
"Do you know? What is she saying to it?" But no one
understands.

Wolverine is telling his little brother to stop his noise.
And the noise does stop. Ki'kwa'ju the Wolverine wraps his
brother up in that nice soft moose-hide, and stuffs him full
of fat. He gives him a good supply of it, and then he turns
to leave. "I must go back for a while," he says to him, "this
joke is not yet over."

So Beautiful Woman Wolverine returns to the camp of
the People, and to the wigwam of his husband to await the
birth of his baby. And when the time of birth has come,
Wolverine speaks to his husband.

"It is the custom of my people that women should give
birth alone," he says. And so this young man leaves the
wigwam, and goes to stay with his father, until the baby has
come. Throughout the camp of the People, women are
listening out for Beautiful Woman Wolverine, in case she
calls to them for help. But Wolverine does not need their
help in delivering this baby. He takes the dead moose calf
and wraps it up in the little robes which the chief's wife has
made for her first grandchild.

And then all those waiting women hear a sound from
inside the wigwam. It is the sound of a baby crying, the
way babies cry when they first come into the world.
"E'e," they say to each other, *"e'e,* the little one is
here." And they rush into the wigwam to help the
mother and to see the baby. The baby's face is
covered. "It is the custom," says Wolverine,
"it is the custom of my people that the
baby's father must be the first to see his
new child." *Weska'qelma'titl.* The
women kiss this little baby outside the blankets, without un-
wrapping him, and they take
him over to the wigwam

where his father waits. "It is a son," they say to him. "Your wife has had a son." Then they hand him the bundle which Beautiful Woman Wolverine has so carefully wrapped up.

He smiles. Already he has given his heart to this child. Very carefully he unrolls the little furs away from its face. Very carefully he pulls them back. *Ai'iiiii,* what does he see? He sees a dried dead moose calf, and he screams with rage and grief. This chief's son picks up his axe, and rushes into his own wigwam. He will kill whoever has done this thing.

But Wolverine has been running as fast as he can. He has been running since those women left the wigwam. He stops by the hollow stump where his younger brother lies. "Why are you lying there when you could be out having a nice little walk?" asks Wolverine, and then they are off and running again.

That chief's son finds his wigwam empty, and so he knows. He knows this is the work of Wolverine. "Come to me, all you men of the People," he screams. "Wolverine has been here. And now he is getting away."

So all the men in that camp of the People are chasing Wolverine down the river. They are getting closer and closer.

But Ki'kwa'ju has Power. He cuts branches, he cuts sticks, he cuts saplings and small trees. He moves fast. He moves like fire through dry leaves, and he builds a dam. He dams up the river above the waterfall until the water stops coming over the drop. And then he sits down below, he sits right at the bottom in the stream bed of that river, and he does a thing.

He changes shape into a waterfall. *"Pu hu hu,"* sings Wolverine, making the noise that a waterfall makes, falling over a cliff. And all those hunters of the People are fooled. They cannot find Wolverine. They cannot see Wolverine. They cannot trail Wolverine, and so they have to go back to camp.

But Wolverine has stayed too long under the waterfall. Above him, the water has built up and up and up. It bursts through the dam, it leaps over the cliff, it falls on the head of Ki'kwa'ju. It crushes him and sweeps him away, down the river toward the sea.

"LET MY BACKBONE BE PPPPPPPPP...." comes the voice of Wolverine from beneath the water. "LET MMMMMM...."

The Weasel Women have a younger brother, *wjiknamual.* And all this time he has been searching for them. He thinks that they are lost. He is trailing them along the seashore when he sees a thing. It is a very dead thing, covered with flies.

"What is that thing?" he says to himself. "It certainly is stinking, and it is full of flies."

A Voice speaks to him. "What do you want?" it asks him. "Nothing in particular," he tells it.

The Voice begins to sing: "*Ntinin, ba ho!* My body, come together." It is Wolverine, calling his body back into being. He calls his arms, he calls his legs, he calls his chest and belly and head. And Wolverine jumps to his feet, shaking off all those flies, shaking off all that rotting flesh. He is Ki'kwa'ju.

He calls his eyes and they come. He calls his teeth and they come. But there is something missing. He calls his testicles, but they do not come. He calls them again. Nothing happens. Ki'kwa'ju Listens. He can hear something. "*Mmmlllmmm,*" it sounds like. What is it? It is his testicles, he can hear them talking together. Once again he calls them, but they do not come. "*Pppllllqqqlll,*" they are saying. He follows the noise. It is coming from under a pile of rocks. His testicles are down in there, under those rocks, talking to each other. They cannot come out, or they will not come out. Maybe they are too busy talking. So there is Wolverine, digging away at those rocks, trying to get them out, and still they are just sitting down under there, talking.

"*Kokja!*" screams Wolverine. "Let them stay down there talking then." And he finds two nice little round stones and straps them on in their place.

Wolverine looks up. He sees someone watching him.

"What are you doing, Skus, Weasel Person?" he says to that young man. "Why are you here?"

"I am looking for my sisters."

"I can help you," says Wolverine. "For I have surely seen them." And then that Ki'kwa'ju gives him all the wrong directions, he sends him off to the wrong side of the river, the very far side of the river.

When he is gone, Ki'kwa'ju takes sticks, two sticks. He throws them into the water and tells them to become a canoe. When that canoe is lying there in the water, he gets in and paddles off, looking for his brother. *Kespi-a'tuksitkik.*

KULU

Wikijik kisiku'k. The Old Ones are in their camps. Out from one of these large camps of the People an old woman is wandering, walking by herself out in the forest. And as she is walking there, she sees something. It is a very strange thing to see, alone under the trees. It is a very small baby, lying on the ground.

"Ai'e," says the old woman. "What are you doing out here?" The baby is so small she can fit it into her mitten, and that is what she does, after she has picked it up. Then she takes it home, still hidden in her mitten. She knows that something strange has come to her from the forest. She knows that Power is here. She must hide it. She must protect it. And then it will protect her.

Now it is morning. The sun has come from beneath the earth, and this old woman is packing up. She ties up some of her things, and very quietly, before the rest of the camp is awake, she leaves her wigwam and disappears into the forest, taking that baby in her mitten. Deep, deep into the forest she goes, until she is well hidden. There she makes a little wigwam, a place to live and raise this tiny child, her gift from the forest.

This old woman has no milk, but she feeds that child. This old woman has Power, and she takes the scrapings from the inside of a piece of rawhide. She scrapes them into her pot, and from them she makes a little soup. That is what she feeds the baby. This baby is a boy-child, and he seems to like that soup. He grows big on it. He grows nice and fat on it. He is a healthy little boy.

Now all this time that old woman is living on rabbits. She has some sinew, and she has made rabbit-snares. She kills rabbits and dresses them and eats them. She makes clothing from their skins. That old woman eats rabbits, and the little baby eats soup made of rawhide scrapings.

Soon this little boy is big enough to run around the camp, to talk and to play. He says to his foster-mother, *"Nukumi', api'j l'tui.* Grandmother, make this for me." He wants her to make him a little bow and a little arrow. He wants to go out hunting.

So his grandmother takes wood and shapes it into a small bow. She strings it with hair. She takes wood and shapes it into a small arrow. The little boy walks around the camp shooting things, and then he goes out hunting. He sees a tiny little mouse, and he kills it with his arrow. Now he is walking home, just like a hunter, very proud. It is his first kill.

"Grandmother, I have killed a huge wild beast," he says. "You must go out to butcher it and drag it home. Take your carrying-strap. Take your knife, and go bring it home. I have killed it."

"E'e," says his grandmother. "I will do that."

So off she goes, until she finds the huge wild mouse lying on the ground. She treats it with great respect; she guts it, ties its legs together, lays it on her back and carries it home.

The child speaks to her. "Grandmother, you must skin my first kill. You must stretch the skin and tan it for a mat, a sleeping-mat. There is Power in it. It can see into the tomorrows, and when we need help, this mat will give it." The old woman does just as he tells her.

Now the boy goes hunting again. Once more he comes back to tell her of the huge kill he has made. *"Westaw-wleyi'kw,"* he says. "We are extremely well-off. I have killed again."

The old woman goes out to fetch home the meat, and she finds a red squirrel lying dead, with the boy's tiny little arrow in it. She guts it; she ties its legs together and carries it home on her back. And then she skins it and tans the skin to make a sleeping-mat, a robe of Power, just as he has told her to do.

The next thing this child kills is a rabbit. He shoots it with his arrow, his small arrow with the sharpened wooden point. He shoots it, and his grandmother makes a third robe from the rabbit skin.

Now this child wants to go after larger animals. He asks his grandmother to see if she cannot find him a proper arrow-head, a stone arrow-head. So she goes out looking, looking through the forest, looking where a hunter might have lost an arrow, and she finds a stone arrow-head. When she brings it home, her grandson is making himself a larger bow and a bigger arrow-shaft. He lashes on the stone arrow-head, and then he is ready.

Now it is morning; the sun is lighting up the world. This boy goes out to hunt, and before nightfall he has killed. He has killed a moose and a caribou, and he brings home a huge back-load of meat. His grandmother's heart is glad. "Fat is my eating," she is singing. "Fat is my eating." There is meat to eat. There is fat to eat, and marrow. There are large warm skins to make into clothing and sleeping-robes.

But in the morning, when her grandson is starting out of the camp, she sees that it is time to speak with him. She must warn him. There are places in the forest where he must not go.

"*Nuji'j,*" she says to him, "Grandchild, I have seen something. The great swamp in this forest, you know where it is? You must not go into that swamp. You must not go through that swamp. You must not cross over it, or great danger will come to us. Promise me that you will not go there."

"*E'e,*" he says to her. "I will not go there." And he sets out to bring back the rest of his two kills from the day before. But all the time he is walking toward them, his thoughts are walking toward that swamp. He wonders what is there. He wonders what the danger is. All the time he is walking one way, the swamp is pulling him another. And finally, he turns around. He goes back to the great swamp and begins to cross it.

It is a terrible swamp, and walking through it is so difficult that at last he gives up. He has gotten half-way across when he gives up and goes back. His clothes are torn and muddy. His skin is scratched and dirty. But even before she sees him, his grandmother knows he has been in the swamp. The robes of Power—mouse, red squirrel, rabbit— these skins have told her so.

Before he can get back to the camp, he meets his grandmother, running to find him. Tears are running down her face.

"Have you crossed over the swamp?" she calls out to him.

"*Moqwe,*" he says. "No. I did not cross over."

"Promise me," she begs him. "Promise me you will not go over to the other side. You will get both of us killed if you do. We will both die. Promise me!"

Once again he promises her. Once again the swamp calls to him and he goes into it. The very next day he goes back into that swamp, and this time he manages to get all the way to the other side.

What does he find there? It is a large camp of the People, a *meski'k wutan.* A large camp, but there are no People in it. They are all gone. And they have left in a hurry. The fires are still burning. The cooking pots are still boiling over the fires. He goes into some of the wigwams. Here is a pot where the food is cooked, but not taken off the fire. Here is a hearth where the food has all been dipped out into dishes, but not eaten. This food is still warm, but no one is there to taste it. This boy begins to sense something feeling very wrong about this place. He does not like it. It is too quiet. So he goes back into the swamp, silently, silently, back into the swamp. He crosses the swamp and returns to his grandmother.

She is mourning. *"Akaia,"* she cries. "I told you not to go there, my grandchild. Why did you go? Now we are all destroyed. Now we must leave this place, this hidden part of the forest, and go to that terrible empty camp. We must go there tomorrow."

Power has found them. Power is calling them. They must pack up all their *wutapsunual,* all their clothes and robes and other belongings. They must cross over that swamp and go to live in the deserted camp of the People. It is a hard crossing for the old woman, and she cannot stop crying.

Now they have come into the camp. It is lonely there, it is too quiet. They walk into one of the big wigwams, and lay down all their things. The grandmother begins to build up the fire, and to cook some of the meat they have brought with them. But her grandson is doing other work.

He is making a very tiny bow. He is making tiny, tiny arrow-heads of stone. He is making six arrow-heads of stone, from the one stone head his grandmother found in the forest. He is making six tiny arrow-shafts to bind them to. He asks his grandmother for a hair from her head, a single hair. He strings his bow with that one hair, and then he is done. His weapons of Power are ready. He puts them aside until he will need them, and then he eats and sleeps.

Now it is morning. The sun is just coming from beneath the earth; the sun's light is just brightening up the world, when that light seems to darken. It darkens because Someone is flying across the sky. Someone With Great Wings. It is Kulu, Great Bird, Giant Bird Person, hovering over the camp, beating his cruel wings, stretching down his terrible claws to clutch, to catch, to kill and eat the People before they wake and leave that wigwam. But the Child Who Was Found In The Forest is ready. He takes his tiny bow, his weapon of Power, he nocks his first small arrow. He shoots his arrow up, up, up into the breast of Kulu, and then he shoots the second, the third, the fourth, the fifth, the sixth arrow. And all these arrows of Power find their mark. They all lodge in the breast of Kulu. Kulu screams a terrible scream. He tries to pull out the arrows, but he cannot. Beating and beating his wings, he lifts up and flies toward his home. He is feeling sick. He is feeling hurt and sick.

Below in the wigwam, the boy is resting. He has used Power; now he rests, waiting for his Power to grow strong again. Tomorrow he will track that Kulu. Tomorrow he will follow it home. He will follow it home and then he will kill it.

Now it is morning. He speaks to his grandmother. "*Nukumi',*" he says, "I am going after our enemy. And you must watch. Watch the skins: the mouse, the red squirrel, the rabbit. Watch your tobacco pipe. If these Things of Power fill up with blood, you will know that I am dead. If they do not, you will know that I am safe. And when I have killed our enemy, I will return to you."

That boy is travelling. He goes over mountains. He crosses many valleys. He fords the rivers and the streams, the big brooks and the rapids. He goes through the marshes and the swamps, until he has almost reached the home of Kulu.

Now he is hearing something. He hears hunters, coming from the Kulu camp, coming through the forest. They are talking and laughing, talking loud until they see him. These hunters stop. They see him, and they begin to weep, to mourn.

"Why do you cry?" he asks them.

"We weep for you," they tell him. "We weep for your parents, your father, your mother, your sister. We weep because tomorrow, when the sun is highest in the sky, Kulu Person is going to eat your kin, kill and eat your kin."

"Is he?" says that young man. "We shall see." And he hastens on through the trees.

Now he is hearing another thing. Young girls are coming

197

through the forest, gathering fir boughs to line the wigwam floors. He hears them laughing and singing, singing little bits of song. They sing until, suddenly, they see him coming, and then they too begin to weep.

"Why are you crying?" he asks them.

"We are weeping for you," they say. "We are weeping for your sister, for your mother and your father. For tomorrow when the sun is highest in the sky, Old Kulu Chief will kill and eat them."

"Perhaps," says this young man, "I shall save him the trouble of coming to fetch me to the meal. Where is his lodge?"

"Our camp is in circles. Kulu Saqmaw, his wigwam is in the very centre. All the other wigwams are built around his, in rings, some in the first ring, some in the second ring outside the first, and some in the third ring, the outermost." This is what they tell him, those young girls gathering fir boughs.

"*E'e,*" says one of them, "he goes round and round the circles, Old Kulu Chief, eating the first one, then the next one, then the next. Round and round the rings, eating us and all our kin."

"So," says the young man. "So." And he walks on toward the Kulu camp, looking for the wigwam of his parents, looking for his mother and father, looking for his sister. And at last he finds them. He pushes back the door-blanket and goes inside.

"My son!" cries his mother. She recognizes him. She knows him, even though she has not seen him since he was a baby. "My son!" And she begins to weep. Her daughter weeps with her; they had thought that he was safe, safely away from old Kulu Person.

"*Akaia,* my son," says his father, "my heart is glad to see you, but it weeps that you have come to us. Tomorrow we will all die, and you will die with us. Tomorrow Old Kulu is going to eat us, kill and eat us. My heart wishes you had stayed away."

"We shall see," says his son. "But first, let us have something to eat ourselves, my father. For I have come a long way to find you."

His mother and his sister begin at once to cook him all the best things in that wigwam. And while he is sitting eating it, and they are all sitting watching him, gazing into his face, someone calls out at the wigwam door.

It is the oldest son of the Kulu Chief. He whines and shuffles around, he does not come in. He only brings a message. His father is very ill, he tells them. His father hears a stranger has come. His father wishes to know if the stranger might have Power, Power to cure the things which are presently making him feel sick. His father wishes the stranger to come to him at once.

"Tell him I am eating," says this young man. "I will come when I have finished."

"And tell him," he goes on, "tell him that when I do come, I will kill him. Instantly. I will kill him at once. Go home. Say to him what I have told you. Go!"

This Kulu boy goes back to the wigwagm where his father is lying in pain.

"My son," says the Kulu Chief, "what did your brother say?"

"He said he is eating. He said he will come when he is done. He said he will kill you when he comes."

"Ah," says Kulu, falling back onto his sleeping-robes.

Now that young man has finished his meat. He rises from his seat by the fire and stretches. He says to his father, "Now I will go to visit the sick."

When he enters the wigwam, he sees the Kulu collapsed onto his fur robes. Six tiny arrows are sticking out of his flesh.

"My brother," says the Kulu, addressing him respectfully, "my chest is paining me. My chest is paining me dreadfully."

"*E'e,*" says the young man. "I shot those arrows into you when you were coming to kill us, to carry us away and devour us. Now I have come to finish what I started. My luck is great. My Power is great. I am killing Kulu." And he raises his axe and strikes. Kulu falls dead.

This young man goes around the wigwam, striking and killing all the Kulu children, all the Kulu women, all the Kulu kin in that wigwam. He kills the whole brood of those Kulu Persons—only one escapes.

One small Kulu boy has hidden himself under the fir boughs which line the wigwam floor. The young man, the Kulu Killer, looks around to see if he has missed any; he sees the fir boughs move. A tiny little movement, barely a breath, but he sees it. He knows someone is there, hiding under the fir boughs.

"Come out," he says. "You are seen. You are discovered. Come out that I may kill you, that I may make an end to all these Kulu Persons."

"*Moqwe,*" says the little one. "I will not. You should not kill me. You should keep me, and use me. I have Power. I

199

can take the Kulu shape. I can be useful; I can carry you through the air on my back."

"Yes," says the young man. "And all the time you will be watching me, waiting to be revenged upon me and all my family, for I have killed your father. I have killed your mother, and all your kin."

"No," says the Kulu, "I will not. And when I am grown, and can fly great distances, I will take you places where you can find the most beautiful women from which to choose a wife. I will take you to the World Above The Earth. I am a Kulu. I can do this. *Na teliaq.*"

"Very well," says the Kulu Killer, "I will let you live. I will let you live if you will do as you have said. You should remember, little Kulu, that if you change your mind, if you plot against my life, I will know it. I will know it the minute that you think it, and I will kill you first."

Now the young man goes back to his father's wigwam. They have great joy to see him, and when he tells them the Kulu Persons are dead, the whole camp of captives rejoices and feasts. He has saved them.

This young man brings home with him the little Kulu, Kulusi's. He hunts for him, he feeds him, and Kulusi's begins to grow. He grows into his man's shape. He grows into the shape of an adult male Kulu, and when he is in that shape he practises, he tries his wings. He learns how to fly, to fly long distances. He learns how to fly high. But always he comes back to his master, to the one who has taken him captive, to the one who spared his life, and he is faithful to the words he spoke.

Now it is morning. The sun is lighting up the world. Kulusi's has eaten. He speaks.

"*Nsi's,*" he says, "my older brother, let me take you into the air on my back." They go out of the wigwam. Kulusi's takes his Bird Shape. His master seats himself on the back of that great bird, and they go up into the air. For hours they are flying, and then they come home again. The next day, they go hunting: the man seated on the bird. They fly over the forest until they see a moose, and the man kills it. He guts it and feeds the offal to Kulusi's. And after the Bird Shape has eaten, the man loads up the moose on his back. And then they fly home.

On the third morning, Kulusi's takes his older brother back across the

200

land to fetch his foster-mother. From high in the sky he sees the old woman sitting in front of the wigwam. The shadow of Kulusi's passes across her face and she looks up in terror.

"Do not be frightened, Grandmother," he shouts down. "I have come to fetch you. Do not be afraid." He helps her pack up all her things, and then he flies with her on the back of Kulusi's, back to the Kulu camp, to the *meski'k wutan* where his parents are living. And there he hunts for her and takes care of her.

Kulusi's comes to him on the fourth day. "My older brother, it is time," he says. "It is time to go up to the World Above The Earth, time to find a wife for you in that land of beautiful women. Let us go to the place where the beautiful women are."

"E'e," says his master, and seats himself on his back. The Great Bird Shape lifts up away from the earth. The great wings beat and beat. The land drops away from them. Up, up, away up, passing through the clouds, until the earth has become so small that it disappears from the sight of the man on the back of Kulu.

Now they have come to another earth, a world surrounded by huge cliffs. Kulu flies even higher, to the very tops of these cliffs, and there he lands. His rider dismounts, safe, on a beautiful plain. And there in front of them is a wigwam, not far from the cliff edge. Kulusi's takes his human shape, and the two men go into the wigwam.

It is a large, well-built wigwam, and inside is an old woman. Inside are her two daughters. The old woman knows why they have come. She knows why they are there. *"Ketaqmu'ka'li, ntlu'suk,"* she says. "Come up, up to the seat of honour, the seat back of the fire. Come up to the back part of the wigwam, my daughter's husband," she says. And so the thing is done. These two men take their seats.

The two daughters are sitting on the women's side of the wigwam, looking at them.

And as is the custom, the first thing to do for guests is to cook them something to eat. This old woman is cooking something. She is cooking scrapings from the inside of an old moose skin. She scrapes them into her kettle and cooks them.

"Do not eat it," whispers Kulusi's to his master, his older brother. "Do not eat it; it is poisoned. Stir it round and round in the dish when she gives it to you."

The young man stirs it and as he does so, it foams up and boils over; he throws it into the old woman's face. Instantly the skin of her face peels off, and she rushes out of the wigwam.

"I cannot," she says, "seem to please them with my cooking; one of you must do it."

One of her daughters rises and begins to cook then. She cooks good pieces of moose meat; she cooks beaver meat; she cooks nice fat caribou meat, and then she sets it before the strangers. They eat. They are satisfied. And then the young man takes one of them. He takes her for his wife.

Before they go to sleep, she whispers in his ear. "My mother will try to kill you again tomorrow. She has already killed a great many men who have come to take us for their wives."

Now it was morning. The sun is shining. The old woman comes into the wigwam and speaks to her daughter's husband.

"We must wrestle," she says to him. "It is the custom. All my other sons-in-law have done this with me."

"*E'e,*" he says to her. "Very well."

This old woman has Power. She puts on her rawhide belt, she ties on her rawhide belt, her *puoinoti,* her medicine belt. She stands close to the cliff. She is going to throw him right over. She is going to kill him. But Kulusi's is watching.

Kulusi's whispers to him, "If she throws you over, I will catch you. I will not let you fall."

"I am ready," says the young man. "You may attack me first." The old woman lunges at him, but she cannot move his feet. He stands firm. Now it is his time to test her. He grasps her, he lifts her, and he throws her over the cliff.

Kulusi's is watching; he is floating out there in the sky. Kulusi's turns his head away. He lets her fall, he lets her pass by. She crashes to the earth below and then she dies.

Those two men return to the wigwam. Those girls are glad that their old mother is dead, and they rejoice. *Welta'sultijik.* The four of them leave that place. They leave that place and move deep into the forest of the World Above The Earth. Here they make a big comfortable wigwam. Here the men hunt and bring home animals. Here the women slice up that meat and dry it, here they take care of the wigwam. That is always the business of women.

Now a baby is born to the man and his wife, a son to them, and they are greatly pleased. The man likes to stay home and play with that baby, but he and Kulusi's must often be away hunting. And one day while they are out in the forest,

Kulusi's is troubled. He is sensing something feeling wrong. He cannot eat.

"What is happening?" says his older brother.

"Something bad is happening at home," he tells him. "Some strange People came there last night. They have stolen the baby. I do not know why. I cannot see who they are."

The baby's father is in a frenzy. He leaps to his feet. Kulusi's tells him to wait until they get to an open space, a space where he can change shape. And when they come to a clearing, he springs into his Great Bird Shape. The other man is ready; he throws himself on the bird's back, and they race for home. The closer they get to home, the louder they can hear the crying of the women, crying for their little baby.

"Who has done this?" says the baby's father.

"We do not know," say those crying women. "They were strangers. They just took the baby and went away again."

"Let us go after them," says Kulusi's.

They track those men from the air, all day they are tracking them. And as night is coming, they see the camp, the camp of those baby-stealers, they see it from the air. It is so dark now that they can sneak up on them unseen.

Here is a large wigwam. Inside these strange men are dancing; around and around the wigwam they are dancing. They have changed the baby, changed him into a man. He is dancing as well. His father cannot tell which one he is, but Kulusi's knows him and points him out. The two men lie by the wigwam door, lying in the dark, waiting their chance to steal back the baby.

"When he comes round again," says Kulusi's. "He is coming ... he is almost here ... Now!"

And they have him. The minute his father's arms touch him, he is a baby again. The father leaps onto the back of Kulusi's in his Great Bird Shape, and they are off and up into the air before those strangers know that anything has happened.

From far away the women can hear the baby, hear him crying, and they know that he is safe.

"He smells of Power," says Kulusi's. "Do not let him nurse. We must destroy whatever Power is still wrapping round him. Do not let him nurse. Take off all his clothes and wash him all over. Give him new clothes, and then let him drink. Do that, and he will be safe."

When the baby is happily nursing, Kulusi's speaks to its father. "They will come after us, you know." And all evening those two men are preparing their weapons. Each one makes himself a bow and six stone-headed arrows.

Now it is morning. The sun's light is just coming over the trees. There is a tiny little noise from outside, a noise like a single breath.

"Shoot," whispers Kulusi's, and he points upward through the smokehole.

His master shoots one of his arrows, and immediately someone groans and falls off the ridgepole. Now Kulusi's shoots, and his arrow strikes its target. Then his master shoots. Then Kulusi's shoots, and each one shoots all six of his arrows, and each time those arrows strike an enemy.

"What now?" asks the man.

"Now we wait," says Kulusi's. "Do not go outside yet."

All of them are waiting, waiting quietly inside the wigwam. Finally Kulusi's goes out. The enemy has all gone home. They have taken their dead and wounded with them, for there is blood on the ground, blood on the wigwam walls.

"They will come back," says Kulusi's. "They will come back with more men, and try to kill us all. So let us eat, and then let us leave this place."

They pack up all their things. Kulusi's carries it all on his back, carries them all on his back, until they come to the old woman's wigwam on the edge of the cliff of the World Above The Earth. The baby's aunt stops there and gathers her clothes and a few other things, and then it is time to leave the World Above The Earth.

The two women, the little baby, the man, all sit on the back of Kulusi's in his Great Bird Shape, and they hold on to all those bundles of furs and things, and Kulusi's leaps from the cliff into the sky, into the clouds. Lower and lower he sails down the wind, until they can see Earth World below. The land rushes up towards them, growing in their eyes until they can see the old Kulu camp, and the wigwam of the young man's family.

The old people are still alive. They are so glad to see their son again. They welcome his wife and her sister, they play with the baby. And all the People in that Kulu camp make a feast. They make a feast for the young man and Kulusi's, and they are eating and dancing and playing. They are eating and dancing all night long.

GHOST
WORLD

PAPKUTPARUT

Kisiku'k wikuomk. Wikijik kisiku'k. It is in the very oldest of the camps of the Old Ones. A *saqmaw* becomes sick. It is a strange sickness; it makes him jerk and spasm like fish do when they are caught on a leister. This *saqmaw* is a man whom the People respect. He has Power. But the sickness is stronger than he is. So all the People are waiting with him as his Power drains away, waiting for him to die. His body jerks and twists, it contracts one last time, and then it lies still. It lies very still, the way all bodies of the People lie in death.

The People begin to mourn him. *Akaia, akaia,* that is what they are crying out. They begin to paint their faces black for him. They begin to unbraid their hair.

And then this man who has died opens his eyes.

E'e, the People are astonished. They are frightened. This is a thing which no one of them has ever seen before, that a man should come back from being dead.

And then this man who has died begins to speak. We all remember exactly what it was that he said, because the Old Ones have passed it down to us.

This man says, "My children, listen to me. My kin-friends, listen to me. Papkuparut has sent me back. The Guardian has sent me back to tell you what it is like in the Ghost World."

"*E'e,*" say the People. "Please continue talking to us. We are listening to what you have to say."

This man speaks. "Every Person has a *skite'kmuj,* a ghost body. For a man or a woman, it looks like a black shadow of a man or a woman. It has hands and feet, a mouth, a head, and all the other parts of a human body. It drinks and eats. It puts on clothes, it hunts and fishes and amuses itself. With a moose or a beaver, it looks like a black shadow of the animal. For a canoe or a pair of snowshoes, a cooking pot, a sleeping-mat, it looks like a shadow of these things, these Persons."

This old man raises himself up a little. "I have been there, in the Ghost World. I have seen these things. I have seen the *skite'kmujk* of those People who have not acted as they should. They are punished. They are given to eat only the bark of rotten trees. They are made to dance and leap without stopping, for as many moons as the Guardian decides they must. He punishes them for not having acted as they should. I have seen the *skite'kmujk* of those People who have done well, who have conducted themselves as they should. Life is good for them in the Ghost World. They have canoes, they have snowshoes, they have bows and clubs and sleeping-mats. The sun shines into their wigwams twice a day. The fir boughs and cedar boughs in their wigwams are always green and fresh. The sun renews them when it shines within. Papkutparut the Guardian watches over them, and they have always much meat to eat—much meat and fat and marrow. Their chins are always dripping with fat. This is how it is, in the Ghost World. I have been sent back to bring you certain of the spirit berries of this world. Papkutparut sends them to you. These are some of the fruits which are eaten in the ghost world. And now, my children and my kin-friends," says the old man, "I am returning there, to that world. It lies so many days' travel away, that way, over the water. Papkutparut has sent me; now he takes me back again. *Na teliaq.* I have finished." And as he finishes saying these things, that old man dies. He closes his eyes and dies. Once more they mourn for him. They paint their faces black. And now they begin to beat on the birchbark cover of his wigwam, to encourage the ghost to come out. *Uey, uey,* they are calling out.

When they see that this time he stays dead, then the People bury him. They bury with him all the things he will need in the Ghost World: clothes, weapons, food and all the other things a man needs, so that the ghosts of these things, these Persons, can accompany him into the Ghost World.

Now the People are thinking all the time about this Ghost World. "He said it lies over there, so many days' journey away, across the water," they say to each other. The young men especially are thinking about it. Could living men travel there? It would be a Great Thing a man could do, to travel to the Ghost World. Their eyes are always looking now in that direction.

Now in the camps of the People, another death occurs. Death comes for the son of one of the hunters. This child is his only son. He has given his heart to this child, and now his child is gone. "My son has gone to the Ghost World," says this man, "and I am going to follow him there. I am going walking to the Ghost World. My kin-friends, will any of you come with me? I am going to the Ghost World to bring back my son."

Now some of the hunters, the young men, are coming to him. "We will go with you," they say. "We will see with our eyes what this Ghost World is like. The People will sing songs about our journey, for it will be a Great Journey. No living man of the People has ever made a journey such as we shall make." So this dead child's father gives presents to all his friends who will go with him. He makes sure their families will have meat to eat while they are away. And soon they are all ready to start.

We are all still astonished at what they did. The Old Ones have told us those things which happened to them.

Each man takes his weapons. He takes his bow, he takes his arrows in their quiver, he takes his war club. Each man takes presents for Papkutparut the Guardian. And each man takes poles, nine or ten feet high.

The way to the Ghost World lies over there. It is many days' journey. Going to the Ghost World is walking many days, endless walking through water. Their feet are walking on the top of the World Beneath The Earth. Their bodies are walking through the Water World. Their heads are walking in the sky. Their eyes are seeing nothing but water; it stretches blue and shining all around them, to the very edge of the edge.

Every night, when it is time for them to sleep, they take their poles and shove the ends down in the sands below the water. They tie these poles together to make a sleeping-platform that rises above the water. And they lie on them through the night, sleeping in the sky above the water. In the morning, they walk on.

Going to the Ghost World is a long journey. It is a hard journey. These men are getting tired, their strength is draining away. They are very hungry now. And some of them begin to die. "We will see you in the Ghost World," say these brave men, making jokes as they are dying. "We will get there before you do." And toward the end of their journey, there are only five or six of them left, of all those hunters who started out. Night comes.

The last men lie down to sleep, on their platforms above the water.

Now it is morning. They wake to see the sun, and then they see another thing. They see the Ghost World rising above the horizon, there in the distance. They see the land curving up above the water like a bow.

"It is the end of our journey," says the dead child's father. "Now I shall find my son." And they hasten to jump down into the water, to untie the poles, and to set off for the land they can now see in the distance.

These men have come to the Ghost World. They look around amazed. It is just as the old saqmawo'q has said. There are dogs there. They see beaver there. They see moose and caribou. They see canoes and snowshoes and wigwams of the People.

And then a moment later, they see something else. They see a thing which fills them with terror. These men see Papkutparut the Guardian. It is his wigwam they have been walking toward, and now he has come out.

Papkutparut takes the shape of a man of the People. But he is as huge as a mountain, he is like a mighty waterfall pouring over a steep cliff, he is a terrible storm and wind. He is Papkutparut the Guardian.

"WHOEVER YOU ARE," says the voice of Papkutparut, "PREPARE YOURSELVES TO DIE. YOU HAVE HAD THE ARROGANCE TO COME TO THE LAND OF THE DEAD ALIVE. YOU HAVE ENTERED THE GHOST WORLD LIVING, AND THIS IS FORBIDDEN. FOR I AM PAPKUTPARUT THE GUARDIAN, THE MASTER OF SOULS, AND I SAY YOU MUST DIE."

Papkutparut is consumed with fury. He rushes toward them, raising his club. And then the dead child's father throws himself on his knees. He opens his robes, he exposes his stomach to death. He offers his death to Papkutparut, but first he speaks.

"Crush me with your club," says this hunter. "Shoot into me all your arrows. For I am dead already. My heart has died when my child died. It is for his sake only that I have come here, and my kin-friends accompanied me because they love me." And the tears roll down his face. He makes no weeping sound, but the tears fall out of his eyes and make tracks in the black with which he has painted his face.

Then this hunter speaks again: "You are the master of my life and death," he says to Papkutparut. "I give myself to your justice. Yet if there is anything of the People still left within you, here in this Ghost World, if any compassion or tenderness for the People lives in your heart, I ask you to accept these presents which we have brought you from the Living World, the Earth World, and to receive us as your friends."

The respectful and polite behaviour of this man, his beautiful way of expressing himself, as well as his bravery and his love for the dead child he has lost—all these things open the heart of Papkutparut toward him. His fury dies away. He lowers his club and receives him as his friend.

"E'e," he says to him, "e'e, nji'nm, you are a brave man of the People. Your heart is strong. I take pity on your sufferings. I honour your courage, and I will forgive you for entering the Ghost World."

"I will do more. I will give you the soul of your child to take home with you."

The heart of this hunter is filled with gladness.

"But first," says Papkutparut, "let us rest a while and amuse ourselves a little. It is not every day that someone comes to visit me from the Earth World. You have Power, and I wish to play against you. I wish to play waltes with you."

This speech gladdens the hearts of all the men who had journeyed with that hunter. They are no longer afraid. They stake against Papkutparut all the things which they have brought with them. And Papkutparut stakes against them three things from the Ghost World. He stakes against them tmawey, tobacco. He stakes against them corn. He stakes against them the spirit berries which the skite'kmujk eat as food in the Ghost World. And then they begin to play.

These men play against Papkutparut from the early morning until the late evening, when the sun goes beneath

STORIES FROM THE SIX WORLDS

the earth. And they win. Playing *waltes,* they win corn. They win tobacco. They win spirit berries.

"You are brave men. You are strong," says Papkutparut. "You have shown your Power. You have won the three greatest things in the Ghost World. It gladdens my heart to give them to you, to take back to the Earth World."

All the time they have been playing, they are hearing the ghosts chanting and rejoicing. And all the time they have been playing, the ghost of the dead child has been there in the wigwam with Papkutparut. Those men cannot see him, but he is there. And now Papkutparut takes this child, he makes him very small, he makes him the size of a nut. He puts this nut into a medicine bag and wraps it up tightly.

"Here," he says, handing the bag to the child's father. "Here is the ghost of your son, the spirit of your son. Return with it at once to your own country, to the Earth World, the land of living Persons. As soon as you are there, build a special wigwam. Place within it the body of your son. Take his soul and put it back into his body. But be very careful. Make sure there is no opening out of which the soul can escape. For he will not wish to leave the Ghost World. He will not wish to enter the body again. And if there is an opening, he will escape and return here. He leaves this world against his will."

This father is filled with joy. He has gotten his son back. He is taking great gifts home to the People. And now Papkutparut shows him the Ghost World. He sees those who have acted as they should, and how the animals allow themselves to be hunted, and to be eaten by them. He sees their wigwams, filled with the fragrance of fir and cedar. He sees the frantic dancing of those who have not acted as they should; he sees them eating rotten bark.

And then those travellers return to their own country. They give to the People the gifts of corn and tobacco. "These Papkutparut sends you," they say. "You must plant them and watch over them." And so it was done, and for many years after that, the People did plant corn and tobacco.

But it is a time of feasting. The travellers have returned. It is a time for stories and dancing. It is necessary to do all these things, to thank Papkutparut.

And so this father will dance. He will chant and dance in honour of Papkutparut. He gives his medicine bag to an old woman, to hold for him, so that he may dance.

This old woman is curious. She opens that bag to see what is inside. And instantly the soul of the dead child flies

out and returns to the Ghost World. And instantly the father of that child dies of grief, and his soul flies off to the Ghost World after him.

And the People bury them both, and weep for them, and tell their story.

Kespi-a'tuksitkik. Na teliaq.

KLUSKAP TELLS THE PEOPLE ABOUT DEATH

Kluskap did many Powerful things on the Earth World, and then he left it. Before he went away from this earth, he spoke to the People.

"There will be white people," said Kluskap, "who will come and take this forest away from you. But I am going north, to make a place for you where no white person can ever come. No white person shall ever enter there. And this place will be a place where you may not come while you are alive. You will only travel there after you die on the Earth World."

"I am telling the People to act always as they should. Those of you who do not act as you should must remember that there is a place of Darkness Forever. Those of the People who do not act as they should will forever have to hunt their game in darkness. There will be no sun for them."

Kluskap told the People that none of them would live to see the ending of the Earth World.

"Do not worry," he said to them. "I will come. I will raise you from the burial mounds. I will call you down from the crotch of the trees. I will call you down from the scaffolds of the air, to go north with me, to live where no white person shall ever come."

SOURCES AND NOTES

When I first began the research for this book, I often wondered whether there were any stories about the origin of stories. John Newell, a Micmac elder at Pictou Landing, had told Wilson Wallis in 1911 that Micmac songs were all based on the songs of birds:

> One old Indian listened to the gull until it had finished its song. Thus he learned its song, and said to the others: "If you people care to dance to it, dance. If not, then merely listen to me." He then took a stick and beat time. But as he sang he wanted to put some words into the tune. He was thinking about a woman who was hunting for something, and accordingly he sang about this. (Wallis, Wallis 1955:118-119)

In a way, this may be an account of the origin of Micmac stories as well: chanting and singing, one added words about whatever thoughts came to mind. Eventually there was a song, a poem, a story. These three categories may actually have been one and the same thing to the Micmac. "The old people," said Charles Leland, "declared that they had heard from their progenitors that all of these stories were once sung; that they themselves remembered when many of them were poems." (1884:iii) He was delighted when one of his collaborators, Mrs. Wallace Brown, recorded "a long Micmac tale" which had actually been sung to her rather than recited.

Certainly many tales partook of the elements of poetry, even if they were not sung. The Micmac language naturally lends itself to rhyme, as the Abbé Maillard was to learn, preaching to the People in the 1700s.

> I ... take care of observing measure and cadence in the delivery of my words.... As nothing enchants those people more than a style of metaphors and allegories, in which even their common conversation abounds, I adapt myself to their taste ... I borrow the most lively images from those objects of nature, with which they are so well acquainted ... I affect, above all, to rhime as they do, especially at each member of a period. (1758:2-3)

Elsewhere he notes, "If I read this [Micmac] to you myself, the rhyming talent of these people would be obvious." (1865:295-296) Micmac use of rhyme and the rhythmic quality of their speech—its measure and cadence, and their habit of repeating phrases, almost like a chorus—may have structured stories as poetry, which easily lent itself to chanted recital. However, the majority of collected stories, beginning with LeClercq's in 1675, seem to have been spoken, rather than sung, although many of them contain songs.

The earliest known Micmac story was recorded between 1675 and 1683, by the Recollet priest, Chrestien LeClercq, who lived with the Micmac during that period on the Gaspé Peninsula of Quebec, the Miramichi and Restigouche Rivers. He was formally adopted as a son, a 'kin-friend,' by a Micmac elder and his wife; he learned to speak Micmac, and undoubtedly he heard many stories during his residence in their wigwam. Unfortunately the story about Papkutparut is the only one he wrote down.

The Reverend Silas Rand, born in Nova Scotia in 1810, also spoke Micmac. He became fascinated with their stories after being told his first one by an old woman named Susan Barss, in 1847. At that time he was in Prince Edward Island. The bulk of his material, however, was collected in Nova Scotia, although he later recorded tales, both Micmac and Maliseet, in New Brunswick.

"I once asked Dr. Rand to do for the Glooskcap Legends what Longfellow has done for those clustering round Hiawatha," wrote his friend Campbell Hardy, who included a few of Rand's tales in a book of his own. "I have his reply, which reached me here in Dover, not long before his death. He was unable to undertake so great a task—his work was Evangelization." (1910 ca III:3-4) Hardy was an English army officer, living in Nova Scotia between 1854 and 1867. He published several of Rand's collected tales in 1855, in his *Sporting Adventures in the New World,* and included therein a few he had recorded himself; these, however, were told to him in English, and were therefore much abridged.

Rand's great body of tales, still the best resource for Micmac stories, was collected between 1847 and his death in 1889. His manuscripts went to the Wellesley College Library, and that institution arranged for their publication in 1894. "The stories were related to him in Micmac, by the native Indians, and then translated and written down by him in English; the translations only have been preserved,

in no case the narration in the original language." (Webster
1894:i)

> The greater portion of these legendary remains were
> written out at first, not in Indian, but in English. I
> never found an Indian, either man or woman, who
> would undertake to tell one of these stories in English.
> I heard them all related, in all cases, in Micmac. I
> usually had pen, ink, and paper at hand; if I came to a
> word I did not understand, I would stop the speaker, jot
> down the word with its meaning, make a few other
> brief notes, and then write out the story in English
> from memory, aided by the brief notes I had made. But
> this was not all; I always read over the story in English
> to the one who related it, and made all necessary
> corrections.... I never found more than five or six Indi-
> ans who could relate these queer stories; and most, if
> not all, of these are now gone. (Rand 1894:i)

Given those circumstances, it is frightening to think how
much would have been lost forever if Rand had not been
able to speak Micmac.

In the summer of 1923, a redoubtable woman named
Elsie Clews Parsons made a trip to Nova Scotia to collect
Black folklore, with side-trips into the tales of other ethnic
groups.

> At Whycocomaugh ... I had the good fortune to make
> friends with a Micmac woman who proved to be an
> exceptionally helpful informant and who invited me to
> camp with her family at the coming mission for St. Ann
> on Chapel Island. The accompanying tales were re-
> corded at that time, also at Whycocomagh and at
> Lequille, a small Indian settlement on the outskirts of
> Annapolis Royal, Western Nova Scotia. (1925:55)

The Micmac woman was Isabelle Googoo Morris; she and
her mother, Mary Madeline Newall Poulet, both told stories to Parsons. Most of them had come from Mary Doucet
Newall, Mrs. Poulet's mother, born ca 1800 in Newfoundland. "Inferably," said Parsons, "several of the tales recorded here throw back to a period but little later than
many of the tales recorded and paraphrased by Rand."
(1925:55)

> One of [Rand's] informants, Susan Christmas, stated
> in 1870 that she had learned her stories from an old
> blind woman on Cape Breton who used to interest her

219

and other children and keep them quiet for a long time, telling them stories. I incline to identify this blind storyteller with Mary Doucet Newall. (1925:55)

Elsie Clews Parsons' collection has been invaluable to me, even though her informants all spoke English when telling her stories. Parsons did not "paraphrase"; she wrote everything down exactly as it came out of the mouth of the speaker. With the exception of Campbell Hardy, she was the first to allow the storytellers their own words. She does not appear to have resorted to euphemisms, either—one of Rand's nineteenth-century habits.

Wilson Wallis, an anthropologist, visited the Maritimes in the summers of 1911 and 1912. He returned in 1950 and 1953 with his wife, Ruth Sawtell Wallis, to gather a few further fragments of stories. Their collection was published in 1955.

▲

Micmac stories have never been static, either as a body of literature, or singly. In looking at those tales documented by the collectors above, between 1675 and 1955, one can see how certain stories accrete episodes like barnacles, around a particular character or set of actions— often episodes from other stories. One character's story-cycle subsumes others, the first growing longer and longer while the rest fade more and more from memory.

The corpus of Micmac myth also changes, through this three-hundred-year period. The character Papkutparut, for example, appears once in a seventeenth-century tale. As Guardian of the Ghost World, this Person was then well known to the Micmac, yet by 1847 he and the tales about him had been forgotten.

Many Micmac stories gradually acquire European elements during this time: servants, kings, palaces, gunboats. European ideas begin to creep in, giving some tales a Christian gloss. The character Kluskap is first recorded about 1850. He goes from being one of many Persons in the traditional Micmac world, to a central position as *the* Micmac spirit-helper, always victorious in encounters with Europeans. His story-cycle annexes other tales, placing him in the starring role. By 1930, he has taken on some of the attributes of Christ: he will raise the People from the dead when the world has ended.

Certain older tales from a world before Europeans drop out of the storyteller's repertoire over the years, to be replaced by tales entirely of European origin. "The Solitary Maiden," which Rand recorded, is a variant of the poem "Berta of Hungary," written about 1270 A.D. by Adenes li Rois. (Retold in Goodrich 1961:102-125) This has little, if any, Micmac content. Obviously it came into the world of the People through the early French settlers. Parsons collected stories about Red Fox and the Daigel [Tiger] from a Micmac boy; he had heard them from a relative who once lived in Florida, picking up these Black folk-tales there. (1925:128)

One can also see how tales have devolved, as the nineteenth century drew to a close and storytelling itself began to die out, replaced by books, and later by radio and television. The story-cycle of Ki'kwa'ju runs to thirty pages, in the version collected by Silas Rand. (1894:160-169, 263-270, 306-321) By 1911, Wallis found only enough material to fill eight pages. (1955:422-430) In 1975, Rita Joe recorded three *paragraphs* about "Key Qua Joo," told to her by the late Harriet Denny of Eskasoni, one of the last great storytellers. (1976:29) And although "Mrs. Rita Joe has had to exclude certain parts that might have been offensive to non-Indian readers," this is still a considerable reduction. Stories collapsed and condensed as detail was forgotten.

There were two categories of stories, according to Micmac hunters interviewed by Campbell Hardy in the nineteenth century. The first was oral history, the *aknutmaqn*, "he tells news." The second type was the *a'tukwaqn*, "stories, treasured up, indeed, and handed down from age to age, and often told for diversion, and to keep in memory the habits and manners, domestic and political, of the 'sahk-ah-waych-kik' [*sa'qwe'ji'jk*], the ancient Indians...." (Hardy 1855:226)

For this collection, I have chosen only the *a'tukwaqn*, and from them I selected twenty-nine stories with little or no obvious European content. Kukwes Grandfather, for example, slays his son's wife with an iron bar; Lamkisn, performing the war-medicine dance, is fired on by Kwetej muskets. These are almost the only concrete intrusions from a European world. There may very well be deeper levels, where certain themes can be shown to be European in origin—if, indeed, they are not universal. Certainly the story "Nuji-Kesi-Kno'tasit" has a very strong flavour, in places, of "Aladdin and the Magical Lamp." My intent, however, was to choose stories which would most clearly show the Micmac world before the arrival of the Europeans, the world of the Old Ones of the People. Therefore, the collection was limited to stories which needed no subtractions, no editing out of European material.

What I *have* done here was to take all the variants of the chosen tales, drawing on the collections of Silas Rand as the core-stories, simply because they are the most complete, and to flesh out the core-tale with any missing details that the variants could provide. Having done this, I attempted to retell the stories in a voice closer to those which the original storytellers might have used, and in language a little less stilted and nineteenth-century in tone.

Silas Rand, for example, writes like this: "After a while soft sleep with dewy fingers pressed down their eyelids; and clasped in each other's arms, they revelled in the land of dreams."(1894:308) The Micmac, however, did not talk like the English Romantic Poets. Rand also keeps bringing the European world into his translations: "Gazing at the stars, they were animated by the natural curiosity so beautifully expressed by the poetess: 'Twinkle, twinkle, little star; How I wonder what you are....' " (1894:308) This sort of thing really interferes with any entering into the world of the Micmac which a reader might hope to do, or any experiencing of the story as a distinctively Micmac work of literature.

Almost all of the documentation of stories of the People were done by those who did not speak Micmac, and who themselves were not Micmac; in many cases, they put their own gloss on certain beliefs or events. I have tried to eliminate these outside interpretations, additions and misunderstandings, keeping the stories ethnographically accurate to the best of my knowledge. I am sure that history will find faults with my efforts as well; I can only hope they will be minor ones. For the stories belong first to the storytellers; theirs must be the last word in any exegesis, yet most of their voices are now forever silent.

Many of these tales exist today only as fragments, as potsherds of literature. Vital elements of plot or detail are missing, yet I have included a number of such short pieces which I know are condensed fragments of much longer epics, simply because of their shattered beauty or the vivid light they still can shed on some part of traditional Micmac life.

In terms of giving the stories a Micmac voice again, I have listened to hours of tapes of Micmac speech—stories being told in both English and Micmac—and I had the good fortune to hear Alietji'jo'q, Harriet Denny, telling stories before she died. I have tried to give my retelling the same sorts of cadences and repetitions of phrases, the same sort of immediacy and graphic imagery which storytellers such as Rita Joe are able to give their audiences in dramatic performances of their art.

I have retained the Micmac names and phrases which occur in older collections, and Bernard Francis of the Micmac Language Institute has corrected them and transcribed them into the Francis-Smith orthography, the modern writing system. Some of these stories contain archaic words whose meanings are now unknown to speakers of modern Micmac. Such words are listed at the end of the Notes on the tale in which they occur, as their original transcription, assigned meaning, or the orthography approximated by Mr. Francis may not be correct.

An explanation of the Micmac alphabet and orthography, with a guide to pronunciation, also by Mr. Francis, appears as an appendix.

WSITIPLAJU
"The History of Usitebulajoo" (Rand 1894:44-58), no informant named.

"Addition One" (Rand 1894:59-60).

"Addition Two" (Rand 1894:60-61); collected 10 October 1870 from Susan Christmas, probably in Yarmouth, N.S., as Rand collected other material from Susan Christmas there on 7 September 1870.

"The Serpent Horn" (Parsons 1925:60-63); collected *ca* 26-31 July 1923, at Chapel Island, N.S., from Isabelle Googoo Morris and Mary Madeline Newall [Noel] Poulet.

"Partridge and His Family" (Wallis, Wallis 1955:441-445); collected by Wilson D. Wallis in the summer of 1911 or 1912 at Shubenacadie, N.S., from Maximius Simon Basque.

Notes: The name Plawej means Birch Partridge, and one of the variants of this story points out that the reason all Birch Partridges have such skinny, meatless legs and backs is because Plawej cut off his own flesh. Information about the natural world is often worked into stories in this way.

Polar bears, for example, have livers that are so full of Vitamin A that they are toxic to humans. Polar bears are often infected with trichina parasites, and eating their undercooked meat—or their livers—can be fatal. Muin Wapskw gives his meat as a means of revenge: his Power speeds up the natural course of events, killing Wijïke'skw and her People between a day and a night. Harold McGee feels that Muin Wapskw is not a Polar bear, however, but a magical bear, whose Power is revealed and emphasized in this story through the fact that he is white. (1988: personal communication)

223

The stratagem used by the two women to slow down the Killer Whale Person chasing their canoe would have been very familiar to a Micmac audience, for it was one which they themselves employed. It was described about 1740 by a shaman-chief named Lkimu, from the Chignecto Isthmus of Nova Scotia.

> [Journeys are] never longer than seven or eight leagues.... These are long journeys for us. We much prefer to make them in calm or good weather since the bad fish [Killer Whales] which often infest these seas do not allow us to sail without worry and fear. All too often these malevolent beings attack the sterns of our canoes so suddenly and without warning that they sink the boat and all who are in it.... If we are caught without our spears, with fear and trembling we throw overboard any pieces of meat or fish we may have, one by one, to distract the fish behind us.... if we have nothing else to throw then we take off our furs and throw them overboard. We have often thrown even our game-bird headdresses to the creatures. At last, when there is nothing left to throw, we take the longest and sharpest of the bones we always have in our canoes and tie them as best we can to the ends of our paddles.... Then we lie in wait to harpoon the creature. (Maillard 1863:308-309)

When Wsitiplaju calls on Keswalqw to help change him into a man, he is calling upon the moon. Rand translated this term as "the Great Spirit, the Creator, literally" (1894:47). He may have thought he was hearing the word *kisu'lkw,* 'he who made us,' which is used as "Creator." Other stories, however, confirm that it is indeed the moon that is meant. *Keswalqw* combines the meanings 'moon' and 'hollowed out' or 'concave': the new moon.

"Whenever they saw the new moon they had prayers. What they asked for, suppose a moose, they would get." (Parsons 1925:89) Parsons' variant of this story, collected in English, reads, "Tonight I am going to stand up this stick outside and I am going to speak to the Moon and ask him [her; there is no distinction in the Micmac language, but they considered the moon to be a woman] that I may be as tall as this stick in the morning." (Parsons 1925:80) The Moon was a powerful ally, having helped the Sun create the world (Maillard 1758:47), and as late as 1950, children were still being taught a formalized greeting or prayer made in Micmac when first seeing the new moon.

The exact meaning of Wsitiplaju is no longer known.

THE MAN WHO MARRIED JIPIJKA'MI'SKW

"A Man Became a Tcipitcjkaam" (Wallis, Wallis 1955:345-346); collected in the summer of 1911 or 1912 by Wilson Wallis, from John Newell [Noel] of Pictou Landing, N.S. John Newell had been born in Cape Breton in the nineteenth century, and lived there for his first twenty years. He was literate in French and English. "I believe I could have become a *buoin* [*puoin*]," he said to Wallis,

224

"and that if trouble had come to my people, I would have had the power. Sometimes, when I was smoking, with my eyes closed, I would feel myself rising, rising to about the height of the house. When I dream, things are as real and as clear as when I am awake. One time I dreamed I was walking over the water, as *buoin* often do, and I saw a wigwam on the bottom, way out there. This does not happen to me as often as it formerly did—it is going from me. If, however, the need came, and any harm befell my people, I think I would have the power to help them." (Wallis, Wallis 1955:160-161)

THE WOMAN WHO MARRIED JIPIJKA'M
"A Woman Marries the Horned Snake" (Parsons 1925:95-96); collected in the summer of 1923 by Elsie Clews Parsons, from Lucy Pictou of Lequille, N.S. She had heard it from her stepfather, a "Mr. Francis, of Botlodek, Cape Breton. He was also called Mieuse (Moose), because his great-grandfather captured moose easily, with a knife (Parsons 1925:95)." [Mius, spelled various ways, is a common Micmac and Acadian surname, originating with the Sieur Phillipe Mius d'Entremont, who settled in Nova Scotia and married a Micmac woman *ca* 1650.]

The earliest recorded variant of this story was collected by John Gyles from the Maliseet who had captured him in 1689.

There is an old story told among the Indians of a family who had a daughter ... so formed by nature and polished by art, that they could not find for her a suitable consort. At length, while this family were once residing upon the head of the Penobscot River, under the White Hills, called *Teddon*, this fine creature was missing, and her parents could learn no tidings of her. After much time and pains spent, and tears showered in quest of her, they saw her diverting herself with a beautiful youth, whose hair, like her own, flowed down below his waist, swimming, washing, &c., in the water; but they vanished on their approach. This beautiful person, whom they imagined to be one of those kind spirits who inhabit the Teddon, they looked upon as their son-in-law; and according to custom they called upon him for moose, bear, or whatever creature they desired, and if they did but go to the water-side and signify their desire, the animal would come swimming to them!" (Gyles 1869:45-46)

THE CHILD FROM BENEATH THE EARTH
"A Little Boy Catches a Whale" (Rand 1894:280-281); no informant or date of collection listed. My retelling of this story was first published in *Six Micmac Stories* (Halifax, Nova Scotia Museum 1988), and appears here by permission.

LAMKISN
"Fox Fire" (Parsons 1925:75-77); collected by Elsie Clews Parsons from Mary Madeline Newall Poulet, who heard it from her mother

Mary Doucet Newall (b. *ca* 1800, Newfoundland), in July 1923, at Chapel Island, N.S.

Notes: When this female shaman hears a cry from a phosphorescent log, she thinks it is ghosts. Such logs are left at burial sites to give light to the spirits (see the story "Fetching Summer"), and it is well known that ghosts get lonely.

As we stood at the mounds, Morris sang the snatch of song the ghosts, *nigelwech* [meaning unknown], are said to sing, because they are lonesome: *kuwe nudaneh kuwe nudaneh kuwe nudahanen.* (Parsons 1926:482)

The caribou feet which the Kwetej wear, and which they lose, probably refer not only to the practice of strapping animal hoofs on to fool trackers, but to the Kwetej ability to shape-change into caribou.

The word *lamkisn* is now unfamiliar, but the initial morpheme *lam* means "inside something."

MIMKITAWO'QU'SK

"The Story of Mimkudawogoosk (Moosewood Man)" (Rand 1894:321-325); collected by Silas Rand from Susan Christmas, Yarmouth, N.S., 7 September 1870.

Notes: Moosewood (*Acer pennsylvanicum*), is the straight-growing supple wood used to make the hoop which binds together the central poles of the wigwam. Tobacco pipe-stems are made from its shoots.

I think Rand has swapped in error the two trees, pine and elm, in the shape-changing contest in this story. Surely elms have many branches, but pines grow to a great height without them, and may best be described as "trees with no branches"—as indeed they are in other stories.

THE COMING OF PLANTS

"Jay's Beak Is Burned; First Plants" (Parsons 1925:81-82); collected by Elsie Clews Parsons, July 1923, from Mary Madeline Newall Poulet of Whycocomaugh, N.S.

Notes: The vivid image of the old woman spotting the moose swimming in the moonlight raises the question of what were those moose eating, if this story takes place before there were plants in the world. "Plants," in this case, may be cultivated plants: corn, beans, squash. "That is the time they started gardens," said Parsons' informant (1925:82). Stealing plants may reflect raids by the Micmac on other tribes practising agriculture.

BRINGING BACK ANIMALS

"Brings-Back-Animals; Variant" (Parsons 1925:71-74); collected by Elsie Clews Parsons in July 1923, from Isabelle Googoo Morris (b. 1877) of Whycocomaugh, N.S., who learned it from Bessie Cremo Morris, her husband's brother's wife from Sydney, N.S. "She is 'pure Indian.'" (Parsons 1925:72)

Notes: This story is one of the clearest teaching-tales; it states very plainly one of the primary laws of the People: that animals which give themselves to the hunter to be killed and eaten must not be wasted or killed indiscriminately. Their remains must also be honoured.

> It was a religious act among our people to gather up all bones very carefully and either to throw them in the fire (when we had one), or into a river where beaver lived. I cannot tell you the reason for this ... I do not know it. I only know that the Ancestors used to tell us that we must throw all the bones of the beaver we ate in rivers where we could see beaver lodges, so that the lodges would always exist. They also told us that our domestic animals must never gnaw the bones because this would not fail to diminish the species of the animal which fed us. None of the shamans, not even I, the foremost one ... could give any other reasons for these practises to our young people, who sometimes asked us questions on this subject. (Lkimu, 1740; in, Maillard 1863:304-304)

The only other context in which I have encountered *nespipaqn,* the smoking material, is in notes made by Nova Scotia Museum Curator Harry Piers in 1926 (NSM Printed Matter File). The bark of Squaw Bush *(Cornus candidissimus),* said Piers, was used as a tobacco, and called "Nes-pe-baw-un." Red Willow (Red Osier Dogwood, Red-twigged Cornel, *Cornus stolonifera)* was used in the same way, and called "Nes-pe-baw-un meg-way-ek" [red *nespipaqn*].

FETCHING SUMMER
"They Fetch Summer" (Parsons 1925:73-75); collected by Elsie Clews Parsons from Lucy Pictou of Lequille, N.S., July 1923.
Notes: This story has a variant which connects it strongly with "The Coming of Plants."

> The birds all met together to consult on which should go to the north after the Summer.... Three little birds go. One of them is Jay.... He finds Summer asleep in a wigwam, between two old women who are guarding him. When [he] sticks his beak through the wigwam wall, they burn it. (Parsons 1925:75)

KOPIT FEEDS THE HUNTER
"The Beaver Magicians and the Big Fish" (Rand 1894:351-353); no informant or date given.
Notes: There were strong associations of the beaver with Power. Shamans, according to the Abbé Maillard (1758:37), saw into the future and into the hearts of men by gazing into a great birchbark dish filled with water "from any river in which it was known there were beaver huts." Many stories told of the alliances of humans and Beaver Persons, such as this tale of the young man who fell asleep waiting by a hole in the ice to catch beavers.

Just as he was about to awake, he heard some one speak to him. "Are you asleep?" the voice said. He opened his eyes and saw a nice-looking young girl standing before him. He looked up and said, "Yes, I fell asleep." "You must be lonely," said the girl. "I am lonely," said the boy. "Come with me and we will go to my home," said the girl. She went to the hole in the ice and dove down in, and the young man followed her. (Nicholas Jerome; in, Michelson 1925:34)

"Those animals like men," the Micmac called the beaver; "they could talk to us if they wanted to, but they refuse." Except every now and then.

SKUN
"The Liver-Coloured Giants and Magicians" (Rand 1894:142-149); collected by Silas Rand from Nancy Jeddore, no date. Rand recorded other stories told by Nancy between 2 December 1870 and 19 February 1872. "She professed to have heard [this one] from some relative of hers many years ago." Others of her stories came to her from her mother, a "real Ninjun [Indian]."
Notes: The enemy *puoin* who takes a shark shape in this tale may very well be a Killer Whale Person, not a Shark Person. Rand recorded the tale in English, and whatever the name given him, he translated it as "shark," and I have left it that way, giving in turn the Micmac name for sharks. Rand, however, confuses elsewhere the words for shark and killer whale, translating Wipitimu'k as "shark."
Killer whales were abundant in the Gulf of St. Lawrence, and were feared by the Micmac. They appear in other stories (see "Wsitiplaju") but there are no stories about sharks. The animal in this story is chasing live fish, and watchers can see his distinctive back fin. As a literary device, the replacement of a Dream Vision whale (Putup) by a real-time killer whale (Wipitimu'k), is much subtler, more dramatic, and very Micmac.

SAKKLO'PI'K
"Caught by a Hair String" (Rand 1894:7-13); no informant or date given. See the Introduction above, for extended comments.
Sakklo'pi, 'hair-string,' is a term no longer in use, although *sekklo'pi,* 'something tied tight,' is still current.

NUJI-KESI-KNO'TASIT
"The Magical Dancing Doll" (Rand 1894:7-13); collected by Silas Rand, who said, "I simply *translate* ... as I wrote it down from the mouth of a Micmac Indian in his own language." He does not give the man's name or date.

MEDICINE BAG
"Upsaakumoode" (Rand 1894:434-437); collected by Silas Rand, no informant or date given.

MI'KMWESU
"The Indian Who Was Transformed into a Megumoowesoo" (Rand 1894:94-98); collected by Silas Rand, no informant or date given.

KLUSKAP AND MI'KMWESU
"Glooscap and the Megumoowesu" (Rand 1894:23-29); collected by Silas Rand, no informant or date given.

KWIMU
"The Loon Magician" (Rand 1894:378-382); collected by Silas Rand, no informant or date given.
Notes: The description of the Kukwes slaying a whole camp of the People, while four terrified survivors hide in the water with only eyes and noses showing, comes straight out of a reality the People themselves had to face, with historic enemies. Contingency plans for escaping sudden attacks were primary concerns, at least during the sixteenth and seventeenth centuries.

[Lkimu] told me he had learned from others older than he that they had been forced to learn quickly how to build canoes because of the constant alarms caused by other tribes, their enemies. So as not to be surprised as they had often been in the past times, they had made very sure they always had with them enough boats to carry them by water from one point or cape of land to another; from their village to another belonging to their tribe; from the coast to another piece of land.... (Maillard 1863:307)

TIA'M AND TIA'MI'SKW
"The Invisible Boy" (Rand 1894:101-109); collected by Silas Rand from Susan Barss [Basque], "and written down from her mouth in Charlottetown, Prince Edward Island, in the winter of 1848, and translated from the original May 1869, by S.T. Rand."
Notes: The portion of this story which deals with the marriage of Tia'm and Wjikii'skw has often been extracted and treated as if it were a Micmac Cinderella story. But Wjikii'skw is almost incidental; this is a tale about the bond between brother and sister, and the passing of Power—the protective Power of the spirit-helper animal—between siblings at the moment of death.
The way in which Tia'm's sister prepares his (moose) body after she kills him parallels both the treatment of the ordinary animal kill, which the People would eat, and the treatment of the bodies of humans after death. Such embalming is described by Chrestien LeClercq, living with the Micmac on the Gaspé *ca* 1675.

Our Gaspesians have never burned the bodies of their dead.... I have learned only this from our Indians, that the chiefs of their nation formerly entrusted the bodies of the dead to certain old men, who carried them sacredly to a wigwam built on purpose in the midst of the woods, here they remained for a month or six weeks. They opened the head and the belly of the dead person, and removed therefrom the brain and the entrails; they removed the skin from the body, cut the flesh into pieces, and, having dried it in the smoke or in the sun, they placed it at the foot of the dead man, to whom they gave back his skin, which they fitted on very much as if the flesh had not been removed. (LeClercq 1910:302)

LeClercq also described a shaman's medicine pouch which had been made from the head-skin of a moose, the entire head, minus the ears (1910:222-223).

The word *tioml,* spelled "teomul" by Rand and glossed as "totem," is no longer familiar to modern Micmac speakers. This spelling is tentative.

PLAWEJ

"Robbery and Murder Revenged" (Rand 1894:1-6); collected by Silas Rand, no informant or dates given.

Notes: This is a story full of Shape-Changers. Plawej is both man and birch partridge; his wife is probably a seal or a beaver, some animal which lives under the ice and has breathing holes.

KITPUSIAQNAW

"The History of Kitpooseagunow" (Rand 1894:62-77); collected by Silas Rand from Susan Barss [Basque]. "The preceeding is one of the first Ahtookwokun I ever heard related. Susan Barss, a woman with a humpback, told it in Micmac; and Jo Brooks interpreted it as she went along. I afterward wrote it down from her dictation, on the shores of the North River, where Brooks was encamped. This was in the summer of 1847." (Rand 1894:77)

"Addition to Legend VIII" (Rand 1894:77-80); collected by Silas Rand from Susan Christmas, Yarmouth, N.S., 10 October 1870.

"Ketpusyegenau" (Parsons 1925:56-59); collected by Elsie Clews Parsons, from Isabelle Googoo Morris of Whycocomaugh, N.S. "Her story was not very well told as I had to get it in fragments." (Parsons 1925:56)

"Kitpusiagana's Beginnings" (Wallis, Wallis 1955:338-339), and "Variant" (340-341); both collected by Wilson Wallis in the summer of 1911 or 1912, the latter fragment from Louis Glode.

Notes: The incident in which the two boys trap their father and leave him to burn to death in the wigwam is one of the most dramatic in any of the Micmac stories. Fire in the wigwam was something all of the People feared; Chrestien LeClercq recorded the destruction of a wigwam by fire *ca* 1680.

Our Indian woman, wife of Koucdedaoui, with whom we had come from Nipisiquit, was encamped in the absence of her husband quite close to the Fort of Monsieur de Fronsac with an Indian woman of her acquaintance, who had an infant at the breast. Through lack of birch bark they covered their

230

camp with branches of fir, and they found it convenient to make use of straw to rest upon during the night. The cold was extreme, and its rigour was increased by a wind from the north-west which blew with all its force, so that these women were compelled to make a much larger fire than usual. They went quietly to sleep without any presentiment of the evil which was coming upon them; but scarcely had these two unfortunate Indian women closed their eyes when the fire caught in the straw, and, making its way to the branches of fir, it consumed and reduced to ashes the entire wigwam. I leave it to be imagined to what extremity these poor women were reduced when they saw themselves completely shut in and surrounded by flames. They uttered at once cries so piercing that these reached our ears almost as soon as they left their mouths.... these poor mothers ... had tried to save their children from these devouring flames. One was lying in the snow with her infant, the other was still at the door of the wigwam without power to come out therefrom, and she suffered a grief so keen that she did not heed the sparks and coals falling continually upon her flesh. Everybody knows that the fir is a tree full of resin, which some call turpentine; and since, through the violence of the fire, this gum fell all in flame upon the body of this Indian woman, it is probable she would have expired along with her son ... if Monsieur Henaut had not, by strength of arm, rescued her [she died later of her burns] ... I entered the wigwam, which was still all on fire, in order to try to save her child; but it was too late, for this little innocent was smothered in the flames and half roasted. He died, in fact, a moment later in my arms.... (LeClercq 1910:182)

The scene with Kukwes Grandmother is very reminiscent of a piece of oral history collected in 1911 by Wilson Wallis (1955:408).

After all the flesh and bones were burned white, so that when touched they would fall apart, the deceased's wife came and uncovered the end of his toe, which was very hot. Two men who were standing there, watching, stirred up the flames, and remained by the body until it was merely ashes. The old man's wife held a piece of his bone on her knee. The men who were watching asked what she intended to do with it. "I want to keep it. I shall wrap it in a rag, put it in a box, and think of him when I see it." [The men said], "I suppose you will eat it." "No, I shall not eat it. He treated me well; I liked him; he will never come back, and I want to have this much of him." "No, you may not keep it. All must be burned." When she saw the men stirring the ashes, she cried.

The exact meaning of Kitpusiaqnaw is lost, although *kitpu* is the term for 'eagle.' Kitpusiaqnaw has been glossed as "Taken-from-Guts" or "Born by Caesarian Section," by collectors of this story.

MISKWEKEPU'J

"The Boy Who Played the Flute" (Parsons 1925:63-65); collected by Elsie Clews Parsons from Mary Madeline Newall Poulet of Whycocomaugh, N.S., July 1923. "The idea of Whale smoking was comical to the narrator's daughter [Isabelle Googoo Morris] who was listening. 'How can a whale smoke?' she exclaimed. '*That day he smoked*,' her mother firmly repeated." (Parsons 1925:63)

No literal meaning for Miskwekepu'j is now remembered.

THE THUNDERS AND MOSQUITO

"Thunder and Mosquito" (Parsons 1925:84-85); collected by Elsie Clews Parsons from Lucy Pictou, Lequille, N.S., in the summer of 1923.

Notes: The word 'thunder' in Micmac is always animate and plural: *kaqtukwaq*. The Thunder Persons live much as men do, eating, drinking, hunting, telling stories. But their Power-shapes are those of great birds, and when they fly and beat with their wings, the People down below on the Earth World have storms. Kaqtukwaq are akin to the Thunderbirds of Northern Woodlands and Plains cosmology; they are often portrayed in stories as helpful to the People.

As birds they flew away up to the skies, making a great deal of rain, a great deal of noise ... a great big noise and with lightning.... [The hunters] walked on two days, they came to another camp late in the day. They found the old lady sitting there, the old man sitting there. The old lady says, "Stay overnight. The boys are not home yet. We've got six boys. You stay overnight." The boys all came home in the evening. The old man says, "You better help these strangers." The boys say, "Are you ready to go?" "Yes." The old woman went out, she told the youngest boy, her pet, "Don't you be too fast, too loud, you are the one who makes the big lightning." Each goes on the back of one of the boys. They went easily. They were thunders. (Parsons 1925:70-73)

MUINI'SKW AND PKMK

Untitled (Hardy 1865:259-262); collected by Campbell Hardy *ca* 1840-1860, from Michael Thomas of Tufts Cove, Dartmouth, N.S.

The Indians have also traditionary [*sic*] stories connected with many of the animals and birds of the country. They tell them in their camps for the amusement of their children; but I have always noticed that they enjoy the narration of them just as much as do the younger portion of the community. "Most all the animal tell the grand story," said an Indian named Michael Tom to me one afternoon, as I sat in his wigwam. [Michael Thomas proceeds to tell Hardy a story about Rabbit, which, as it is so obviously post-contact, I have left out of this collection.] "Well, we say to the rabbit, we say,

'What makes you so white, Mr. Rabbit?' 'Well, I just tell you how it was,' the rabbit he say, 'We been dinin with um wedding; we cover all over with the white ribbon.' 'And what makes you so short tail, sir?' 'You see, I tell you friend what make me so short tail. We use to dine 'long with the gentlemen long time ago, and we use to set in the chair great deal when we go into the parlour; so the tail wore almost right off....' Absurd though the story was, and so delighted did all the inmates of the camp appear, (Michael himself could hardly tell it for his risibility), that I could not help joining in the universal burst of merriment. "Oh, dear! Oh, dear!" continued the narrator, wiping his eyes and puffing dense clouds of "Tamawee" [tmawey: tobacco]. "That rabbit queer fellow!"

THE NAMES OF STARS

Untitled (Dennis 1936:96,107).

Notes: Dr. Clara Dennis collected this story from "an Indian," while touring Nova Scotia in the 1930s, researching her book *Down in Nova Scotia*. Her anonymous informant may have been Peter Wilmot, formerly Chief at Pictou Landing. She visited him at his house in Truro (her photographs of Chief Wilmot taken on that occasion are now in the Nova Scotia Museum collection; one of them appears in her book).

If Chief Wilmot were her informant, he had a remarkable stretch of history on which to draw: he was born ca 1826, and still retained his baptismal certificate dated 26 July [St. Anne's Day] 1826. At his death in December 1932 he was at least 106 years old, his mind still sharp. "Our old people used to teach us about the sky," her informant told Dennis (1934:96). If these were Peter Wilmot's "old people," they would have been born in the eighteenth century.

Although Dennis's collection is late, and contains many errors (Little Marten is referred to as Kluskap's niece, for example), I have included her information about the stars because of the possible antiquity of the names given therein, and because some of those names do not appear elsewhere.

The earliest star-name lists for the Micmac come through Chrestien LeClercq, and were collected between 1675 and 1683.

[The Micmac] have some knowledge of the Great and the Little Bears, which they call, the first *Mouhinne* [*Muin*], and the second *Mouhinchich* [*Muinji'j*], which mean exactly in our language the Great and the Little Bears. They say that the three guards of the North Star is a canoe in which three Indians are embarked to overtake this bear, but that unfortunately they have not yet been able to catch it. (LeClercq 1910:135-136)

Charles Leland included in his *Algonquian Legends of New England* (1884:379) an unreferenced song in which the Milky Way is referred to as a "spirit road," and the three hunters chasing the bear are mentioned.

233

STORIES FROM THE SIX WORLDS

We are the stars which sing,
We sing with our light;
We are the birds of fire,
We fly over the sky.
Our light is a voice;
We make a road for spirits,
For the spirits to pass over.
Among us are three hunters
Who chase a bear;
There never was a time
When they were not hunting.
We look down on the mountains.
This is the Song of the Stars.

Silas Rand also wrote a short paragraph on star-names; his editor quotes it in the introduction to Rand's *Legends of the Micmac* (1894:xli).

They have some knowledge of astronomy. They have watched the stars during their night excursions, or while laying in wait for game. They know that the North Star does not move, and call it *okwotunuquwa kulokuwech* [*oqwatnukewey kloqoej*], the North Star. They have observed that the circumpolar stars never set. They call the Great Bear, *Muen* (the Bear), and they have names for several other constellations. The morning star is *ut'adabum* [see "Oaklahdahbun"; neither variant is now remembered, so the correct orthography cannot be given], and the seven stars *ejulkuch* [the meaning of this word, as spelled by Rand and Dennis, is now unknown as well]. And "What do you call that?" asked a venerable old lady a short time ago, who, with her husband, the head chief of Cape Breton [John Denys or Denny], was giving me a lecture on astronomy, on Nature's celestial globe, through the apertures of the wigwam. She was pointing to the Milky Way. "Oh we call it the Milky Way, the milky road," said I. To my surprise she gave it the same name in Micmac.

Apart from Dennis's account, retold in this collection, the lists above are the only ones I've found. Star Persons were prominent in Micmac stories. Through thousands and thousands of dark nights they were guides and friends to ancestral hunters and travellers of the People. It would be nice to think that Peter Wilmot's eighteenth-century "Old Ones" are herein still teaching us how to speak of them.

KLUSKAP
Untitled (Dennis 1934:94-97); collected by Clara Dennis *ca* 1930, from "an Indian" in Nova Scotia.

KI'KWA'JU AND SKUSI'SKWAQ
"The Two Weasels" (Rand 1894:160-168); collected by Silas Rand from Ben Brooks [possibly Louis Benjamin Brooks, who provided

Rand with other stories, most of them passed down by his maternal grandfather, Chief Louis Benjamin Peminuit Paul, who died in 1843]. Ben Brooks was living in Falmouth, N.S. "He understood English very well for an Indian; I read to him the translation, or rather, the story as I put it down in English,—and he pronounced it correct. He is confident that the story is of Indian authorship, of which there can be no reasonable doubt. He thinks it has been handed down from ancient times; of this there is internal evidence, particularly in the polygamy which it presupposes, and the confident belief in magic."

"The Badger and the Star Wives" (Rand 1894:306-320); collected by Silas Rand from Susan Christmas, 7 September 1870. "She professed to have learned this story, and many more, when she was a small child, from an old blind woman on Cape Breton. The old blind woman used to interest her and other children and keep them quiet for a long time, telling them stories." [Possibly Mary Doucet Newall]

"Badger and His Little Brother" (Rand 1894:266-269); collected by Silas Rand from Ben Brooks, 9 December 1869. "He had heard it many times, and ever so long ago."

"Crane Betrays Badger and Other Adventures of Badger" (Parsons 1925:68-69); collected by Elsie Clews Parsons in the summer of 1923 from Mary Madeline Newall Poulet, Whycocomagh, N.S.

"Star Husbands; Sucker Man" (Parsons 1925:65-68); collected by Elsie Clews Parsons from Mary Madeline Newall Poulet, who had heard it from her mother, Mary Doucet Newall.

"Rabbit and Wolverine Visit Kitpusiagana" (Wallis, Wallis 1955:424-430); collected by Wilson Wallis in the summer of 1911 or 1912, from Louis Glode and Thomas Meuse.

Notes: Silas Rand called Ki'kwa'ju a Badger, as did Frank Speck and Elsie Clews Parsons, apparently relying on Rand's identification. Yet there are no badgers east of Ohio. (Fred Scott, Nova Scotia Museum, personal communication)

Mary Madeline Newall Poulet told Parsons several "Kigwa'ju" stories, "but my informant could not translate the word, she seemed to think it meant a bird of some kind." (Parsons 1925:67)

"The story was started after I read the last two incidents of the Badger story recorded by Dr. Speck, either from Joe Julian or from John Joe.... 'Everybody here knows the story about Badger,' said another man, 'that's a hell of a long story, most of it too dirty to tell you.'" (Parsons 1925:68) Informants seem to be accepting the collectors' English translation, all based on Rand.

But most of Rand's informants spoke little English. Perhaps he based his translation on a *description* of a similar animal, one which would not leap to his mind, as it had become extinct in Atlantic Canada. Perhaps Ki'kwa'ju is that "very fierce and mischievous creature, about the bigness of a middling dog, having short legs, broad feet, and very sharp claws" described by John Gyles (1869:40). Sounds like a badger, doesn't it? But it is the description of a wolverine. And wolverines, according to the seventeenth-century French sources, are called "Quincajou" by the Micmac. Clara Dennis (1934:168) collected a variant of Rand's "Badger and His Little Brother," about Wolverine and his little brother. Ki'kwa'ju is a wolverine.

Wolverine's acts of what were seen as wanton mischief against humans were legendary among the Micmac.

The wolverenes [sic] go into wigwams which have been left for a time, scatter the things abroad, and most filthily pollute them with ordure. I have heard the Indians say that this animal has sometimes pulled their guns from under their heads while they were asleep, and left them so defiled. An Indian told me that having left his wigwam, with sundry things on the scaffold among which was a birchen flask containing several pounds of powder, he found at his return, much to his surprise and grief, that a wolverene had visited it, mounted the scaffold, hove down bag and baggage. The powder flask happening to fall into the fire, exploded, blowing up the wolverene, and scattering the wigwam in all directions. At length he found the creature, blind from the blast, wandering backward and forward, and he had the satisfaction of kicking and beating him about. This, in a great measure, made up their loss, and then they could contentedly pick up their utensils and rig out their wigwam. (Gyles 1869:40-41)

Doesn't this sound exactly like something Ki'kwa'ju would do? Perhaps that wolverine screamed "Let my backbone be preserved," as the gunpowder blew him up. Gunpowder, of course, quickly spelled the end for all wolverines in the Maritimes. Humans had absolutely no love for them, but the Micmac have given them their immortality in all those stories of Ki'kwa'ju.

We are indebted to Elsie Clews Parsons for telling us exactly what it was that Younger Sister did to that neck-bone. Silas Rand, with customary nineteenth-century delicacy, says merely, "This bone the younger sister was not careful to treat with respect, but kicked it around and in other ways treated it with contempt." (1894:165) In a variant of the story, he writes, "The younger girl was inclined to insult it, and despite the warnings of her companion, treated it with great indignity." (1894:319)

Parsons evidently was not a woman to baulk at the word "piss," and that is just what her informant, Mary Madeline Newall Poulet, said that Younger Sister did. "Mrs. Poulet first said that Younger Sister sat on the stone; but she accepted the correction of her daughter who was present [Isabelle Googoo Morris]. 'Nicer to say "sit,"' she commented." (Parsons 1925:65)

KULU
"The Small Baby and the Big Bird" (Rand 1894:81-93); collected by Silas Rand from Susan Barss, at Charlottetown, P.E.I., in the winter of 1847-1848. "In the tale that follows there figures a

remarkable bird, a monster in size, into the form of which certain sanguinary chiefs, who are wizards, powwows [*sic; puoinaq*] and cannibals, are able to transform themselves, retaining their intelligence, and able at will again to resume the shape of men.... These birds are described in some legends as able to carry a great number of men on their backs at once, with immense piles of fresh meat; they have to be fed every few minutes with a whole quarter of beef, which is thrust into the mouth while they are on the wing." (Rand 1984:82,89)

Notes: Kulu Persons were known to both Micmac and Maliseet, the earliest account of them being recorded in New Brunswick by John Gyles, between 1689 and 1698 (1863:37).

[Of] two stories which were related and believed by the Indians ... the first, of a boy who was carried away by a large bird called a *Gulloua,* who buildeth his nest on a high rock or mountain. A boy was hunting with his bow and arrow at the foot of a rocky mountain, when the *gulloua* came diving through the air, grasped the boy in her talons, and although he was eight or ten years of age, she soared aloft and laid him in her nest, food for her young....

PAPKUTPARUT

Untitled (LeClercq 1910:207-213); collected by Chrestien LeClercq from Micmac on the Gaspé Peninsula, between 1675 and 1683.

Notes: LeClercq provided a context for this story, in his account of Micmac burial practices for his area and time.

When the dying person has drawn his last breath, the relatives and friends of the deceased cover his body with a fine skin of elk, or a robe of beaver. In this he is enshrouded and bound with cords of leather or bark in such a manner that the chin touches the knees and the feet the back. Hence it comes about that their graves are quite round, of the form of a well, and four to five feet deep. Meanwhile the leading person and the chiefs give directions that the bark of the wigwam of the dead man be struck, the words *Oué, Oué, Oué,* being said for the purpose of making the soul come forth. Then certain young Indians are appointed to go and announce to all the people ... the death of their relatives and friends ... inviting them to assist in his funeral.... The relatives and the friends of the deceased ... go into mourning, that is to say, they smear their faces with black, and cut the end of their hair; it is not permissable for them to wear this in tresses, nor to adorn it with strings of beadwork and of wampum during the period that they are in mourning, which lasts a year altogether.... It is only a very short time ago, that in the Isle of Tisniguet, a noted place and an ancient cemetery of the Gaspesians of Restigouche, we found in the woods a grave built in the form of a box, containing a quantity of skins of beavers and of moose, some arrows, bows, wampum, beadwork, and other trinkets. These had been buried by the Indians with the dead persons, in the thought which possessed them, that the spirits of all these articles would bear him company and do him service in the Land of Souls. (LeClercq 1910:300-303)

"Papkutparut the Guardian" appears in no other surviving Micmac story. His name is no longer remembered or translatable, although Bernard Francis points out (personal communication 1987) that the initial morpheme *papk* is the same for the Micmac word *papkwesetmay:* "I am lighting my [pipe]." 'Papkutparut' is probably a verb-phrase, as were many traditional Micmac names, having something to do with smoking or the tobacco pipe. The letter 'r' does not appear in the modern Micmac alphabet; even in LeClercq's day, the People found it hard to distinguish between 'r' and 'l' sounds. But I have left it Papkutparut (LeClercq spells it Papkootparoot), instead of modernizing it all the way to Papkutpalut.

KLUSKAP TELLS THE PEOPLE ABOUT DEATH
Untitled (Dennis 1934:97); collected *ca* 1930 by Clara Dennis, from "an Indian" in Nova Scotia.
Notes: "I'll call you down from the crotch of the trees and from the scaffolds of the air," refers to Micmac burial practices.

If an Indian dies during the winter at some place remote from the common burial-place of his ancestors, those of his wigwam enwrap him with much care in barks painted red and black, place him upon the branches of some tree on the bank of a river, and build around him with logs a kind of little fort, for fear lest he be torn by wild beasts or birds of prey. In the spring the chief sends the young men to fetch the body, and it is received with the same ceremonies which have just been described. (LeClercq 1910:303)

One method of preserving the bodies of the dead was to place them on scaffolding to dry in the sun, or to be smoked. (See the Notes for "Tia'm and Tia'mi'skw.") These exposed burials are the "scaffolds of the air" to which Kluskap refers in the story.

APPENDIX: MICMAC ALPHABET AND ORTHOGRAPHY

The Micmac language has twenty-seven or so distinctive sounds. Only one is not found in English, while English has some not used in Micmac. The Francis-Smith orthography—a system for writing Micmac developed by myself and Douglas Smith—is used in these stories.

The system represents all twenty-seven possibilities with a combination of eleven consonants, six short vowels, and five long vowels created by adding an apostrophe after a, e, i, o and u, to indicate that these are long. Long vowels in Micmac are held for two beats, instead of one.

A *schwa* sound is also used in Micmac, represented in the Francis-Smith system by a character called a "barred i," simply an i with a hyphen struck through it. It is one of the six vowel sounds mentioned above.

Micmac consonants are p,t,k,q,j,s,l,m,n,w, and y. The Francis-Smith system organizes them in this order. Speakers of English tend to find the letter q difficult to pronounce properly in Micmac, since English does not have the velar, better known as the guttural, sound. The closest to it, as an example, is the *ch* in *loch,* a loan-word from Gaelic.

The key to learning the system, and the pronunciation of the Micmac names and terms in this collection of stories, is by memorizing the vowel sounds. The consonants, even if misprounounced, will generally not affect meaning—only accent. The vowels do not change sounds, whether one finds them in the initial, medial or final position within a word. Here is a guide to their pronunciation:

a as the u in b*u*d	*a'* as the o in b*o*ss
e as the e in b*e*t	*e'* as the ay in pl*a*y
i as the i in s*i*ck	*i'* as the double e in s*ee*
o as the o in b*o*at	*o'* as the o in g*o*
u as the u in p*u*	*u'* as the double o in sch*oo*l
ɨ as the i in s*i*r	

There is an absolute one-to-one correspondence between letter and sound, and sound and letter. For every one sound there is one letter, and vice-versa.

Bernard Francis
The Micmac Language Institute
Sydney, Nova Scotia

239

BIBLIOGRAPHY

Brasser, Ted
1987 "By the Power of Their Dreams" *The Spirit Sings* Toronto: McClelland and Stewart 93-132
Dennis, Clara
1934 *Down in Nova Scotia* Toronto: Ryerson
Goodrich, Norma Lorre
1961 *Medieval Myths* New York: New American Library
Gyles, John
1869 *Memoirs of Odd Adventures, Strange Deliverances, etc.* Cincinnati, n.p.
Hallowell, A. Irving
1960 "Ojibway Ontology, Behaviour and World View" *Culture in History* Stanley Diamond, ed. New York: Columbia University Press 19-52
Hardy, Campbell
1855 *Sporting Adventures in the New World Vol 2*. London: Hurst and Blackett

———

ca 1910 "In Evangeline's Land" MS, Nova Scotia Museum Printed Matter File
Joe, Rita
1976 "Key-Qua-Joo" *Tawow* Canadian Indian Cultural Magazine, Vol. 2, No. 5:29. Ottawa: Indian and Northern Affairs
LeClercq, Chrestien
1910 *New Relation of Gaspesia* Tr. and ed. by W.F. Ganong. Toronto: The Champlain Society
Leland, Charles
1884 *The Algonquian Legends of New England* Boston: Houghton Mifflin and Company. 2d ed. 1968 Detroit: Singing Tree Press
Loudon, John
1987 "Book Review: Joseph Campbell's The Inner Reaches of Outer Space: Metaphor as Myth and as Religion" *Parabola Vol XII No. 1* 101-104
Maillard, Abbé Antoine Simon Pierre
1758 *An Account of the Customs and Manners of the Mikmakis and Maricheets, Savage Nations, Now Dependant of the Government at Cape Breton* London: S. Hooper and A. Marely

———

1863 "Lettre à Madame de Drucourt" *Les Soirées Canadiennes* Québec: Brousseau Frères Translated for this publication by M.A. Hamelin, Nova Scotia Museum
Parsons, Elsie Clews
1925 "Micmac Folklore" *Journal of American Folklore* 38:55-133

1926 "Micmac Notes" *Journal of American Folklore* 39:460-485
Phillips, Ruth
1987 "Like a Star I Shine" *The Spirit Sings* Toronto: McClelland and Stewart 51-92
Rand, Silas T.
1894 *Legends of the Micmacs* New York: Longmans, Green & Co

1902 *Micmac-English Dictionary* Jeremiah Clark, ed. Charlottetown, PEI: Patriots Publishing Company
Red Hawk
1983 "Towards the Glorious Sun of Infinity" *Journey of the Medicine Man* Little Rock, Arkansas: August House
Speck, Frank
1926 "A Wawenock Myth Text from Maine" Bureau of Ethnology Annual Report 43:165-197
Vastokas, Joan
1977 "The Shamanic Tree of Life" *Stone, Bones and Skin* Toronto: The Society for Art Publications 93-117
Wallis, W.D. and Wallis, R.S.
1955 *The Micmac Indians of Eastern Canada* Minneapolis: The University of Minnesota
Webster, Helen, ed.
1894 see Rand, Silas T. *Legends of the Micmacs* i-xlvi.
Whitehead, Ruth Holmes
1987 "I Have Lived Here Since the World Began" *The Spirit Sings* Toronto: McClelland and Stewart 17-50

ACKNOWLEDGEMENTS

I would like to express my grateful thanks to Bernard Francis, of the Micmac Language Institute, for the light his translations have shed on the stories, and for long conversations about Power and the way it shapes the world.

I would also like to thank Dr. H.F. McGee, Jr., of Saint Mary's University, for lending me his entire library, and for sharing his knowledge of the Micmac. Dr. Ralph Pastore, Dr. Ruth Phillips, and Dr. Graham Whitehead also read the manuscript and gave me helpful criticism. Thanks also to Fred Scott of the Nova Scotia Museum, who told me that Ki'kwa'ju was not a badger, and to Sarah Denny and Rita Joe, for their great kindness to me over many years. Working on these stories has been an honour and a deep and lasting pleasure. I hope the book will enable the Micmac to share them, in all their beauty and terror, with a much wider audience. I am grateful to Dorothy Blythe of Nimbus Publishing for suggesting that this be undertaken, and to Elizabeth Eve and Kathy Kaulbach for the execution of it.

03/9